M 11/21

PIGEON
ENGLISH

WITHDRAWN

PIGEON
ENGLISH

STEPHEN KELMAN

HOUGHTON MIFFLIN HARCOURT
BOSTON   NEW YORK
2011

For information about permission to reproduce selections from this book,
write to Permissions, Houghton Mifflin Harcourt Publishing Company,
215 Park Avenue South, New York, New York 10003.

www.hmhbooks.com

First published in Great Britain in 2011 by Bloomsbury Publishing

Library of Congress Cataloging-in-Publication Data
Kelman, Stephen, date.
Pigeon English / Stephen Kelman.
p. cm.
ISBN 978-0-547-50060-7
1. Boys—Fiction. 2. Ghanaians—England—London—Fiction.
3. Immigrant families—England—London—Fiction. I. Title.
PR6111.E524P54 2011
823'.92—dc22
2010050114

Printed in the United States of America

DOC 10 9 8 7 6 5 4 3 2 1

For the traveller

I'd rather learn from one bird how to sing
than teach ten thousand stars how not to dance
                                    E. E. Cummings

MARCH

You could see the blood. It was darker than you thought. It was all on the ground outside Chicken Joe's. It just felt crazy.

Jordan: 'I'll give you a million quid if you touch it.'

Me: 'You don't have a million.'

Jordan: 'One quid then.'

You wanted to touch it but you couldn't get close enough. There was a line in the way:

POLICE LINE DO NOT CROSS

If you cross the line you'll turn to dust.

We weren't allowed to talk to the policeman, he had to concentrate for if the killer came back. I could see the chains hanging from his belt but I couldn't see the gun.

The dead boy's mamma was guarding the blood. She wanted it to stay, you could tell. The rain wanted to come and wash the blood away but she wouldn't let it. She wasn't even crying, she was just stiff and fierce like it was her job to scare the rain back up into the sky. A pigeon was looking for his chop. He walked right in the blood. He was even sad as well, you could tell where his eyes were all pink and dead.

*   *   *

The flowers were already bent. There were pictures of the dead boy wearing his school uniform. His jumper was green.

My jumper's blue. My uniform's better. The only bad thing about it is the tie, it's too scratchy. I hate it when they're scratchy like that.

There were bottles of beer instead of candles and the dead boy's friends wrote messages to him. They all said he was a great friend. Some of the spelling was wrong but I didn't mind. His football boots were on the railings tied up by their laces. They were nearly new Nikes, the studs were proper metal and everything.

Jordan: 'Shall I t'ief them? He don't need 'em no more.'

I just pretended I didn't hear him. Jordan would never really steal them, they were a million times too big. They looked too empty just hanging there. I wanted to wear them but they'd never fit.

Me and the dead boy were only half friends, I didn't see him very much because he was older and he didn't go to my school. He could ride his bike with no hands and you never even wanted him to fall off. I said a prayer for him inside my head. It just said sorry. That's all I could remember. I pretended like if I kept looking hard enough I could make the blood move and go back in the shape of a boy. I could bring him back alive that way. It happened before, where I used to live there was a chief who brought his son back like that. It was a long time ago, before I was born. Asweh, it was a miracle. It didn't work this time.

I gave him my bouncy ball. I don't need it anymore, I've got five more under my bed. Jordan only gave him a pebble he found on the floor.

Me: 'That doesn't count. It has to be something that belonged to you.'

4

Jordan: 'I ain't got nothing. I didn't know we had to bring a present.'

I gave Jordan a strawberry Chewit to give to the dead boy, then I showed him how to make a cross. Both the two of us made a cross. We were very quiet. It even felt impor tant. We ran all the way home. I beat Jordan easily. I can beat everybody, I'm the fastest in Year 7. I just wanted to get away before the dying caught us.

The buildings are all mighty around here. My tower is as high as the lighthouse at Jamestown. There are three towers all in a row: Luxembourg House, Stockholm House and Copenhagen House. I live in Copenhagen House. My flat is on floor 9 out of 14. It's not even hutious, I can look from the window now and my belly doesn't even turn over. I love going in the lift, it's brutal, especially when you're the only one in there. Then you could be a spirit or a spy. You even forget the pissy smell because you're going so fast.

It's proper windy at the bottom like a whirlpool. If you stand at the bottom where the tower meets the ground and put your arms out, you can pretend like you're a bird. You can feel the wind try to pick you up, it's nearly like flying.

Me: 'Hold your arms out wider!'

Jordan: 'They're as wide as I can get 'em! This is so gay, I'm not doing it no more!'

Me: 'It's not gay, it's brilliant!'

Asweh, it's the best way to feel alive. You only don't want the wind to pick you up, because you don't know where it will drop you. It might drop you in the bushes or the sea.

In England there's a hell of different words for everything. It's for if you forget one, there's always another one left over. It's very helpful. Gay and dumb and lame mean all the same. Piss and slash and tinkle mean all the same (the same as greet the chief). There's a million words for a bulla. When I came to my new school, do you know what's the first thing Connor Green said to me?

Connor Green: 'Have you got happiness?'

Me: 'Yes.'

Connor Green: 'Are you sure you've got happiness?'

Me: 'Yes.'

Connor Green: 'But are you really sure?'

Me: 'I think so.'

He kept asking me if I had happiness. He wouldn't stop. In the end it just vexed me. Then I wasn't sure. Connor Green was laughing, I didn't even know why. Then Manik told me it was a trick.

Manik: 'He's not asking if you've got happiness, he's asking if you've got a penis. He says it to everyone. It's just a trick.'

It only sounds like happiness but really it means a penis. Ha-penis.

Connor Green: 'Got ya! Hook, line and sinker!'

Connor Green is always making tricks. He's just a confusionist. That's the first thing you learn about him. At least I didn't lose. I do have a penis. The trick doesn't work if it's true.

Some people use their balconies for hanging washing or growing plants. I only use mine for watching the helicopters. It's a bit dizzy. You can't stay out there for more than one minute or you'll turn into an icicle. I saw X-Fire painting his name on the wall of Stockholm House. He didn't know I could see him. He was proper quick and the words still came out dope-fine. I want to write my own name that big but the paint in a can is too dangerous, if you get it on yourself it never washes off, even forever.

The baby trees are in a cage. They put a cage around the tree to stop you stealing it. Asweh, it's very crazy. Who'd steal a tree anyway? Who'd chook a boy just to get his Chicken Joe's?

When Mamma puts her phone on speaker it sounds like they're far away. It makes Papa's voice go proper echoey like he's trapped in a submarine at the bottom of the sea. I pretend like he has one hour of air left, if he doesn't get rescued by then it's all over. It always freaks me out. I'm the man of the house until Papa escapes. He even said it. It's my duty to look after everything. I told him about my pigeon.

Me: 'A pigeon flew in the window. Lydia was even scared.'

Lydia: 'How! No I was not!'

Me: 'She was. She said his wings were making her crazy. I had to catch him.'

I put some flour in my hand and the pigeon landed on it. He was only hungry. I tricked him with the flour. You have to walk proper slow, if you go too fast the pigeon will just get scared and fly off again.

Lydia: 'Hurry up! It's going to bite somebody!'

Me: 'Advise yourself! He only wants to get out. Shut up or you'll scare him.'

His feet felt scratchy on my hand like a chicken's. It was lovely. I made him my special pigeon. I made a proper good look at him to remember his colours, then I let him out on the balcony and he just flew away. You don't even need to kill them.

Papa: 'Good work.'

Papa's voice was smiling. I love it when his voice is smiling, it means you did good. I didn't need to wash my hands after, my pigeon doesn't have any germs. They're always telling you to wash your hands. Asweh, there's so many germs here you wouldn't believe it! Everybody's scared of them all the time. Germs from Africa are the most deadliest, that's why Vilis ran away when I tried to say hello to him, he thinks if he breathes my germs he'll die.

I didn't even know I brought the germs with me. You can't feel them or see them or anything. Adjei, germs are very tricky! I don't even care if Vilis hates me, he's a dirty tackler and he never passes the ball to me.

Agnes loves to blow spit bubbles. She's only still allowed because she's a baby. I even want her to blow lots of them. As many as she wants and forever.

Me: 'Hello, Agnes!'

Agnes: '**O!**'

I swear by God, when Agnes says hello it makes your ears ring like a crazy bell! You love it anyway. When Agnes says hello Mamma cries and laughs at the same time, she's the only person I know who can do it. Agnes couldn't come with us because Mamma has to work all the time. Grandma Ama looks after her instead. It's only until Papa sells all the things from his shop, then he's going to buy some more tickets and we'll all be together again. It's only been two months since we left, you only start to forget them after one year. It won't even be that long.

Me: 'Can you say Harri?'

Papa: 'Not yet. Give her time.'

Me: 'What's she doing?'

Papa: 'Just blowing more bubbles. You better go now.'

Me: 'OK. Come soon. Bring some Ahomka, I can't find any here. I love you.'

Papa: 'I lo

That's when the calling card ran out. I always hate it when that happens. It's always a shock even if it happens every time. It's like at night when I'm watching the helicopters and they go quiet, I always think they're going to crash on me. Asweh, when the engine comes on again it's a mighty relief!

I saw a real dead person. It was where I used to live, at the market in Kaneshie. An orange lady got hit by a trotro, nobody even saw it coming. I pretended like all the oranges rolling everywhere were her happy memories and they were looking for a new person to stick to so they didn't get wasted. The shoeshine boys tried to steal some of the oranges that didn't get run over but Papa and another man made them put them back in her basket. The shoeshine boys should know you never steal from the dead. It's the duty of the righteous to show the godless the right way. You have to help them whenever you can, even if they don't want it. They only think they don't want it but really they do. You only get to be righteous if you can sing every church song without looking at the words. Only Pastor Taylor and Mr Frimpong can do it and both the two of them are proper old. Mr Frimpong's so old there's spiders in his ears, I've seen them with my own two eyes.

At church we said a special prayer for the dead boy. We asked that his soul would be carried into the arms of the Lord and the Lord would soften the heart of his killers so they'd give themselves up. Pastor Taylor made a special message to all the children. He said if we knew anybody with a knife to tell about them.

Lydia was peeling the cassava for fufu.

Me: 'You've got a knife! I'm telling about you!'

Lydia: 'Gowayou. What shall I peel them with, a spoon?'

Me: 'You can peel them with your breath. It's like a dragon.'

Lydia: 'Your breath's like a dog. Have you been licking bumholes again?'

It's our favourite game to see who can make the best abuse. I'm usually the winner. So far I have a thousand points and Lydia only has two hundred. We only play when Mamma can't hear. I chooked myself with the fork. It was only in my arm. I wanted to see how much it hurt and how long the holes would last. I was going to tell everybody they were my magic marks from when I was born and they mean I can see inside your mind. But they disappeared after one minute. It still hurt like crazy.

Me: 'I wonder what it feels like to be chooked for real. I wonder if you see stars.'

Lydia: 'Do you want to find out?'

Me: 'Or fire. I bet you see fire.'

My Mustang has fire. I've got four cars: a Mustang and a Beetle and a Lexus and a Suzuki jeep. My best is the Mustang, it's just dope-fine. It's blue with fire on the bonnet and the fire is in the shape of wings. It has no scratches because I never crash it, I only look at it. I can still see the fire when I close my eyes. That's what dying must be like, except the fire isn't beautiful anymore because it actually burns.

Manik's papa showed me how to tie my tie. It was my first day at my new school. I hid my tie in my bag, I was going to tell them it got stolen. But when I got to school I got scared. Everybody was wearing a tie. Manik's papa was there with Manik. The whole thing was his idea.

Manik's papa walks to school with him every day. He has to guard Manik from the robbers. Manik had his trainers stolen one time. One of the Dell Farm Crew stole them. When they didn't fit they put them up a tree. Manik couldn't get them down again because he's too fat to climb the tree.

Manik's papa: 'Let them try it again. It'll be a different story next time, little bastards.'

Manik's papa's quite hutious. He's always red-eyes. He knows swordfighting. Asweh, I'm glad I'm not Manik's enemy! Manik's papa put my tie on for me and made the knot. He showed me how to take the tie off without un-tying it. You just make a hole big enough to get your head through then you take the tie off over your head. That way you don't have to tie the tie every day. It even works. Now I'll never have to tie my tie my whole life. I beat the tie at his own game!

There's no songs in my new school. The best bit about my old school was when Kofi Allotey made up his own words:

Kofi Allotey: '*Before our Father's throne*
We pour our ardent prayers.
Please don't burn me on the stove
Or push me down the stairs.'

Asweh, he caught so many blows we called it the Kofi Stick!

At first me and Lydia stayed together at breaktime. Now we stay with our friends. If we see each other we have to pretend we don't know each other. The first one to say hello is the loser. At breaktime I just play suicide bomber or zombies. Suicide bomber is when you run at the other person and crash them as hard as you can. If the other person falls over you get a hundred points. If they just move but don't fall over it's ten points. One person is always the lookout because suicide bomber is banned. If the teacher catches you playing you'll get a detention.

Zombies is just acting like a zombie. You get extra points for accuracy.

When you're not playing games you can swap things instead. The most wanted things to swap are football stickers and sweets but you can swap anything if somebody wants it. Chevon Brown and Saleem Khan swapped watches. Saleem Khan's watch tells the time on the moon, but Chevon Brown's is chunkier and it's made of real titanium. They're both bo-styles. Everybody was happy with the deal but then Saleem Khan wanted to swap back.

Saleem Khan: 'I changed my mind, that's all.'
Chevon Brown: 'But we shook on it, man.'
Saleem Khan: 'I had my fingers crossed, innit.'
Chevon Brown: 'Pussy clart. Two punches.'
Saleem Khan: 'No, man. One.'
Chevon Brown: 'On the head though.'
Saleem Khan: 'The shoulder, the shoulder.'
Chevon Brown: 'Rarse.'

Chevon Brown punched Saleem Khan proper hard and gave him a dead arm. It was his fault for going back on the deal. He was only scared for if his mamma got red-eyes.

I don't have a watch yet, I don't even need one. The bell tells you where to be and there's a clock in the classroom. When you're outside school you don't need to know the hour, your belly tells you when it's chop time. You just go home when you're hungry enough, that way you never forget.

I was the dead boy. X-Fire was teaching us about chooking. He didn't use a real knife, just his fingers. They still felt quite sharp. X-Fire says when you chook somebody you have to do it proper quick because you feel it as well.

X-Fire: 'When the knife goes in them you can feel where it hits. If it hits a bone or something it feels disgusting, man. You're best going for somewhere soft like the belly so it goes in nice and easy, then you don't feel nothing. The first time I shanked someone was the worst, man. All his guts fell out. It was well sick. I didn't know where to aim yet, I got him too low down, innit. That's why I go for the side now, near the love handles. Then you don't get no nasty stuff falling out.'

Dizzy: 'The first time I shanked someone the blade got stuck. I hit a rib or something. I had to pull like f— to get it out. I was like, give me my blade back, bitch!'

Clipz: 'Innit. You just wanna stick him and get the f— outta there. No messing around.'

Killa didn't join in. He was just quiet. Maybe he hasn't chooked anybody yet. Or maybe he's chooked so many people that he's bored by now. That must be why he's called Killa.

I was the dead boy because X-Fire picked me. I just had to stand still. X-Fire didn't like it when I moved. He kept pulling me. I felt quite sick but I had to keep listening. I even wanted to listen. It was like when I first tasted mushy peas: it was disgusting but I had to finish it because wasting food is a sin.

I could still feel his fingers in my ribs even after he was gone. It felt very crazy. X-Fire's breath smells like cigarettes and chocolate milk. I wasn't even scared.

We always go to the market on Saturday. It's all outside so you get proper cold waiting for Mamma to pay, you have to keep your mouth closed to stop your teeth escaping. It's only even worth it for all the dope-fine things you can look at like a remote-control car or a samurai sword (it's only made from wood but it's still proper hutious. If I had the means I'd buy it like that, I'd use it to chase the invaders away).

My favourite shop is the sweets shop. It sells every kind of Haribo you can think of. It's my ambition to try every style there is. So far I've tried about half. Haribo comes in a million different shapes. Whatever there is in the world, there's a chewy Haribo version of it. Asweh, it's true. They make cola bottles, worms, milkshakes, teddy bears, crocodiles, fried eggs, dummies, fangs, cherries, frogs, and millions more. Cola bottles are the best.

I only don't like the jelly babies. They're cruel. Mamma has seen a dead baby for real. She sees them every day at work. I never buy the jelly babies for if it would remind her.

Mamma was looking all over for a pigeon net. I said a prayer to myself that she never found one.

Me: 'It's not fair. Just because Lydia's scared of them.'

Lydia: 'Gowayou! I'm not scared!'

Mamma: 'We can't have pigeons flying in the house all the time, it's dirty, they'll mess everywhere.'

Me: 'It was only one time. He was hungry, that's all.'

Mamma: 'Don't make squeeze-eyes at me, Harrison, I'm not arguing with you.'

Some people put nets over their balcony to stop the pigeons getting in. I don't even agree with it, they're not hurting anybody. I want my pigeon to come back. I even hid some fufu flour in my pant drawer specially for him. I don't want to eat him, I want to make him tame so he'll go on my shoulder. In the end my prayer was answered: they don't even sell pigeon nets at the market. Asweh, it was a mighty relief!

Me: 'Don't worry. If he comes back I'll tell him to find another home.'

Mamma: 'Don't put any more food out for it. Don't think I haven't seen the flour all over the balcony, I'm not stupid.'

Me: 'I won't!'

I hate it when Mamma reads my mind! From today onward going I'll just wait till she's asleep.

I pretended like I didn't see when Jordan stole the lady's phone. I didn't want Mamma to think I agreed with it, she already hates Jordan because he spits on the stairs. I was at Noddy's clothes stall. I saw the whole thing while Mamma was paying for my Chelsea shirt. It was X-Fire and Dizzy who actually got the lady's phone. They were very tricky: they waited until she was talking, then they bumped her to make her drop the phone. They made it look like an accident. The phone fell on the ground, then Jordan came from nowhere, picked the phone up and ran off with it. He squeezed into the crowd and was gone in one second. It was like he was a ghost, he just disappeared. The lady looked around for her phone but it was already gone, there was nothing she could do. It was a clean getaway. Jordan doesn't get paid for helping them, he just gets some cigarettes or one week of freedom where they don't try to kill him. It's not even a good deal. If it was me I'd want a tenner every time.

My new Chelsea shirt is a bit too scratchy. I had to put a plaster on my nipples to stop them getting rubbed off. It's still bo-styles though. The dead boy loved Chelsea as well. He had the proper shirt with Samsung on it, even the away kit. I hope Heaven has proper goals with nets on them, then you don't have to run miles to get the ball every time you score a goal.

There's a million dogs around here. Asweh, there's nearly as many dogs as people. Most of them are pit bulls because they're the most hutious, you can use them as a weapon for if your gun ran out of bullets. Harvey's the worst. He belongs to X-Fire. He makes him bite the swings in the playground, that's how he keeps him extra hutious. He actually hangs off them with his teeth and swings around in the air like a crazy helicopter. Whenever I see Harvey coming I just hold my breath so he can't smell my fear.

My favourite dog is Asbo, he's just funny and friendly. I first met him when me and Dean Griffin were playing football on the green and a dog came and took our ball. It was Asbo. We chased him and tried to tackle him but he was too fast. He burst the ball by mistake. Now we only have my plastic ball left. It always flies away because it's too light. It's very vexing. I'm getting a proper ball soon, it will be made of skin so it won't fly away.

Did you know that dogs can sneeze? Asweh, it's true. I saw it with my own two eyes. Asbo did a big sneeze. It was a shock at first. Nobody suspected it. He did about a hundred sneezes. He couldn't stop after the first one, it was like a machine gun. Every sneeze made a new sneeze. Even Asbo was surprised. He couldn't stop for donkey hours.

Terry Takeaway: 'He's allergic to beer, innit.'

Terry Takeaway put some beer in his hand and gave it to Asbo to drink but Asbo wouldn't drink it. He just made a sad face and turned his head away and that's when he started sneezing. The bubbles went up his nose.

He's called Terry Takeaway because he always takes things away. It's just another name for a thiefman. Every time you see him he's carrying the last thing he stole. It's mostly DVDs or a mobile phone, they're the easiest. He asks you if you want to buy it even if you're just a kid and you have no means.

Terry Takeaway: 'Wanna buy these? Proper copper, worth a bundle.'

Dean: 'What are we gonna do with a load of copper pipes?'

Terry Takeaway: 'I dunno. You could sell 'em.'

Dean: 'Why don't you sell them?'

Terry Takeaway: 'That's what I'm trying to do, innit.'

Dean: 'I mean why don't you sell them to someone who wants them?'

Terry Takeaway: 'Alright, son, cool your boots. I was only asking.'

We weren't even wearing boots! Asweh, Terry Takeaway is dey touch. It's because he drinks beer for breakfast.

I love easing myself after Mamma puts bleach in the toilet. The bleach makes mighty bubbles, then it's like easing yourself on a cloud. I save up a long one for specially. Nobody's allowed to flush the cloud away until I've done my special piss on it. I pretend like I'm God easing himself on his favourite cloud. I saw on top of a cloud. It was when we were in the aeroplane. We were actually above the clouds. Do you know what's there? Just more sky. Asweh, it's true. Just more and more sky that never runs out. Heaven only comes after.

Mamma: 'You can't see Heaven until you're ready. That's why God hides it with the sky.'

Me: 'But it's still there somewhere.'

Mamma: 'Of course!'

I wanted to see it now. I wanted to see what Grandpa Solomon was doing.

Me: 'I bet he's playing rock, paper, scissors with Jesus.'

Lydia: 'I bet he's cheating.'

Me: 'How! It's not even cheating!'

Lydia: 'Advise yourself!'

Grandpa Solomon says scissors actually beats rock because in the end the rock is so tired from all the chooks that it falls apart. Anybody who says rock beats scissors is just too lazy to wait until the end. It's the only thing I can remember him saying because he died when I was still a baby. It's still true though. Anybody who says it's cheating is just a fool.

Lydia thought the aeroplane was going to crash. It was on the second plane, the one from Cairo to England. We were sitting right next to the wing. You could see it wobble as you went along. I wasn't scared. If an aeroplane crashes the best place to be is next to the wing, that's where it's the strongest. Even Papa said it. The wobbling's normal.

Me: 'Look at it! It's wobbling even more! It's going to fall off!'

Lydia: 'Stop it!'

Mamma: 'Harrison! Stop that palaver. Put your belt on.'

We didn't even crash. I prayed for it before we left the ground.

When I came home from school there were police outside the flats. There were two police cars and a hell of cops all looking in the bushes and bins like they lost something special. One of the cops was a lady. Asweh, it felt very crazy. She even wanted to be a man. She had the same cop clothes on and everything. She was asking the kids questions, nobody could go home until they'd been interviewed.

It was brutal. I think lady cops are a very good idea. They just talk to you instead of hitting you all the time.

A pisshead: 'Do you wanna show me how them handcuffs work? I've been a naughty boy, I think I need a spanking.'

Lady cop: 'Watch it!'

The lady cop just asked us about the dead boy. Did we know where he was that day and if anybody was after him. Did we see anything strange. We just said no. We didn't know anything. We wished we knew more but there was nothing we could do.

Dean: 'Have you got any leads?'

Me: 'She's not a dogcatcher!'

Dean: 'Criminal leads, dumb-arse.'

Lady cop: 'We're working on it.'

Dean: 'If we hear anything we'll text you. What's your number?'

Lady cop: 'Cheeky.'

Then the cops had to go. Harvey was trying to bite the door mirror off one of the cop cars. X-Fire was even making him do it. Killa and Dizzy were cheering him on. They only split when the cops got their acid spray out and went to spray it in Harvey's face. It only makes people go blind but it kills dogs in five seconds.

Me: 'I saw where the dead boy got killed, the blood was everywhere.'

Dean: 'I wish I'd seen it.'

Lydia: 'I don't want to see it.'

Me: 'Yes you do. You're only vexed because you didn't see it. It was like a river. You could even swim in it.'

Lydia: 'Advise yourself.'

I even wanted to jump in it like a fish. If I held my breath long enough I could dive right down to the bottom and if I came up again and I was still alive it would be like the dead boy was still here. He could be my air or the light I saw when I opened my eyes again. I held my breath and tried to feel my blood going round. I couldn't even feel it. If I knew my blood was going to run out in five minutes, I'd just fill that five minutes with all my favourite things. I'd eat a hell of Chinese rice and do a cloud piss and make Agnes laugh with my funny face, the one where I make my eyes go crooked and stick my tongue right up my nose. At least if you knew you could be ready. It's not fair otherwise.

Paradiddle just means a drum roll. It's my favourite word of today. In Music we played the drums. A drum roll is when you hit the drum proper quick with two sticks and make it last a long time. I love paradiddle because it sounds like the sound it makes. Asweh, it's very clever.

The big drum at the bottom (bass drum) has a pedal. You actually play it with your foot. It's brutal. Most people hit the drums too hard like they're trying to break them. It's just a game to them. I only hit them hard enough to make a good sound. I showed Poppy Morgan how to move your foot so the bass drum keeps the same pattern. It's easier if you count in your head. You always count up to four. You hit the pedal on every one. Like this:

1 2 3 4
1 2 3 4

And you just repeat it for as long as it feels right. Or you can hit the pedal on one and three to make a faster rhythm:

1 2 **3** 4
1 2 **3** 4

But that one's a bit too fast, it makes you feel crazy like you're going to fall off. When I was showing Poppy Morgan how to play the bass drum I smelled her hair by mistake. I got too close and then I just smelled it. It was honey flavour. Poppy Morgan's hair is yellow like the sun. When she smiles to me it makes my belly turn over, I don't even know why.

You can only see the car park and the bins from my balcony. You can't see the river because the trees are in the way. You can see more and more houses. Lines and lines of them all everywhere like a hell of snakes and smaller flats where the old people and never-normals live (never-normals is what Jordan's mamma calls the people who are not right in the head. Some of them were born like that and some of them went like it from drinking too much beer. Some of them look just like real people only they can't do sums or talk properly).

Mamma and Lydia were both snoring like crazy pigs. I put my coat on and got some flour. It was very late. The helicopters were out looking for robbers again, I could hear them far away. The cold wind bit into my bones like a crazy dog. The trees behind the towers were blowing but the river was asleep. Papa and Agnes and Grandma Ama were all dreaming me, they were watching like I was on TV. The pigeon could feel me waiting for him, he was going to come back tonight, I just knew it.

I waited for the wind to move, then I put a nice big pile of flour on the handrail. I spread it out proper long so the pigeon could see it from miles away. Adjei, the wind came back quick quick and blew it off! I just had to hope he'd smell my plan and come back. I like their orange feet and the way their heads move when they're walking like they're listening to invisible music.

I love living on floor 9, you can look down and as long as you don't stick out too far nobody on the ground even knows you're there. I was going to do a spit but then I saw somebody by the bins so I swallowed it back up again.

24

He was kneeling on the floor by the bottle bank. He was poking his hand under like he dropped something there. I couldn't see his face because his hood was up.

Me: 'Maybe it's the robber! Quick, helicopter, here's your man! Shine your torchlight down there!' (I only said it inside my head.)

He pulled something from under the bin. It was all wrapped up. He looked all around and then he unwrapped the wrapping and I saw something shiny underneath. I only saw it for one second but it had to be a knife. It's the only thing I can think of that's shiny and pointy like that. He wrapped it up again and put it down his pant, then he ran away sharp-sharp towards the river. It was some funny thing. The helicopters didn't even see him. They didn't follow him or anything, they were too high up. He runs proper funny like a girl with his elbows all sticking out. I bet I'm faster than him.

I wanted to keep watching for if something else happened but I had to greet the chief too bad. I waited as long as I could. I don't know why the pigeon never came. He thinks we're going to kill him but we're not. I just want something that's alive that I can feed and teach tricks to.

*I watched the sun come up and saw the boy off to school,
I start every day with the taste of his dreams in my mouth.
The taste of all your dreams. You look so blameless from
up here, so busy. The way you flock around an object of
curiosity, or take flight from an intrusion, we're more alike
than you give us credit for. But not too alike.*

*This is me nine storeys up, perched on a windowsill
quietly straining the remnants of my last millet meal. This
is me pitying you, that your lives are so short and nothing's
ever fair. I didn't know the boy who died, he wasn't mine.
But I do know the shape of a mother's grief, I know how
it clings like those resilient blackberries that prosper by
the side of a motorway. Sorry, and everything. Now watch
your heads, I need to. There she blows. Don't shoot the
messenger.*

Every time somebody shuts their door too hard my flat
shakes. You can even feel it. When one person shuts a
door everybody else feels it as well. It's even brutal, it's like
you're all living in the same big house. You can pretend
like it's an earthquake. Mr Tomlin said an earthquake only
happens in the parts of the world where the rocks are too
ticklish. Everybody laughed. Mr Tomlin is very funny. He
even makes better jokes than Connor Green.

I only don't like it when the shouting gets too loud. It
makes me jump right out of my skin. It sounds like invaders

coming to kill us. When the shouting gets too near I just turn the sound up on the TV to hide it.

If any invaders come it's my job to send them away. That's what the man of the house is there for. We always keep the chain on the door and the locks locked up so the invaders can't get in. If they get inside we have to chook them with a fork (you can't chook them with a knife because it's murder. Forks is not. Forks is just self-defence). I'll stand in front of Lydia to protect her. And Mamma as well if she's home. While I'm fighting the invaders Lydia or Mamma are calling the police. I'd aim for the eye because it's the softest part. It would just make them blind. Then when they can't see anything I'd push them outside and into the lift. The lift is safe.

It's only if invaders come. It might not even happen.

I looked through the spyhole. It was only Miquita and Chanelle. I unlocked the locks and let them in.

Miquita: 'What's this, security?'

Lydia: 'Just let them in, Harrison.'

Me: 'Don't call me Harrison, you're not Mamma.'

Asweh, Lydia always acts like the boss when her friends come around. She's always bluffing and telling me to go to my room and do my homework. I don't want to go to my room. She only wants me to go so they can watch Hollyoaks. They think it's the greatest. It's only people kissing all the time. Sometimes it's even a boy kissing another boy! I swear by God, it's true! They're just disgusting.

Me: 'I'm telling Mamma you were watching kissing. It's disgusting.'

Then Lydia shuts the door in my face. She waits until I'm proper close, then she shuts the door. It's very mean. She never used to shut the door in my face. Now she does it all the time just so her stupid friends can laugh at me.

Me: 'Let me in!'

Lydia: 'Miquita doesn't want you to come in. You keep pinching her behind.'

Me: 'Don't bring yourself! No I don't.'

It's not even true. I've never pinched Miquita's behind. I'd rather put my fingers in a fire ants' nest. Miquita and Chanelle are both dey touch, they're always bluffing about all the boys they've sucked off (it means harder kissing). Miquita has a cherry lipstick. It actually tastes like cherry. She's always putting it on her lips. She says she wants to taste nice and sweet for when she kisses me.

Me: 'You're never going to kiss me. I'll just split.'

Miquita: 'Where to? There's nowhere to run. Don't be scared just 'cause you love me too much.'

Me: 'I don't even love you. I wish you'd fall down a hole.'

Miquita could be pretty if she kept her mouth shut. She sat on my hand and I went all hot. It was only an accident, I didn't mean to feel her behind. Anyway she bluffs too much, she's always abusing our TV just because it's made of wood and it's very old. We got it from the cancer shop, it used to belong to a dead person. The picture doesn't come straight away, you have to wait for it to warm up. When the picture first comes it's proper dark, then the real colours come after. The whole thing takes donkey hours. You can even go and greet the chief in the time between turning the TV on and the picture coming. I even tried it and it works.

Miquita isn't going to the dead boy's funeral. She didn't know him.

Miquita: 'What's the point, man? All funerals are the same, innit.'

Me: 'It's only for respect.'

Miquita: 'But I don't respect him. It's his own fault he got killed, he shouldn't have been fronting. You play with fire you get burned, innit.'

Me: 'You don't know what you're talking about, you weren't even there. He didn't even front anybody, the killer just wanted his Chicken Joe's.'

Miquita: 'Whatever. You don't know shit, you're just a kid.'

Me: 'You don't know either. Asweh, you're just a fool.'

Miquita: '*Asweh, asweh! Asweh by God!* You sound like a little yappy dog. Get out of my face now, you're vexing me.'

Me: 'Well your face is vexing me, fish lips.'

I just split before I got too red-eyes. If Miquita ever sucks me off I'll kill her. She's too disgusting and she's got fat hands.

The shopping centre doors open by magic. You don't even have to touch them. There's a big sign with all the rules written on it:

NO ALCOHOL
NO BICYCLES
NO DOGS
NO SKATEBOARDS
NO SMOKING
NO BALL GAMES

Underneath the real rules somebody has written a new rule in pen:

NO FUGLIES

A fugly is a girl who always wants a baby from you. Dean Griffin told me about them.

Dean: 'If you kiss a fugly she'll have a baby every time. You only need to look at 'em for too long and you'll put a bun in their oven, I swear. They're rancid, man, stay well away.'

You don't even want to get too close, they have scabs on their face and they smell like cigarettes. Their babies smell like cigarettes as well. We pretended like the fuglies were going to get us. They were zombies and they were all after us, we had to get away. If one of them kissed us we'd change into a fugly zombie. It was very funny. We got away just in time.

Dean's my second-best friend. He's my best friend at school and Jordan is my best friend outside of school. It's Dean who told me to put my dinner money in my sock so the robbers can't find it. He does it all the time, now he never gets robbed anymore.

I tried it but it felt too lumpy. I couldn't walk properly. I just keep my dinner money in my pocket. Nobody will rob me anyway, I haven't done anything to them.

Me: 'Do you think it's the dead boy's own fault they chooked him? That's what my sister's friend said. I don't believe her. I think she might be a fugly. Do you think they'll catch who did it?'

Dean: 'Don't bet on it, the coppers round here ain't got the skills. They should get CSI on the case, they'll crack it in no time.'

Me: 'What's a CSI?'

Dean: 'They're like the top detectives in America, they know the best tricks and they can find the clues that no one else has even thought of. It's not just on telly, it's real. I seen this one, there was this gang going round busting people up, like just with baseball bats and stamping on their heads and stuff.'

Me: 'Why?'

Dean: 'I dunno, just for a laugh. And there was no witnesses or nothing but CSI got this special computer program that can tell what kind of trainers you've got just from the pattern on the bottom, yeah? And they matched the footprints on the dead man's face to the killer's footprints, that's how they got him. It was well smart.'

Me: 'That is well smart. They should do the same thing here. Maybe we could find the footprints.'

Dean: 'Maybe, but our technology's shit though, innit. We ain't even got the right equipment. Oi, watch it!'

Terry Takeaway nearly crashed into us. He was running like a maniac. He didn't even see us. He had a big tray of chickens under his arm. I knew it was too heavy. The tray slipped and some of the chickens fell off. Terry Takeaway didn't even stop, he just carried on running. His eyes were all big from concentrating, it was very funny. We had to jump out of the way.

Butcher: 'Come back here you little f—er!'

The butcher tried chasing him but he was too fat. He just gave up. The other pissheads were waiting outside on the big library steps. They all took a chicken and went running off in every direction. Even Asbo ran away. He just thought it was a game. He was barking like crazy. We even wanted them to get away. Asweh, it was very funny. Dean said we should come this way every day. We made it a new rule.

I don't even know where the real chickens are. Everybody just buys them already dead and plucked. It even feels crazy. I miss their faces. Their dead eyes were lovely, like they were dreaming of all the good times when they were running around in the sunshine pecking each other in the head.

Chicken: 'Peck peck peck peck!'

Other chicken: 'Peck off!'

When a baby dies they have to give it a name or it won't get into Heaven. Sometimes they're too sad to think of a name. Then Mamma thinks of a name for them. She usually gets them from the Bible. If the mamma doesn't believe in the Bible then she gets a name from the newspaper instead. One baby died today. It was ectopic.

Mamma: 'That's when it grows outside the womb. There's nothing you can do about it. Sometimes they just get lost.'

Mamma had to give the dead baby a name. She called it Katy after a lady in the newspaper. The baby's mamma was very pleased. She loved it.

Me: 'Next time a baby dies you can call it Harrison. She'd love it.'

Mamma: 'I can't do that, it's bad luck.'

Me: 'How?'

Mamma: 'It just is. Harrison is your name. I don't want anybody else to have it.'

A name is so Jesus will find you. Otherwise Jesus won't know who he's looking for and you'd just float in space forever. That would be hutious. What if you fell into the sun, you'd get burned up like human toast!

It's OK, the dead babies grow up in Heaven. Asweh, it was a mighty relief. I'd hate it if I had to stay a baby forever. You'd never learn how to read or talk. You'd be useless. I can't even remember what it feels like to be a baby. I was asleep most of the time. It was very boring. If I was like that forever I'd probably go crazy from head to toe.

There should be footprints by the bins, they should have stuck like when you jump in the puddle and jump out again. I looked for them before school but they were gone. Maybe the killer was wearing special trainers with no pattern, or maybe he just didn't press hard enough for it to work. I always press hard, it's how you make the best shapes. Breaktime can be for puddle-jumping, especially if it's rainy and there's too many teachers around for suicide bomber. I did a massive one. Then I went frozen for if the pigeon did a shit on me, but he just went past. I couldn't tell if it was my pigeon, he was too far away. In England bird shit is good luck. Everybody agrees.

Me: 'Even if it does it on your head?'

Connor Green: 'It don't matter where it does it as long as it lands on you. It can be anywhere.'

Me: 'What if it goes in your eye? What if it goes in your mouth and you eat it?'

Connor Green: 'It's still good luck. All shit's good luck. Everyone knows that.'

Vilis: 'Harri must be lucky then because he smells of shit.'

Asweh, I got red-eyes like a maniac when he said that. I wanted to destroy him but there were too many teachers around. I had to hold it in.

Dean: 'We weren't talking to you, spaz. Go and pick some spuds with your mum.'

Connor Green: 'Go and f— a cow.'

Vilis just said something in his language and ran away, he ran right through the puddle and ruined the game. The next time he abuses me I'm going to kick him in the nuts.

My coffin would be an aeroplane. The dead boy's coffin was just normal except it had the badge of Chelsea on it. It still looked bo-styles. All his family were very sad. It felt proper dark because of the rain and all the black they were wearing. There was no singing.

Mamma: 'God rest him.'

Mamma was squeezing me and Lydia the whole time. You couldn't tell her to stop. You couldn't dance because nobody else was dancing and anyway the rain made it too slippy. They wouldn't let us inside the church because we didn't know him enough. We had to wait outside. You couldn't see much for all the people in the way. I saw the cameraman from the TV. The lady who was telling the news kept stopping to get her hair fixed. She was taking donkey hours. It was very vexing. I just wanted her to shut up so I could hear what the speakers were saying.

Me: 'I wonder what songs they'll play.'

Bigger kid: 'Dizzee Rascal! They should play Suk My Dick, innit!'

Another bigger kid: 'You know it, man!'

TV news lady: 'Can you moderate your language please, we're filming here, thanks.'

Bigger kid: 'Modify this, bitch!'

He pretended to grab his bulla and pointed it at the lady. She didn't even see it, she was already turned around. He was only bluffing. He didn't even say it loud enough for her to hear.

Another bigger kid: 'Rarse!'

Where I used to live, some people have a special coffin in the shape of a real thing. It's something they loved the most when they were alive. If the lady was always sewing then her coffin would be a sewing machine. If the man loved beer it would be a beer bottle. I've seen them all. The coffin tells you what the person loved the most. One time the coffin was a taxi. The man who died was Joseph the taxi driver. I greeted the funeral. I was just coming back from taking the bottles to Samson's Kabin, one of the funeral ladies pulled me and made me dance with her. It was brutal fun. Everybody was happy. Everybody was allowed to join in. I even forgot that somebody died.

Me: 'They should have made his coffin a football boot. That would be even better.'

Mamma: 'Quiet, Harrison. Show respect.'

Me: 'Sorry!'

I'd have an aeroplane because I've never seen one like that before. Mine would be the first.

The dead boy's blood is all gone now, the rain washed it off. There was nothing you could do to stop it. I wanted to see his body, especially the eyes. I wanted to see if they were like the chickens and what dreams they gave away but the coffin was already closed before I got there.

I sneaked away from Mamma and Lydia, they didn't even know I was gone. Dean was waiting for me in the car park. We were spies. We watched the crowd for suspicious activity. That's when people act sneaky because they've got something to hide, Dean learned it from the real detective shows.

Dean: 'Sometimes the killer comes back to watch the funeral, he wants to rub the cops' noses in it. It's like saying you can't catch me, dumb-arses. It's like giving them the finger. He don't wanna get caught though, he's not that dumb. Look out for geezers with their hoods up.'

Me: 'Everyone's got their hood up, it's raining cats and dogs.'

It was true: all you could see was a hell of hoods like boats on the sea. They were at the back, the people near the front who actually loved the dead boy were sharing umbrellas instead. I wonder if opening an umbrella in church would give you double bad luck. It probably would. You'd probably fall down dead on the spot. At least you'd be in the right place, they could have your funeral straight away before the flies could even get to you!

Dean: 'Alright, and what colour hoodie was your geezer wearing? No, forget that, he'd have dumped it by now. Think, think.'

Me: 'I know, we could greet everybody and whoever doesn't shake our hand must be hiding something. Who wouldn't shake your hand at a funeral? We'll just go to everybody and say congratulations and see who doesn't join in.'

Dean: 'Commiserations, not congratulations.'

Me: 'Whatever. We'll just say sorry. Follow me.'

We squeezed into the back of the crowd where the hoods were all standing smoking fags and hiding from the TV camera for if it snapped them. We pretended like we were the official greeters, we went down the line shaking everybody's hand and saying sorry. Most of them just shook our hands and said sorry back, they knew it was serious and they had to show respect. It was proper quick and quiet.

Me and Dean: 'Sorry.'

Hoodie: 'Sorry.'

Me and Dean: 'Sorry.'

Next hoodie: 'Sorry.'

Some of them were black and some of them were white. Some of them even dropped their fag before they shook hands like it was the only right thing to do in the circumstances. Only a few of them didn't join in.

Me and Dean: 'Sorry.'

Ten or eleven hoodie: 'You taking the piss?'

Me: 'No. It's for commiserations.'

Dean: 'You got a problem with that?'

Ten or eleven hoodie: 'F— off, you cheeky little c—.'

We were going to make him a suspect except it was the butcher and he was too fat to be the killer. He's just mean with everybody. We had to give up after that because they were bringing the coffin out again. They nearly dropped it, one of the carriers was in his bottle and he nearly fell over. Everybody held their breath but they got themselves straight again just in time. There was nearly a ruckus at the end. Killa came along on his bike. He couldn't get through all the cars in the car park. He went all wobbly trying to get in between them and the funeral car nearly ran him over on its way out. It only stopped at the last minute. Killa slipped in the rain and fell off his bike.

Funeral man: 'Watch where you're going!'

I thought there'd be blows or at least Killa would give the man his dirty finger but he just got back on his bike and rode away quick quick. He went wobbly again when he went past the back of the car where the coffin was. The flowers on the coffin said Son and Forever. But it felt like Forever was already finished. It felt like somebody took it away when they killed the dead boy. It's not supposed to happen. Children aren't supposed to die, only old people. It even made me worried for if I was next. I spat out the rest of my Atomic Apple Hubba Bubba for if I swallowed it by mistake and my guts all got stuck together.

*   *   *

The steps outside the cafeteria belong to the Dell Farm Crew. Nobody else is allowed to sit there. They're the best spot in the whole school. They're under the roof so you don't get wet when it rains and you can see the whole school from there so your enemy can't sneak up on you. Only Year 11 can even go near there and only if X-Fire invites you.

If you sit on the steps without permission you'll get dirty blows. Even if there's enough room for everybody, you don't own the steps. The Dell Farm Crew own them. They won them in a war. Now the steps belong to them forever.

They're called the Dell Farm Crew after Dell Farm Estate. X-Fire is the leader because he's the best at basketball and fighting. Everybody agrees. He has chooked the most people. He stole my bag. I was only walking past. I wasn't even suspecting it.

Dizzy: 'Chuck it on the roof, man.'

X-Fire: 'Do you want it?'

Me: 'Yes.'

X-Fire: 'What you gonna do for it?'

Everybody was watching. I stopped trying to get my bag back. I knew I'd never reach it because his arm was too high. I was just going to tell the teachers that an eagle came down and stole it.

X-Fire: 'What country you from anyway?'

Me: 'Ghana.'

Dizzy: 'Do the cops have guns there? They do, innit.'

Clipz: 'They make their houses out of cowshit, innit. I seen it.'

X-Fire: 'Don't be a dick, man. He's alright. Tell you what, you can have your bag back if you do a job for me.'

Me: 'I don't need a job. I just lock the doors and carry the heavy things.'

Killa: 'What's he on about? You're funny, man.'

Dizzy: 'If you roll with us we'll show you the times. We'll look out for you, innit.'

X-fire can throw the basketball miles. He always scores. I can't even score because the basketball's too heavy. I think they put a rock inside it to trick you. I just dribble then pass it to Chevon or Brayden. When I'm Year 11 my muscles will be big like X-Fire's. I'm already the fastest. I could be the strongest as well.

X-Fire gave me my bag back in the end. It was a mighty relief.

X-Fire: 'Keep it real, Ghana. You get any shit, you come to me, yeah?'

I didn't want any shit, I just wanted to get my chop before Manik stole it all. You're not allowed to eat with your fingers, you have to use the fork or the dinner ladies will ban you. I still use my fingers sometimes, just to make the pile on the fork. Nobody can stop you, it's a free country.

One lady who lives in the never-normal flats drives a chair car. It's just a chair on wheels. You just sit in it and drive it like a car except instead of a steering wheel it has handlebars. I'd love to drive it one time. It only goes slow though.

She was going to the shops. I was going home. Two smaller kids came from nowhere. I wasn't even suspecting it. They came running out of the alley and jumped on the back of her car. I saw it with my own two eyes. Asweh, it was very funny. They held on all the way to the shops.

The lady didn't even know them. She tried to get them off but they wouldn't listen.

Chair car lady: 'Oi, what you playing at? Get out of it!'

But they didn't even care. When they got to the shops, they just jumped off and ran away. They didn't even say thank you for the ride! It was the funniest thing I've ever seen.

It's the lady's own fault. She's not even sick. She can talk and everything. She only needs the chair car because she's too fat to walk.

Chair car lady: 'What are you looking at? Why didn't you stop 'em, eh?'

I didn't say anything. I didn't even want a ride. I'd rather run, it's quicker and you can't get slaps for it.

I don't have a favourite raindrop, they're all as good as each other. They're all the best. That's what I think anyway. I always look up at the sky when it's raining. It feels brutal. It's a bit hutious because the rain's so big and fast and you think it will go in your eye. But you have to keep your eyes open or you won't get the feeling. I try to follow one raindrop all the way down from the cloud to the ground. Asweh, it's impossible. All you can see is the rain. You can't follow just one raindrop, it's too busy and all the other raindrops get in the way.

The best bit is running in the rain. If you point your face up to the sky at the same time as running, it nearly feels like you're flying. You can close your eyes or you can keep them open, it's up to you. I like both. You can open your mouth if you want. The rain just tastes like water from the tap except it's quite warm. Sometimes it tastes like metal.

Before you start running, find an empty bit of the world with nothing in the way. No trees or buildings and no other people. That way you won't crash into anything. Try to go in a straight line. Then you just run as fast as you can. At first you're scared of crashing into something but don't let it put you off. Just run. It's easy. The rain on your face and the wind makes it feel like you're going superfast. It's very refreshing. I dedicated my rain run to the dead boy. It was a better present than a bouncy ball. I kept my eyes closed the whole time and I didn't even fall over.

One time me and Lydia were in the lift when it broke down. It stopped for about one hour. It wasn't even hutious. Lydia was screaming like a maniac. I had to stop her going crazy with rock, paper, scissors. I saved the day all over again.

Lydia: 'Advise yourself! I didn't scream!'

Me: 'Yes you did. This was Lydia: Make it go, make it go! I hate being stuck!'

Lydia: 'Shut up Harrison. He's lying.'

We were showing Auntie Sonia our lift. Auntie Sonia says she doesn't have a lift where she lives, only stairs. It didn't even feel fair.

Me: 'It only makes your belly turn over at the beginning. You won't get sick.'

Lydia: 'Advise yourself, she's seen a lift before. She's been to America. They go up to one hundred over there.'

Me: 'How! I don't believe you!'

Auntie Sonia: 'It's true. They call them elevators. They even make your ears go pop like on the aeroplane.'

Me: 'Cool!'

Auntie Sonia's been everywhere. She's met a hell of famous people. One time she made Will Smith's bed (he's in I Am Legend). They're not in the room when she's making their bed, they wait outside. Sometimes they give you a tip. One time they gave Auntie Sonia a twenty dollars. One time a hotel man gave Auntie Sonia a hundred dollars just to shag it up with him. She said no because he was too ugly. Mamma went proper red-eyes when she told her. She hates shagging talk.

Mamma: 'Not in front of them!'

Me and Lydia: 'We don't mind!'

Next time Auntie Sonia goes to America she's bringing back some Fruit Loops. They're the sweetest of all the cereals. I'm going to have them for breakfast every day for the rest of my life.

Mamma: 'Are you planning another trip then? You just got here.'

Auntie Sonia: 'It's been six months.'

Mamma: 'And your feet are itchy already?'

Auntie Sonia: 'It's not my feet I'm thinking of.'

Mamma looked at Auntie Sonia's fingers where they were all black and cracked. You had to pretend like you didn't know about them and everything was normal. My favourite word of today is fuzzy-wuzzy. Mamma and Auntie Sonia were smashing the tomatoes for palaver sauce. It was like a race to see who could kill them first. Asweh, it made me glad I'm not a tomato!

Mamma: 'So she says to Janette, are there any other midwives there? And Janette ask her why. And she says it's her first baby, do I know what I'm doing. She says she don't want no fuzzy-wuzzy just got off the boat.'

Auntie Sonia: 'Fuzzy-wuzzy? That's a new one.'

Mamma: 'I swear by God. I said I didn't come on a boat, I came on a plane. They have planes now where I come from. I shouldn't have said anything really. I had to apologise to her.'

Auntie Sonia: 'How! You had to apologise? I would rough her. I'd tell her I gave her a juju curse, her baby will come with two heads. She'd probably believe it.'

Mamma: 'You can't say that, it's not professional.'

Auntie Sonia: 'Fuzzy-wuzzy. I'll have to remember that one.'

Me: 'What's a fuzzy-wuzzy?'

Mamma stopped smashing the tomatoes. You wanted them to escape while they had the chance. Run for your lives!

Mamma: 'It's what they call you when you're new at the hospital. Sometimes if you're new the patient doesn't trust you to do the job. It just means somebody who's new.'

Me: 'Why fuzzy-wuzzy though? I don't get it.'

Mamma: 'I don't know. Don't disturb.'

Auntie Sonia: 'It's for the noise the nurse's shoes make. When they're new they squeak on the floor. The noise just sounds like fuzzy-wuzzy, that's all.'

Me: 'How come your shoes don't make that noise in here?'

Mamma: 'It only works on shiny floors.'

It sounded quite crazy. It could be true. Next time I get new shoes I'm going to try it. The corridors in the flats have proper shiny floors. I bet they'll make the dope-finest squeaking you've ever heard.

Next time we're going to Auntie Sonia's house. She lives in Tottenham, you have to go on the tube. Connor Green says the tube police have machine guns and if you run away they shoot you. I'll just have to hold my running in, that's all. It's only until I get to the other side.

Jordan doesn't go to school. He got excluded for kicking a teacher. Excluded means thrown out. I didn't believe it at first, but even his mamma said it was true. She thinks it's brutal. Jordan's mamma smokes black cigarettes. The paper is liquorice flavour. Jordan's lighter than me because his mamma's obruni. I told you, everything's crazy around here!

Jordan: 'My mum's trying to get me in another school but no one wants me, innit. I don't even care man, school's shit anyway.'

Me: 'What do you do instead?'

Jordan: 'Play Xbox. Watch DVDs.'

Me: 'Does your mamma make you do jobs?'

Jordan: 'No way! Why, does yours?'

Me: 'Sometimes.'

Jordan: 'That's so gay.'

Me: 'Only the man's work. Locking the doors, checking for invaders, things like that.'

Jordan: 'It's still gay.'

We greeted the rubbish pipe (it's a special pipe where the rubbish goes. Inside is metal and it smells like shit, it goes all the way down to Hell). We have to greet it every time for luck, it's a tradition. Just stick your head in and shout:

Me and Jordan: **'Bollocks!'**

and it makes a dope-fine echo. Only don't stick your head in too far for if it sucks you in. Jordan jumped on my back and tried to push me down the pipe but I spun around just in time. Then I had to hold the lift door while Jordan did a big spit all on the buttons. When he got out Fag Ash Lil got in. We waited for the doors to close. We could hear her when she pressed the button Jordan did a spit on. She didn't know about the spit.

Fag Ash Lil: 'Bloody hell!'

She said bloody hell! It was very funny. I only felt scared after. Fag Ash Lil killed her husband and ate him in a pie. Everybody agrees. That's why her eyes are all mad and watery, it's from eating human meat.

Jordan: 'Bloody hell bloody hell! Stupid bastard!'

Me: 'Bastard!'

You can say bastard, it just means somebody who doesn't have a papa. Fag Ash Lil's papa died a hundred years ago so it's not even lying. Bollocks are just the same as nuts.

In Art Tanya Sturridge was absent and Poppy sat in her chair instead. Then she was almost right next to me. She stayed there for the whole lesson, she didn't even move away. It made me go all hot. I couldn't concentrate because I wanted to see what Poppy was doing. She was painting her fingernails. She actually used the paint for pictures to paint her fingernails with. I watched her the whole time. I couldn't even help it.

She painted one fingernail pink and the next fingernail green, and then the next one pink again, in a pattern. It took a very long time. She was very careful, she didn't make a single mistake. It was very relaxing. It made me feel sleepy just watching it. I used Poppy's hair for my yellow. Mrs Fraser says inspiration for your mood picture can come from anywhere, from the world or inside you. I got my inspiration from Poppy Morgan's hair. I only didn't tell her for if it ruined it.

Colour Theory teaches you about using different colours to mean different moods or to tell a story. The colours tell them what you felt like inside. It doesn't need a shape, it can just be colours. It doesn't have to look like anything. Mine is made of green, yellow and red. The yellow is sunshine and Poppy Morgan's hair. The green is for the time Agnes was crawling on the grass in children's park and she saw a cricket and tried to catch him. That was very funny. You should see her face when the cricket jumped away, she was very surprised. She wasn't suspecting it in a million years. When he landed she tried to catch him again. She didn't give up, she just carried on trying and trying. In the end I caught the cricket for her. She squeezed his leg. She squeezed too hard at first and nearly broke it off but after that she just touched it nice and gentle. Her fingers are very tiny but fat at the same time. I love them the most. Only babies can be tiny and fat at the same time, they're very lucky like that.

The red is the dead boy's blood. I couldn't get it dark enough so I mixed some black with it, just a little bit at a time. It still didn't look how it was in my head. I couldn't get it to match. Asweh, it was very vexing.

45

Mrs Fraser: 'You'll wear a hole in the paper if you carry on like that!'

In the end I just gave up. My eyes were all blurry and Poppy was looking at me funny like she thought I was a spaz. That's when I knew it was time to give up.

There are warnings everywhere. They're only there to help you. They're very funny. The big fence around the front of school has hutious spikes on top to stop the robbers climbing over. There's a sign on the fence:

Asweh, it's very funny. There are signs all over school telling you to turn off your mobile phone:

Connor Green: 'It's 'cause the teachers are all robots and the signal from the phones messes with their circuits, innit.'

Nathan Boyd: 'There should be a warning sign on you. No talking to this boy. Serious risk of bullshit.'

Connor Green: 'F— off.'

We found another crazy sign by the river:

We love that sign. It's our new alltime favourite.

Me: 'We should dare Nathan Boyd to eat the watercress.'

Dean: 'Good idea. He'll never do it.'

The river is behind the trees. It's only dark. It's too small for swimming and the water is acid, if you fell in all your skin would burn off. There's a platform that goes over the shit pipe that's big enough for both the two of you to sit on. You can just sit there and watch all the things in the river go past. It's usually just sticks or cans or paper. Whoever sees a human head first gets a million points.

We were looking for the knife the dead boy got killed with. It's called the murder weapon. If we see it, we're going to fish it out and take it to the police.

Me: 'Keep your eyes peeled, it could be anywhere.'

Dean: 'Roger that. I'm on it, Captain.'

We're proper detectives now. It's a personal mission. The dead boy even told the rogues to leave me alone one time when they were hooting me for wearing ankle-freezers (that's when the legs of your trousers are too short).

47

I didn't even ask him, he just helped me for no reason. I wanted him to be my friend after that but he got killed before it came true. That's why I have to help him now, he was my friend even if he didn't know about it. He was my first friend who got killed and it hurts too much to forget. There'd be fingerprints and blood on the murder weapon. If we found it we could identify the killer, that's what Dean said. He's seen all the shows.

Dean: 'And if we help catch the killer we'll get a reward, innit.'

Me: 'How much?'

Dean: 'Dunno. A grand. Maybe more.'

A grand is a thousand. It sounded like too much. If I got a grand I'd buy a ticket for Papa and Agnes and Grandma Ama and if there was any left over I'd buy a proper football made of skin that doesn't fly away.

Me: 'Keep looking. He definitely came this way.'

Dean: 'Are you sure it was a knife?'

Me: 'Yes! It was this big.'

I showed him how long with my hands.

Dean: 'Right you are, Chief.' (That's how detectives talk. It's just a rule.)

If the killer threw the knife in the river it could be gone to the sea by now. It could already be too late. Asweh, it was very nervous. I didn't want them to get away with it. We went quiet again for better searching.

There's even no fish in the river. It made me feel proper sad. There should be fish even if they're not tasty ones. There's no ducks left either, the smaller kids killed them with a screwdriver. The babies just got crushed. We didn't see the murder weapon. We only saw a wheel from a bike all rusty and bent up. Next time we'll bring torchlights and gloves for digging in the sharpest weeds.

APRIL

The launderette is a shop just for washing machines. It's at the bottom of Luxembourg House. The washing machines don't belong to any one person, they're for everybody who lives in the flats. You have to pay them money to make them work. Every machine is big enough to fit a person inside. One day I'm going to try it. I'm going to sleep inside it, it's one of my alltime ambitions.

You can use any machine, it doesn't have to be the same one every time. My favourite is the one nearest the window, somebody wrote a poem on it:

> *Round and round my skivvies go,*
> *Where they stop, nobody knows.*
> *Round and round go my smalls,*
> *A lovely hammock for my balls.*

We have to pretend we didn't see it or Mamma will make us use another machine.

The clothes take donkey hours to wash. Me and Lydia play a game. We watch the clothes going round in the other people's machines. Whenever we see a pant it's a hundred points. If we see a bra it's a thousand. You have to be very quiet when you call them out so Mamma doesn't find out about the game. You have to shout in a whisper.

Me: 'Pant!'

Lydia: 'Where?'

Me: 'There, look! The white ones.'

Lydia: 'They're the same ones!'

Me: 'No, those had little flowers on. These are plain, see. A hundred points!'

Lydia: 'Confusionist!'

One time I saw a pair of cowboy boots. They were pink. The lady was actually washing them in the washing machine! It was brilliant. It was a million points. Lydia will never beat me now. You'll never see pink cowboy boots again as long as you live.

Altaf is very quiet. Nobody really knows him. You're not supposed to talk to Somalis because they're pirates. Everybody agrees. If you talk to them you might give away a clue to where you keep your treasure and the next thing you know, your wife has been strangled alive and they're throwing you to the sharks. Me and Altaf don't have to go to RE. Mamma doesn't want me to hear about the false gods, she says it's a waste of time, and Altaf's mamma thinks the same thing. Instead of doing RE we go to the library. You're supposed to study but normally we just read a book. It was me who started talking first. I just wanted to know what Altaf thinks. Would he rather be a robot or a human.

Me: 'I think a human's better because you get to eat all the fine food. Robots never get to eat any of it, they don't need food.'

Altaf: 'But a robot's better because you can't get killed.'

Me: 'That's true.'

In the end both the two of us decided we'd rather be a robot.

Altaf's going to design cars when he grows up. You should see his drawings, they're bo-styles. He's always drawing cars and crazy things. He drew a 4×4 with a gun at the back.

Altaf: 'It's so the enemies can't get you. It's a special gun that never runs out of bullets. And all the windows and the body's all bulletproof too, a tank could even drive over it and it wouldn't get squashed.'

Me: 'Nice! If they make a car like that I'll definitely buy it!'

I don't think Altaf can be a pirate if he can't even swim. He's scared of the water even with armbands on.

Mamma doesn't like the shows, she says there's too much jibber-jabber. Her only favourite show is the news. Somebody dies on the news every day. It's nearly always a child. Sometimes they're chooked like the dead boy and sometimes they're shot or run over by a car. One time a little girl got eaten by a dog. They showed a picture of the dog and he looked just like Harvey. The little girl must have pulled his tail. Dogs only attack people who are cruel to them. Somebody should have told her to never pull a dog's tail, they don't like it. Nobody told her and that's why she's dead.

Mamma likes it best when it's a child who died. That's when she prays the hardest. She prays proper hard and squeezes you until you think you're going to burst. Grown-ups love sad news, it gives them something special to pray for. That's why the news is always sad. They haven't found the dead boy's killer yet.

Newsman: 'Police are still appealing for witnesses.'

Me: 'What do you think the killer looks like?'

Mamma: 'I don't know. He could be anybody.'

Me: 'Do you think he's black or white?'

Mamma: 'I don't know.'

Me: 'I bet it's one of the junkies from the pub.'

Mamma: 'Where did you get that from? Lydia, why do you tell him these things?'

Lydia: 'How! I didn't tell him anything!'

A killer is the same all over the world, they never change. They have little piggy eyes and smoke cigarettes. Sometimes they have gold teeth and spiderwebs on their neck. Their eyes are red. They're always spitting and they get their blood from the shadows. The pub is probably full up of killers but we'll only look for the one who killed the dead boy, he's the only one we knew. If we caught him it would be like getting Forever back. It would be like everything still works the way it's supposed to. I'll wait until Dean comes with me so he can be my backup. Detectives only work in pairs, it's just safer like that.

If a dog attacks you, the best way to stop it is to put your finger up its bumhole. There's a secret switch up the dog's bumhole that when you touch it their mouth opens automatically and they let go of whatever they were biting. Connor Green told us. After he told us, everybody called Connor Green a pervert because he goes around putting his finger up dogs' bumholes.

Kyle Barnes: 'Pervert!'

Brayden Campbell: 'Dogf—er!'

Nathan Boyd can get three jawbreakers in his mouth at the same time. Everybody knows if you swallow one you'll die but he doesn't even care. Nathan Boyd isn't scared of anything. We always try to think of a bigger dare for him to do. It always has to be bigger than before.

Kyle Barnes: 'You have to run through the whole school shouting hairy bollocks.'

Me: 'You have to throw somebody's pen out the window.'

Connor Green: 'You have to lick that crack spoon.'

There was a spoon on the grass near the main gate. It was all bent and burned. It was the most disgusting spoon in the world.

Connor Green: 'You have to put it all the way in your mouth and suck it.'

Nathan Boyd: 'I'm not sucking that, it's got crack on it.'

Kyle Barnes: 'Pussy.'

Nathan Boyd: 'F— off. Can I wipe it first?'

Connor Green: 'No, you have to suck it like that.'

Nathan Boyd: 'Why don't you suck it? You're used to sucking dicks.'

Kyle Barnes: 'Don't try and pussy out. You can't ask us to dare you and not do the dare.'

Me: 'You asked us.'

Nathan Boyd: 'F— it then.'

Nathan licked the spoon. He gave it one good lick then he threw it away. I thought he was going to puke but he didn't.

Kyle Barnes: 'That wasn't even a suck, that was only a lick!'

Nathan Boyd: 'You suck it then.'

Nobody else would suck the spoon. Nobody else would even touch it again. Nathan Boyd is the bravest in Year 7, it's even official. But even Nathan Boyd wouldn't dare to set the fire alarm off. When the alarm goes off for real, the firemen have to come to put out the fire. Even if there's not really a fire they still have to check. If it's a false alarm and they find out who did it they go to jail. It's a crime to set off the alarm if there's no real fire because while the firemen are checking there could be a real fire somewhere else and somebody could die.

X-Fire: 'You sure you ready for this? You ain't gotta do it if you ain't got the balls.'

If I was in the Dell Farm Crew Vilis couldn't abuse me anymore. If I wanted to swap my trainers the other person would have to do it and there'd be no swapping back. I gave my cheesecake to Manik. I got out first. There were some people in the library but the corridor was empty.

X-Fire: 'Just break the glass, innit. It's easy, it's only plastic.'

Me: 'What if it doesn't break the first time?'

Dizzy: 'Just keep going till it does. We need to know you've got what it takes.'

X-Fire: 'We'll back you up, innit. I'll tell you if someone's coming.'

It's best to use the side of your hand and not the knuckles. I can't run until the alarm has gone off. Everything went proper quiet. I could feel my heart going proper fast like a crazy drum, my mouth tasted like metal. Some people came past. I had to wait until they were gone. Hurry up hurry up hurry up! Sharp-sharp! I wanted to ease myself but there was no time.

X-Fire and Dizzy were waiting at the doors.

X-Fire: 'Go on! Put some hustle in it!'

I bashed the alarm. I did it proper hard but the glass wouldn't break. It just made my hand go funny. I tried pressing the glass with my thumb but it wouldn't do anything. I wanted a hammer. I wanted to run. I looked around for help but X-Fire and Dizzy were gone, all I could hear was them laughing in the distance.

Dizzy: 'Pussy boy!'

I just went red-eyes. I bashed the glass again. It was no good. I just didn't have the blood. I just wanted to get away before somebody saw me. I ran down the stairs. My legs went like rubber. I thought I was going to crash but I kept going. I ran all the way down the stairs and under the bridge to the Humanities block. I made it to the toilets. Safe. My belly felt proper sick. I think the Dell Farm Crew are my enemy now. That's what happens when you fail your mission. Adjei, my hands are too soft for everything!

Mr Frimpong is the loudest singer in church, even if he's the oldest. He always sings the hardest from all of us. He just wants his voice to be the first one that God hears.

It's not even fair. What if he sings so loud that God can't hear anybody else? Then Mr Frimpong will get all their favours as well. It's not fair when you think about it. He gets proper sweaty because he always wears a tie and his top button buttoned up.

Lydia: 'He probably wears a tie in the bath.'

Me: 'Don't be disrespectful!'

Lydia: 'Shut up, creep!'

Mr Frimpong got so sweaty he actually fell down. He went asleep and everything. The aunties all fought each other to be the first one to help him. Pastor Taylor had to slap his face to wake him up. When he woke up the aunties said Praise God. But I think it was God who sent him asleep in the first place. He probably didn't like his singing anymore, it's too loud.

That's why they put cages on the windows. It's not to stop the rogues throwing stones, it's to stop the windows breaking from Mr Frimpong's singing.

We said another prayer for the dead boy's mamma and one for the police that God will give them the insight to catch the killer.

Me: 'What's insight?'

Pastor Taylor: 'It means wisdom. It is a great gift God has given us.'

Mr Tomlin is probably the wisest person I know. I have him for Science. He can make a battery out of a lemon. I'm not even bluffing, he really did it: all you do is put the penny in one end of the lemon and the nail in the other end. The acid in the lemon juice is electric. The penny and the nail are conductors. Conductors make the electricity come alive. When we connected four lemons together they made enough power for the light to come on. It was quite amazing. Everybody cheered. If Mr Tomlin worked for the police they'd catch the killer in no time.

I prayed for the insight so I'd ask the right questions. Dean doesn't believe in it so I prayed for both the two of us.

Dean: 'Can you do one for us not getting our heads kicked in?'

Me: 'We'll be alright, don't worry. They won't kill us today, they're too busy getting boozed.'

It was very risky but interviewing suspects is all part of the job. If you're going to get scared all the time then you've got no business being a detective, you should just hand in your badge and go home. The pub smelled like all the beer in the world even from outside. We tried not to breathe in for if we got boozed (Dean says it clouds your judgement). Everybody who went in or came out could be the killer. They all looked at us like a hungry vampire. We just stayed by the door. As long as we keep one foot on the pavement we're safe.

Dean: 'Who are we looking for exactly?'

Me: 'I don't know. I think he was black but I'm not sure. I only saw one hand when he bent down to get the knife. It could have been a glove. I was quite far away.'

Dean: 'Let's just start with the black ones then. What about him?'

Me: 'No, too tall. Our man was shorter.'

Dean: 'Roger that. Alright, this one?'

There was a man by the fruit machine (it doesn't actually give you fruit, it's just a game they play in the pub. You feed the machine some money and it makes all the lights flash). He didn't have any spiderwebs but he did have an earring and his eyes looked deadly like he wanted to destroy everybody. He was shaking the machine to make the lights come on and swearing. Killers always have a quick temper.

Me: 'Could be. What shall we ask him? Did you do it?'

Dean: 'Don't be a retard, you can't just ask it straight out. You have to try and trap him. Ask him if he knew the victim and just see what his eyes do. If he looks away it means he's guilty.'

Me: 'Will you ask him? I'll be backup.'

Dean: 'I'm not asking him. It was your idea, you ask him.'

Me: 'I'm not going in there. I'll wait until he comes out.'

Dean: 'I knew you'd do this. I'm not waiting here all day.'

Me: 'Go and ask him then.'

Dean: 'In a minute. Let's just see what he does first. Don't let him see you watching him, we want him to act natural.'

We got back behind the door and peeked through the glass. The killer finished his fruit machine game and bought another glass of beer. The other men drank their drinks or texted or just watched the boobs of the bar lady even if she was old and looked like a scarecrow. All the time the smell of beer was getting in our noses and making us crazy. It gave Dean ants in his pant. When the suspect came out we had to stop ourselves from running away. You can't show fear, they can smell it like a wasp.

Suspect: 'What's up lads, you looking for someone?'

Dean: 'We're just waiting for my dad.'

Suspect: 'You don't want to hang around out here, there's too many arseholes about.'

It was a trick. He was trying to get rid of us before he gave the game away. He lit a cigarette: another telltale sign!

Me: 'Did you know the boy who died?'

Suspect: 'Do what?'

Dean: 'The one who got stabbed. He was his cousin.'

Suspect: 'No, I didn't know him.'

Me: 'Do you know who did it?'

Suspect: 'I wish I did. These f—ing kids, they need drowning at birth.'

Dean: 'How do you know it was a kid who did it?'

Suspect: 'It's always kids, innit. You wanna stay away from all that shit, boys, it only ends one way. Be smart, yeah?'

Me: 'We are.'

His smoke was going in our eyes. It was another trick to make us blind so we couldn't pick any clues up. I'm telling you, they're very clever. In the end we just had to give up.

Dean: 'They're never gonna tell us nothing. As soon as they know they're being interviewed they just mug us off. We're not gonna get anywhere by asking, we have to find out for ourselves.'

Me: 'How?'

Dean: 'Surveillance and evidence, it's the only way. CSI-style, fingerprints, DNA. That shit don't lie.'

I made a thinking face like I knew what he was talking about. Dean's the brains because he's seen all the shows. I washed all the beer smell off before Mamma got home from work. She says a man who smells of beer is a mess waiting to happen.

Violence always came too easy to you, that's the problem.
It always felt too good. Remember the first time you trod
on an ant, and with an infant stamp made the moving still,
the present past? Wasn't that a sickly sweet epiphany? Such
power in your feet and at your fingertips such temptation!
It would take some act of charity to give all that good stuff
away. You'd need to be something greater than just another
invention of a spiteful god.

Kyle Barnes stuck his compass in Manik's leg. Manik
screamed like a girl even if there was no blood. Everybody
laughed.

Manik: 'What did you do that for?'

Kyle Barnes: 'So you'd do that.'

Kyle Barnes chooked him again. Manik screamed again.
He was like a squeaky pig. It was like the compass was a
fork and Kyle Barnes was testing to see if he was done yet.
Asweh, it was very funny. Kyle Barnes loves it when we
have a supply teacher. Most of the time they don't even do
the lesson, they just read the newspaper. That's when Kyle
Barnes comes after you with the compass. You have to not
get chooked but you're not allowed to get off your chair.
It's proper hard. I've been chooked about three times. It
doesn't really hurt, it just gives you a crazy surprise. There's
never any blood.

The best weapon would be an umbrella that's really a
poison gun. You think it's just an umbrella but actually it

62

shoots poison bullets out the end. We were talking about what the best weapons are.

Kyle Barnes thinks the best weapon is an AK-47.

Dean thinks it's a knuckleduster with extra long spikes.

Chevon Brown thinks the best weapon is a crossbow. But you have to be very strong to shoot it because it's proper heavy. The arrows are called bolts. They're longer than you.

Brayden Campbell: 'You couldn't shoot a crossbow. You couldn't even pick it up.'

Chevon Brown: 'F— off, man. You couldn't even shoot an AK-47, the recoil would knock your head off.'

Brayden Campbell: 'Bullshit. I could do it one-handed.'

Me and Dean: 'My arse.'

Me and Dean: 'Jinx!'

We said jinx straight away. The curse can't even touch us.

I know nearly all the rules now. There's over one hundred. Some of them are to keep you out of danger. Some of them are just so the teachers can control you.

Some of them are so your friends know what side you're on. If you follow those rules, they'll know they can trust you and then you can roam with them. One rule is, if you and your friend say the same thing at the same time you have to say jinx or you'll be cursed. If you don't say jinx you'll shit yourself for one day after.

Some rules I have learned from my new school

No running on the stairs.

No singing in class.

Always put your hand up before you ask a question.

Don't swallow the gum or it will get stuck in your guts and you'll die.

Jumping in the puddle means you're a retard (I don't even agree with this one).

Going around the puddle means you're a girl.
The last one in close the door.
The first one to answer the question loves the teacher.
If a girl looks at you three times in a row it means she
    loves you.
If you look at her back you love her.

He who smelt it dealt it.
He who denied it supplied it.
He who sensed it dispensed it.
He who knew it blew it.
He who noted it floated it.
He who declared it aired it.
He who spoke it broke it.
He who exposed it composed it.
He who blamed it flamed it.
(All these are just for farts.)

If you look at the back of a mirror you'll see the devil.
Don't eat the soup. The dinner ladies pissed in it.
Don't lend Ross Kelly your pen. He picks his arse klinkers
    with it.
Keep to the left (everywhere). The right is out of bounds.
The library stairs are safe.
If he wears a pinky ring he's a gay (a pinky ring is a ring
    on your little finger).
If she wears a bracelet on her ankle she's a lesbian (shags
    it up with other ladies).

There are more but my memory ran out. My arse means
you don't believe it. It's just the same as calling them a liar.

X-Fire wouldn't let us past. They were waiting outside
the cafeteria. They were all standing in our way and they
wouldn't move. You didn't know if it was a trick or for real.

Dizzy: 'What's up, pussy boys?'

Clipz: 'I heard you failed the first test. That's weak, man!'

I wanted to be a bomb. I wanted to knock them all down. That's what it felt like. I kept waiting for him to laugh but his face was still hard like he meant it. Like we were enemies.

X-Fire: 'Don't worry, Ghana. I'll think of something easier for you next time, you'll be alright. What you got then, Ginger?'

Dean went all stiff. My belly went cold.

Dean: 'I ain't got nothing.'

Dizzy: 'Don't lie to us, man. What's in your pockets? Show me.'

We couldn't move. He had to show them or we'd never get past. It wasn't even fair.

Dean: 'I've got a quid, that's it. I need it.'

Dizzy: 'Yeah well, shit happens, innit.'

He took Dean's quid. There was nothing you could do to stop it. He was very sad, you could tell. He should have put it back in his sock after dinner. I wished I had a quid instead but Mamma only gives me the correct money and no extra.

Dean: 'F—ing hell, man.'

Dizzy: 'Don't be fronting me you little bitch, I'll batter you.'

In the end they let us past. I felt sorry for Dean for having his quid stolen but I couldn't help admiring it. I wish I could make them do what I say. If I was the big fish all the little fish would be scared of me. They'd get out of my way so I had the sea all to myself and all the food in it. I'd only let my favourite little fishes work for me, like when the pilot fish eats all the seadust off the shark to stop his gills getting blocked up (I read about it in my Creatures of the Deep book, only 10p from the market).

Me: 'It's only because I'm black. If you were black they'd let you in the gang as well.'

Dean: 'I don't wanna be in their stupid gang, all they do is rob people. Don't go with them, they're numpties.'

Me: 'I was only pretending so they wouldn't rough us too bad.'

Dean: 'I hate them, man.'

Me: 'Me too.'

Somebody left an old mattress on the green. There were a hell of smaller kids already playing on it. We told them to get off.

Dean: 'Piss off or we'll batter you!'

We let the smaller kids watch. I did about ten flips. Dean did about five. It was nearly as good as a real trampoline. I got really high. I was the only one who could nearly do a double flip. Some of the smaller kids cheered. It was brutal. We were there for donkey hours. You forgot about being hungry, you just wanted to get higher every time.

We were going to own the mattress. We were going to charge the smaller kids 50p to jump on it. It was Dean's idea.

Dean: 'We'll need some rules though. Only two people on the mattress at the same time and you have to take your shoes off.'

We were going to make a million. Then Terry Takeaway came and Asbo eased himself all over the mattress. Then you didn't want to bounce on it anymore.

Me: 'Asbo, you dirty boy! We were using that!'

Terry Takeaway: 'Sorry boys! A dog's gotta do what a dog's gotta do!'

I made the roof for Papa's shop proper strong. Papa loved it, you could tell. He said it would last longer than him and me put together. It will keep everything dry when it rains and Papa nice and cool when it's sunny. We made the roof out of chemshi and wood. Papa made the frame of wood and then we put the chemshi on top. I put the bolts on. He only helped me with the first one, I did the rest on my own. It was easy. When it rains the noise is mighty loud. It makes the rain feel even stronger. You feel safe under the chemshi. You feel strong because you made it yourself.

It took donkey hours to build the roof. When we finished, the shop looked more dope-fine than before. Me and Papa drank a whole bottle of beer to celebrate. Papa had most of it but I had one bit. I didn't get boozed, it was just lovely, it made my burps taste like burning. Mamma and Lydia and Agnes and Grandma Ama all came to greet the new shop. They loved it as much as we did, you could tell. Everybody was smiling from ear to ear.

Mamma: 'Did you make that all yourself? Clever boy.'

Me: 'Papa helped me.'

Grandma Ama: 'Was he a good worker?'

Me: 'He's a bit lazy.'

Papa: 'Eh! Gowayou!'

Me: 'I'm only joking.'

We hung a lantern from the roof so the shop can stay open at night. The lantern was Agnes's favourite bit. Babies always love things that hang or swing. They always try to touch it even if it's hot. She cried when the lantern burned her fingers. I sucked them all better again. I'm the best at sucking them better, my spit has healing in it.

Papa makes the best things. His chairs are always the softest and his tables are strong enough to stand on. He makes them all from bamboo. Even if the drawers are wood, the frame is still bamboo. Bamboo is the best material because it's very strong and light at the same time. It's easy to cut with a machete or a saw. You have to saw with care so you make a straight cut. You have to imagine everything you make is your best.

Papa: 'If you can saw bamboo straight, you can saw a leg off. It's the same thing. This is good practice. Pretend the bamboo is somebody's leg. You want to make the cut as straight as you can so it will heal properly.'

Me: 'But I don't want to cut off their leg.'

Papa: 'You might have to. A doctor doesn't get to choose his patients. They're relying on you.'

It was ages ago, when I still wanted to be a doctor. I sawed with extra care. I pretended like it was for real, I was even trying not to hurt them. When I sawed all the way through and the bamboo fell, I even tried to catch it. I thought it was their leg.

Papa: 'Now sharp-sharp, put it in some ice! We can give it to somebody else.'

Me: 'But the leg's bad.'

Papa: 'One man's trash is another man's treasure. We'll give it to a bush man, they won't know the difference.'

Asweh, it was very funny.

I don't know why Mamma has to work at night as well. It's not even fair. Why can't babies just be born in the daytime.

Mamma: 'They come whenever they feel like it. You were born at night. You were waiting for the stars to come out.'

Lydia: 'And there was a full moon, that's why you're dey touch.'

Me: 'No I'm not!'

I just wish Mamma was here so Miquita wouldn't keep coming round all the time. I only let her in after she promised not to suck me off.

Miquita: 'OK, OK. I promise. Why you playing so hard to get?'

Me: 'Stop disturbing me!'

Miquita: 'Don't be like that, Juicy Fruit. I'm sorry.'

I unchained the chains and unlocked the locks. I had the potato smasher behind my back for if I needed to chase her away.

Miquita and Lydia are testing their costumes for the carnival. Both the two of them are parrots. You can only tell from the feathers. Most of the costume's just a body-stocking. The first time Lydia put it on she looked like a chicken who'd been plucked. The feathers she stuck on aren't even real, they came from Dance Club. Some are pink. You can't get a pink parrot.

Lydia: 'Yes you can, I've seen it.'

Me: 'That's a flamingo. You can't get a pink parrot, I'm telling you.'

Miquita: 'You can get a pink tongue though. Look.'

Miquita showed her tongue to me. She wriggled it around like a big nasty worm. It was disgusting.

If a girl has an earring in her tongue it means she's slack. Everybody agrees.

Miquita kept showing me her dancing. I didn't want to watch it. She kept shaking her behind in my face. Adjei, I just had to give up. I went to my room to put the CD player on (only a fiver from the watch doctor at the market). Ofori Amponsah makes the best music for burying Miquita's stupid voice with.

Miquita: 'Where you going Harri, you gonna make your lips nice and soft for me? You wanna borrow my Chapstick?'

Me: 'No thanks, Pigface! I'd rather kiss my own behind!'

Asweh, Miquita looks stupid in her costume. It makes her boobs look too close up like they're going to jump out and eat you. I even wish there was no such thing as boobs, then you wouldn't want to squeeze them all the time.

I only had to come out again to greet the chief, I couldn't hold it in anymore. Miquita was going. She gave Lydia a Nisa bag. They were looking inside it like it was some kind of crazy treasure. When she saw me she tried to hide it but it was too late. Both the two of them made a face like I'd broken some special secret. Then Miquita just split. Lydia put the bag in the black sack with the washing. She poked her head outside and started looking around like for enemies.

Lydia: 'Stay there, I won't be long.'

Me: 'Are you going to the launderette? I'm coming! I go beat you at the washing game again.'

Lydia: 'Too late!'

Lydia shut the door in my face. I wasn't going to take it lying down: I counted to ten, then I opened the door proper slow. I saw the lift doors closing. I ran down the stairs and watched Lydia get out at the ground floor. I followed her proper carefully all the way to the launderette. I hid around the corner where I could still see through the window.

Nobody else was in there. Lydia took just the things from the Nisa bag and put them in my favourite machine. Then it was some funny thing – she got Mamma's bleach from the washing sack and squeezed it all in the machine, all over the things inside. She did everything proper fast like it was a mission. Her hands were going so fast she couldn't even get the money in at first. You have to push the money slot in proper hard, if you do it too soft it just springs out again and you have to start from scratch. It took her about five goes to get it right. Then when the machine was going round she took the sack with the real washing still inside and split. She nearly crashed into me outside.

Lydia: 'How! Why did you follow me? I told you to stay indoors.'

Me: 'What was in the bag?'

Lydia: 'Nothing!'

Me: 'I saw it already.'

Lydia: 'I don't care. What is it then?'

Me: 'Just some stupid things.'

Lydia: 'Don't bring yourself, you don't even know. It's only leftover bits from the costume. They were no good, we got paint on them.'

You always know when Lydia's lying because her face goes angry (I always smile when I try to lie. I can't help it. I just have to give up. It's too risky and it makes me feel sick after). I saw the things in the bag and they didn't belong to a costume, they were the wrong colour and the material wasn't shiny. It was boy's clothes. I could see the hood and the Ecko rhinoceros. There was red all over. It was too dark for paint and too light for Shito. My belly went all cold.

X-Fire was coming with Harvey. When Lydia saw him she went proper quiet. Harvey pulled at his lead and licked his lips like a hungry wolf. I got my finger ready behind my back for if I needed to stick it up his bumhole. You won't be eating me today, mean dog! I've got a trick for you!

X-Fire: 'Did anyone see you?'

Lydia: 'No.'

X-Fire: 'Best get going, Ghana. He's hungry, innit.'

Harvey was pulling and sniffing all around like the air was made of meat. Me and Lydia just split before he got too crazy.

Me: 'Mamma go sound you when she finds out you used all the bleach.'

Lydia: 'I'll just tell her it was you. I'm not the one who has to ease myself on a cloud all the time.'

Me: 'No I don't.'

I don't have to do it all the time. I only wanted to see what God felt like.

The number one best trainers are Nike Air Max. Everybody agrees. They're the most bo-styles of all.

Adidas is number two. Or if you like Chelsea it can be number one because Adidas makes the Chelsea kit.

Reebok's number three and Puma's four. Puma makes the Ghana kit. Nobody believes me but they do. K-Swiss is also bo-styles. K-Swiss could even be number one if more people knew about them.

My trainers are called Sports. They're white all over. I got them from Noddy's shop in the market. They're very fast. Everybody calls them pants but they're just vexed because they go faster than them.

Connor Green always blames his trainers when he spoons the ball. It's never his fault, it's always his trainers.

Everybody: **'Spoon!'**

Connor Green: 'I can't help it, man! It's my trainers! They're not meant for football, they're only for running! At least they're not trampy like Harri's Sports!'

Me: 'Shut up, at least I can run faster than a snail!'

In football nobody used to pass to me. I thought it meant they hated me. Then I found out it's because I used the wrong command. Instead of saying pass to me you have to say man on. Apart from that the rules are the same as where I used to live. Vilis still doesn't pass to me but I don't care. Where he comes from (Latvia) they burn black people into tar and make roads out of them. Everybody agrees. I don't even want the ball from him, he can keep it. I still close my eyes when I go to head the ball. I can't help it. I always think it will hurt.

Vilis: 'You're so gay!'

Me: 'Gowayou, Potato House!' (Because he lives in a house made from potatoes.)

In Maths a wasp came to visit me. He was hanging out on my desk for donkey hours. I was sitting next to Poppy. Poppy was nearly crying. She kept thinking the wasp would sting her.

Poppy: 'One stung me when I was a baby. Now I'm allergic.'

Me: 'Don't worry, he's only visiting. I won't let him sting you.'

I tried to make Poppy feel better but it wouldn't work. She wanted me to smash the wasp but I just made him go on my exercise book, then I let him out the window. Dean opened the window and I let the wasp fly out. Everybody clapped. Poppy was very relieved, you could tell. I stopped her being scared.

Poppy: 'Thanks Harri.'

Me: 'That's OK. Piece of cake!' (That's what you say when something was easy.)

I've only loved one girl before. It was where I used to live. Her name's Abena, she's Lydia's friend. I only loved her for one day. She's very stupid. She thought if she slept with soap flakes on her face she'd wake up obruni in the morning. She even tried it. She wanted to be white for one day. She thought if she was white she'd get the diamonds like the lady in the American film.

Abena is in love with diamonds. She's never even seen one.

She put the soap flakes all over her face like paint. It didn't work, she was still black in the morning. It just made her skin go proper peely. We called her Peely Face. She hated it.

Everybody: 'Peely Face, Peely Face!'

She said it was only a joke but really she wanted it to work, you could tell. Abena's very stupid. I'm glad she didn't come with us. Her eyes are too small and she screams if you throw cocoa pods at her like they're bombs or something. In the end it just got too vexing so I stopped loving her.

You can use the Computer Club computers for home-work or email or the internet. You can't use them for chat room anymore because everybody kept asking each other what colour pant they were wearing. Now chat room's blocked. You can still do instant messages.

Me: 'Go on, ask her. Ask her what colour pant she's wearing.'

Lydia: 'Why do you want to know? Do you still love her?'

Me: 'How! No way, she's stupid! I was only joking!'

Lydia and Abena only chat about England and boys. Abena's news is always boring. It's only ever about another blackout or

Lydia: 'They found the twins.'

Me: 'My God! Are they alive?'

Lydia: 'Hang on, I can't type that fast.'

The twins were lost before we came here. Everybody was very worried. They always kill twins. People in the north think twins are cursed by the devil so they kill them before the juju gets them.

Lydia: 'They only found the skeletons. They were hold-ing hands.'

Me: 'God rest them.'

You had to be sad for one minute. I could see the bones. I pretended like a snake was coming out of the eyehole. I wanted to be sad but it wouldn't come out enough. All

I could think about was Poppy Morgan's lips. They're lovely and not too fat like Miquita's. I even watch them when she's talking to me, they make me go sleepy like a magician. If I had to suck anybody off it would be Poppy Morgan. I decided it today.

Me: 'Can we go now? The hunger idey kill me!'

Lydia: **'In a minute!'**

Me: **'Don't roar at me!'**

Asweh, Lydia's always roaring at me now. I don't even know how it happened. England makes people go crazy like that, I think it's from too many cars. When we used to go to the market in Kaneshie the smoke from all the cars and tro-tros made your head go proper blurry, and they were only about a hundred. Around here they're about a million. One time I crossed the road behind a bus and the smoke went right in my face: I swear by God, I felt like puking for two days after. I even went red-eyes with every-body. That's probably the reason why. From today onward going I'm just going to hold my breath.

Pounds looks quite stupid. The Queen looks too funny like she's not even taking it seriously. She looks like she was trying not to smile when the picture was taken, like somebody told a funny joke and she was trying to hold a laugh in. Mamma always goes serious when she pays the money to Julius, I saw it one time when she left the kitchen door open. Her hands go proper fast like there's dirt on the money and she doesn't want to get it on her fingers. Julius was watching proper carefully. Even when Mamma finished he counted the money again. He doesn't believe Mamma can count right but she can.

Mamma: 'It's all there.'

Julius: 'Hold on.'

He licks his fingers before he counts the money. His hands are quite hutious, they're too big and his rings look proper heavy. He finished counting and put the money in a special paperclip made from silver. There was a hell of other money already there. Asweh, Julius has more means than the president. He drives a Mercedes-Benz. It's dope-fine. It's the same car I'm going to buy when I'm older, the seats are the softest and you can all fit in the back and not even get chooked by their elbows. I even went in it when Julius took us to our new flat.

Me and Lydia played a game: every time you saw a white person you had to say **obruni!** proper loud. You got one point for every time you said it.

I won because I'm the best looker and the fastest teller. We saw nearly as many white people as black people. Asweh, it was the most I've ever seen in my whole life. It felt very crazy. I loved it.

Lydia: 'Ob

Me: **'Obruni!** Too slow!'

Lydia: 'That's not fair! That was my one, I saw him first!'

Me: 'But I said it first. One more point for me!'

Asweh, when I saw the towers for the first time I even went dizzy. We tried to guess which tower was ours. Lydia guessed the middle one and I guessed the one on the end furthest away.

I was right.

Then we had to guess what number floor would be ours. Lydia guessed 7 because 7 is her lucky number. I guessed top because top is the coolest.

None of us was right. It was 9.

Me: 'I think the door will be blue.'

Lydia: 'I think it will be green.'

Both the two of us were wrong. The door was brown. They're all brown.

It was my job to test everything. I won the job because

I asked first. If you snooze you lose. First I tested all the lights. They all came on straight away. Then I told it:

Me: 'Lights working!'

Then I tested all the taps. They all worked. You didn't even have to wait donkey hours for the water, it came straight away. I tested the taps in the kitchen, then the bathroom. Then I told it:

Me: 'Water working!'

Then I tested the floor for loose bits or holes. I did it by jumping all over. I jumped on every bit of floor. It took donkey hours. I made it go faster by dancing a little bit. Then I told it:

Me: 'Floors good!'

Then I checked all the roofs for holes where the rain might come in. All I had to do was look at the roofs. It was easy.

Me: 'Roofs good!'

Lydia: 'Shut up, I've got a headache!'

Then I tested for furniture and other things. I went around looking for things and whenever I found them I just told it:

Me: 'Got a sofa!'

Me: 'Got a table!'

Me: 'Got a bed!'

Me: 'Got another bed!'

Me: 'Got a fridge!'

Me: 'Got a stove!'

I told everything I found, even if it was only small. I opened all the cupboards and drawers and told what was inside:

Me: 'Got knives!'

Me: 'Got forks!'

Me: 'Got spoons!'

Lydia: 'I go sound you! Shut up!'

Me: 'Got plates!'

Me: 'Got bowls!'

Me: 'Got a smasher!'

Asweh, there were so many new things it even made my eyes go blurry. I never suspected to see so many new things just in one day. I even forgot Papa wasn't there. I only remembered at night when Mamma was snoring. When Papa's there he rolls her on her side like a big sausage so she can't snore anymore (Mamma says she doesn't snore but how would she even know, she's asleep!).

The carpet in my room wasn't big enough to reach all the floor. You can still see some wood underneath. I lifted up the carpet to look for money. Somebody wrote a greeting on the floor:

Fuck you

I don't think the greeting was for me. Nobody even knew I was coming.

I don't know what the money's for. It isn't for rent because Mamma got our flat from Ideal Lettings. I don't know what Julius does except he drove us to our new flat and he's in love with Auntie Sonia. He's always slapping her behind. She just lets him do it even when she nearly fell through the door. Grown-ups are stupid like that. They even like it when it hurts.

Auntie Sonia: 'See you, kids!'

Julius: 'Come on, let's go!' (Slap on the behind.)

Auntie Sonia: 'Ow!'

Then Mamma's face goes all hard and she smashes the tomatoes like she's trying to kill them. She says I can't get a ring like the ones Julius has because only bogahs wear them.

Me: 'Not just bogahs, the president as well.'

Mamma: 'Advise yourself! Only bogahs. Now stop making squeeze-eyes at me.'

If I had a ring like that everybody would think I'm the ironboy. If they roughed me I'd just blow them with the ring hand. It's so heavy it would knock them into the middle of next week.

I woke up when the boy did, flew straight over through the bluster and the branches. We watched the wind do its thing and then later we dreamed together. We dream each inside the other. We pass on our goodwill messages, they send us their requests and we put a word in, for seashells if not for speedboats. We live and breathe within the boundaries of our charges; we reach out for them when the bridge between them and their god is blocked.

A tree fell down on the green. It must have happened in the night. It was proper rainy and windy last night, I watched it all with my pigeon. He flew away when I went to open the window but I knew it was him.

Me: 'See you later, pigeon! Don't be a stranger!'

The tree just blew over. It fell on top of somebody's house. It didn't go through, it just landed on the roof. You could see the roots and everything. I climbed up about halfway to the top. It's easier when the tree's already fallen, you just walk up it. It's even too easy. Some smaller kids were trying it but they couldn't get that far. I was going to show them how but if you're late for Registration your name goes in the black book. If your name's in there three times you get a detention and the teacher's allowed to rape you (it's the same as dirty blows but even worse).

I saw a bird nest in the tree. It was very sad. The birds all fell out when the tree came down. They must be dead by now. The tree had squashed them. I just knew it.

Me: 'When we get out of school I go climb to the top and check the nest. If there's any birds still inside I go adopt them.'

Lydia: 'Advise yourself, you don't know how to look after them.'

Me: 'It's easy, you just feed them worms until they're strong enough to fly again.'

The babies only eat worms. They can't tell the difference from a real worm and a Haribo worm. It's only until they're big enough to fly on their own. I love all the birds, not just pigeons. I love them all.

If you're a policeman and somebody needs to ease themself really bad you have to let them do it in your hat. Connor Green told me.

Me: 'How! I don't believe it!'

Connor Green: 'Swear to God.'

Dean: 'It's true, man.'

Me: 'What about a soldier? Can you do it in their hat?'

Dean: 'I dunno. I don't think so.'

Me: 'What about a fireman?'

Connor Green: 'No, I think it's just police.'

Me: 'You're pulling my leg!'

Connor Green: 'Ask him then, go on.'

Me: 'You ask him.'

Mr McLeod: 'Shhh! Keep it down over there!'

It was a special assembly. The policeman was talking about the dead boy, how if we knew something we shouldn't be scared to tell. Nobody will get you for it. The policeman won't let it happen.

Policeman: 'You can stop this person doing the same thing to someone else. We've got to work together to stop him. So if you can help us, tell your parents or your teacher or ring the number on the poster, and we'll treat anything you say in the strictest confidence.'

You didn't know to trust him or not because he was too fat. It just didn't feel right. A fat policeman is just a liar, he can't even chase the bad guys properly. Somebody in the back row shouted pig, except they disguised it like a cough. The policeman didn't even catch the trick, his detective skills are proper low.

Dean: 'He's useless, man, we could do his job better than him. He probably just works in the control room. He probably just sits at a desk all day eating Pot Noodles.'

Me: 'He'd never catch the killer in a million years.'

You didn't believe the killer could be a kid. It just felt too crazy. We looked around at all the faces for if they had killing eyes. It was too hard. Everybody just looked normal. It couldn't be them.

Me: 'Did you see anybody?'

Dean: 'Not really. Did you?'

Charmaine de Freitas has piggy eyes but that's just her style. They're not red.

Me: 'Girls can't be killers, can they?'

Dean: 'Sometimes. They usually just push 'em down the stairs though or poison 'em. They don't usually stab 'em, it's not their MO. I don't think we'll find the killer here, someone would've heard something by now.'

Me: 'Back to the drawing board.' (It just means you have to start again.)

Connor Green: 'Traffic warden's another one. You can piss in their hat.'

Dean: 'Yeah, that's another one. I knew I forgot one.'

I was going to talk to the policeman but I had to stay undercover. If the killer's friends saw us together they'd know I was on the case, and if you grass they flush your head down the toilet. We just asked the policeman if we could try on his handcuffs instead. He wouldn't let us for if we used them on each other. (He was right. We were going to put them on Anthony Spiner and chain him to the fence but he guessed it and ran away before we could capture him.)

Scars look better on white people. You couldn't see my scars very good because my skin's too dark. They still looked bo-styles. You just had to be near.

I made them in Citizenship. We were supposed to do the test but we were finished already (it only asks you things about what happens in England, like what side of the road do they drive on and what meat is safe to eat). I only used the felt tip, I didn't use the marker pen because the fumes make you high. It's easy to draw a scar. It's just one line with little lines going through it like this:

$$\cancel{|||}$$

The big line is the cut and the lines going through it are the stitches. It's the correct way to draw a scar. It's what most scars look like, even a zombie's.

Connor Green draws his scars like this:

$$\overset{\bullet\ \bullet\ \bullet}{\underset{\bullet\ \ \bullet\ \ \bullet}{\rule{2cm}{0.4pt}}}$$

The big line is still the cut. The dots are where the stitches were. The stitches have been taken out. The dots are where the needle went in.

I like my way the best. I just think it's better, that's all.

Connor pretended like he got his scars from fighting a terminator. I pretended like I got mine from fighting asasabonsam.

Connor Green: 'What the f— is that?'

Me: 'He's a kind of vampire. He lives in the trees. He eats you if you go too far in the forest.'

Connor Green: 'Wicked.'

There's a forest outside my school, you go past it every time you have to run a lap around the field. The apples that grow from the trees are poison, you're not allowed to eat them. Asweh, all the tree fruits around here are either poison or disgusting. Even the mushrooms are too dirty to eat. Connor Green ate them once and he fell asleep for three whole days, when he woke up he forgot what his name was or his favourite Poptart flavour, he had to learn it all over again. I don't think it's fair. Why have a fruit tree if you can't eat the fruit? It's just a mean trick.

I couldn't even climb on the tree. When I got there it was already too late, the sawmen were cutting the branches off and putting them on the back of their truck. They had chainsaws. Everybody had to stand back. It was proper vexing. I hated the sawmen. They were very mean, you could tell. It felt like the tree was being tortured. A smaller kid was watching with me. He loved it. His eyes were all big. He even wanted them to cut the branches off.

When the sawmen got to the branch where the bird nest was they stopped the chainsaws and one of them climbed up and got the bird nest out. He put it on the bonnet of the truck and let me look inside.

There was nothing inside. Not even eggs. There was nothing.

Smaller kid: 'I knew there'd be nothing there. A cat must've got 'em.'

Asweh, I wanted to kill him on the spot. The blood just came from nowhere and made me proper red-eyes. A cat didn't get them. They were only babies.

Me: 'A cat didn't get them! Stupid!'

I pushed the smaller kid over. He fell down in the mud. He wasn't even suspecting it. He just got up and ran away. It was brutal. I even wanted him to cry, he deserved it.

I wanted to take a branch to remember the tree with. I was going to plant it to see if the tree came back to life but the sawmen wouldn't let me. They thought the tree belonged to them.

Sawman: 'Sorry, matey. We need it.'

Me: 'Why?'

Sawman: 'It's just the rules. Sorry.'

They're just stupid. The tree doesn't belong to them, it belongs to everybody. I only let them take it because they had chainsaws. The hole where the tree used to be just felt too crazy. It made me proper sad, I don't even know why.

Sellotape can do lots of different detective jobs. You can catch fingerprints in it or hairs. You can use it to make traps. You can stick your notes down so they don't blow away. You can even catch the criminals themself if you have enough, like if you made it into a spiderweb. Only it would take all the sellotape in the world to hold a fully grown person.

We tested it first with our fingerprints. It worked a treat. You could see all the tiny patterns. Everyone's patterns are different.

Dean: 'Sweet. I told you it'd work.'

We were back at the river. We were checking all the surfaces for if the killer left his fingerprints there when he was disposing of the murder weapon. We were going to check the murder scene first but Chicken Joe chased us away, he thought we were going to steal the new flowers the dead boy's mamma planted in the railings. Someone already stole the beer bottles, it was probably Terry Takeaway.

Chicken Joe: 'Get out of it, you little sickos! Have some f—ing respect!'

Me and Dean: 'We've got respect, we've got respect! We're only helping!'

Chicken Joe: 'F— off before I call the coppers!'

Dean: 'Your chicken's rancid! It's got maggots in it!'

That's why we were checking at the river instead. Fingerprints only stick to some surfaces like metal and plastic. They don't stick to leaves or grass. We split up to make us go faster. You just had to stick a piece of sellotape on every surface that the killer might touch. If any fingerprints got stuck it meant the killer was there.

Dean: 'We'll get a sample from the murder scene later. If we can match a fingerprint from where the boy was killed to one from where the knife was hidden it means whoever you saw must be the killer.'

Dean knows what he's talking about, he's seen all the shows. I started with the watercress sign. I had to reach up on my toes to get the sellotape on there. Nothing got stuck. No fingerprints here.

Dean tried the lamppost. No luck.

I tried the path but pavement doesn't work for fingerprints. Dean tried a big leaf for just in case. Asweh, some of the leaves by the river grow bigger than me. It's like a jungle. No wonder the killer came this way, it's the perfect hiding place.

Dean: 'There was poppies here last year. They had to cut 'em down 'cause everyone kept smoking 'em. I smoked one. It was well crazy.'

Me: 'What happened?'

Dean: 'It just makes you tired. Your head goes all weird like you're far away. I only smoked the seeds. You just mix 'em up with some baccy. I think you're s'posed to use more, I only used a few.'

I was the lookout while Dean collected samples. He got some mud from the side of the river. We both looked at it proper carefully but we didn't see any blood in it. Then we swapped and Dean was the lookout while I looked for footprints like on CSI. I was very careful. It felt lovely searching. It made everything go quiet like you were on an important mission and you were the only one who could fix it.

Dean: 'See anything?'

Me: 'Nope!'

Dean: 'He's probably covered his tracks. And it's been raining. All the evidence probably got washed away. We just need to find some more leads, that's all.'

Me: 'What will you buy with your half of the reward?'

Dean: 'A Playstation 3 probably. And a new bike and a shitload of fireworks.'

Me: 'Me too.'

Dean's the best partner a detective can have, he knows all the tricks. I don't even care if he has orange hair. That's what makes him so brainy (a detective's best skill).

I swear by God, I thought I was dreaming at first. It didn't even feel real. I thought under the ground was just mud and bones and the creatures who live there, when I saw the tunnels and all the lights and people, I just had to pinch myself. There was even a man playing a violin. He had long hair in a ponytail even if he was a man. Asweh, the whole thing just felt brutal. Have you ever been on the tube? There's a million people everywhere all going too fast. They don't talk to you, they just chook you out of the way with their elbows. The stairs you go down are moving, they're the same as the ones at the airport. You can pretend like it's asasabonsam's teeth trying to eat you. They put blocks all the way down the middle so you can't slide down. It's very vexing. Asweh, if I ever see an escalator with no blocks, I'm going to slide all the way down to the bottom! It's even my new ambition.

I wanted to run through the tunnel but there were too many people in the way. I just made an echo instead. I made the loudest echo I could and made it last for donkey hours:

Me: 'We are in the **tuuuuuuuuuuuube!**'

It felt brutal. Everybody jumped. You could hear my echo on the other side of the world. I pretended like Papa and Agnes and Grandma Ama heard it. I pretended like they shouted back:

Papa and Agnes and Grandma Ama: 'We heard you! We hope you like it!'

There's a funny smell when the train comes. It's like a wind. It's hot and it smells crazy. It feels nasty when it blows on your face.

Me: 'It's farts.'

Lydia: 'Advise yourself. No it isn't.'

Me: 'It is. It's the farts of all the people on the train. They just went on your face. Now you have a farty face.'

When the train comes everybody starts pushing. They can't wait to get on the train. They're panicking for if there's no room. Advise yourself! There's plenty of room for everybody! The train is as long as the whole tunnel! When the train started it made my belly turn over like on the aeroplane, I nearly fell over. Everybody was bumping everybody. Asweh, it was brutal.

I wanted Mamma to stand up with us but she wouldn't stand up. She likes sitting better. The lady sitting next to her had pink hair. It felt lovely.

Where Auntie Sonia lives looks the same as where I live. It didn't even feel far away. There are still towers but they're not as tall as mine, only like the never-normal flats. Auntie Sonia lives in a house. It's in a big line of them, they all look the same except some of the doors are a different colour and some of the gardens are just pavement.

Some people put their cars on the garden. The car was right next to the window. It felt like the car was waiting to come in but nobody would let it in. I pretended like the car was a dog. He'd been sent out to the garden to ease himself, now he wanted to come back in but nobody was listening. Asweh, it was very funny. I even felt sorry for him.

At first I thought Auntie Sonia's house was one big house but it's actually two flats inside. Auntie Sonia's flat is at the bottom, and there's another flat up the stairs. Auntie Sonia's TV is massive. It's proper skinny and it hangs on the wall like a picture. Everything in her flat looks brand new. Auntie Sonia even has a tree inside a pot. It's only tiny. A tree inside felt crazy, I didn't like it. I was worried for when the tree got bigger and hit the roof. Then it would die.

Me: 'What will happen when it grows up?'

Auntie Sonia: 'It won't grow up, it stays like that all the time. It's a special kind of tree that never grows.'

It's like a baby who dies when it's still a baby. It's very mean to make a tree like that. If I was the tree I'd roar all the time until somebody came and let me outside.

Auntie Sonia made kenkey and fish. I got so fed up I thought my belly would pop. I even had a cup of tea with two sugar. Auntie Sonia dropped the spoon on the floor. It made a mighty crash. Her face went hard.

Me: 'Is it because of your fingers?'

Mamma: 'Harrison.'

Auntie Sonia: 'It's OK. They're not babies, they should know.'

Lydia: 'I want to know. You're always keeping secrets from us.'

Mamma: 'Lydia.'

It's true though, Mamma does keep secrets. I found her lottery tickets when I was looking in the secret drawer for chocolate. Mamma always says the lottery's for foolish people and you might as well throw the pound down a well.

Auntie Sonia: 'Where's the harm? I don't want to lie to them.'

Mamma let out a big breath. That means she's given up trying. She just carried on washing up the plates proper fast like it was a race against the clock. I love it when Auntie Sonia wins. She tells the best stories. They're even true.

Auntie Sonia burned her fingers on the stove. It's the easiest way.

Auntie Sonia: 'There's nothing to it really. You just keep your fingers on the stove until all the skin has burned away.'

Me and Lydia: 'Did it hurt?'

Auntie Sonia: 'It's quite scary the first time. You can smell your skin cooking. You have to pull your fingers off before they get stuck for good. It's the only time I cried.'

I felt sick when I thought about it. I loved the story so much already.

Auntie Sonia: 'You hardly feel it really. It's easier when you're boozed. Like most things.'

Mamma: 'Don't tell them that.'

Lydia: 'Do they feel funny?'

They look funny. Auntie Sonia's fingers are all black at the end and shiny. It looks like it hurts. It looks like a zombie's fingers.

Auntie Sonia: 'Sometimes. I can't feel the close-up of things anymore.'

Lydia: 'Like what things?'

We tested Auntie Sonia's fingers. We gave her a hell of different things to feel and she had to say if she could feel them or not. We tried the remote control from her TV. She couldn't even change the volume at first.

Auntie Sonia: 'The buttons are too small.'

She wasn't even lying. Lydia made her feel the pattern on her top. It's only little stars on the sleeve. Auntie Sonia made a concentrating face. It wasn't working, you could tell.

Mamma: 'That's enough now. Leave her alone, she's not an animal at the zoo.'

Lydia: 'Adjei, I don't know how you could do it. I could never do it.'

Auntie Sonia: 'You do what you have to.'

Mamma: 'You didn't have to do that.'

Auntie Sonia: 'I thought I did at the time. This is where your Mamma and me will never agree.'

Mamma: 'It's not the only thing.'

Auntie Sonia: 'But you still love me, don't you?'

Auntie Sonia burned her fingers to get the fingerprints off. Now she has no fingerprints at all. It's so if the police catch her they can't send her away. Your fingerprints tell them who you are. If you have no fingerprints, you can't be anybody. Then they don't know where you belong so they can't send you back. Then they have to let you stay.

Auntie Sonia: 'I did it the easy way. Some people do it with a lighter or a razor. It takes donkey hours that way. Just get it over and done with, that's what I did.'

Every time her fingerprints grow back she has to burn them off again. It feels very hutious. Auntie Sonia says she'll stop burning them when she finds the perfect place. When she can stay in that place forever and there's nobody to ruin it or send her away, then she'll let her fingerprints grow back for good.

Me: 'It could be here.'

Auntie Sonia: 'It could be. We'll see.'

Me: 'I hope it is, then we can come round to your house for Christmas. If I get a Playstation we can play it on the big TV, I bet it will look dope-fine.'

Auntie Sonia hasn't even done anything bad. She's never killed anybody or stolen anything. She just likes to go to different places. She likes to see the different things there. Some of the countries won't let you in if you're black. You have to sneak in. When you're in you just act like everybody else. Auntie Sonia only does the same things as them. She goes to work and shopping. She eats her dinner and goes to the park. In New York it's called Central Park. It's big enough to fit a hundred children's parks inside and it even has ice skating.

Me: 'If you fall over on the ice you have to fold your fingers in so they don't get sliced off. My friend Poppy told me.'

Auntie Sonia: 'Does Harrison have a girlfriend?'

Me: 'No! And it's the same with firemen, when they can't see because of the smoke they have to feel around instead. They always feel with the outside of their hands, if you feel with the insides and you find a wire your fingers automatically grab on it and that's how you get electrocuted.'

Auntie Sonia: 'Is that right?'

Me: 'Absolutely!'

Asweh, I'd love to go ice skating. I'd even burn off my fingerprints to get there. I'd do it on the stove, it's quicker. It's not really cheating, I'd still pay for my skates like everybody else. Auntie Sonia bought me a proper football made from skin. Lydia got a Tinchy Stryder CD. Auntie Sonia always knows what you want the most, she can read your mind.

We had to go when Julius came back. He had his baseball bat but no ball so we couldn't play a game. Julius calls his bat the Persuader. He always brings it home from work with him. He pats it and talks to it proper gentle like it's a good dog. You can pretend like all the scratches in it are from where it got in a fight with another dog.

Julius: 'He earned his keep today. Give him his bath, eh?'

Auntie Sonia took the bat to the kitchen to wash it. She had to pretend like it was a dog as well. You only can't ask why because too many questions give Julius a headache. You just have to let him drink his kill-me-quick in peace.

Julius: 'Harri, want some?'

Me: 'No thanks!'

Julius: 'The only friends a man needs, his bat and a drink. One to get you what you want, the other to forget how you got it. You'll see what I mean one day. Just stay good for as long as you can, eh? Just stay the way you are.'

Me: 'I will!'

On the tube coming home I saw a lady with a moustache. At first I thought it was just dirt but when I looked again it was definitely hair. It wasn't thick like Mr Carroll's but you still knew it was there. I wanted to laugh but I held it in.

We couldn't see a barber on a bike, I don't think they have them here. Kwadwo was my favourite barber where I used to live, his bike had a radio as well and he always warned you before he used the razor on your neck so you had time to get ready. We had to go to a shop instead. The barber was called Mario. He's quite grumpy. When he moved my head it was too rough. He did it too fast. And his fingers were too hairy. Mario didn't even talk to me. He even hates cutting people's hair.

Dean: 'He's only a barber so he can sell all the old hair to China. They make it into clothes, innit.'

At first I asked Mamma if I could have cornrolls.

Mamma: 'Why, so you can look like a bogah?'

Me: 'No. I just like it. It's bo-styles.'

Lydia: 'He only wants cornrolls because Marcus Johnson has them.'

Me: 'Gowayou. No I don't.'

Mamma: 'Who is Marcus Johnson?'

Lydia: 'He's in Year 11. He thinks he's the ironboy. They get the younger ones to do tricks for them. They have them all running around. It's very sad. He calls himself X-Fire.'

Me: 'It's not X-Fire, fool. It's Crossfire. It only looks like X-Fire when he paints it on the wall.'

Lydia: 'Whatever. It's still sad.'

Me: 'Is not. At least nobody tells him what to do all the

time, not like you keep making me kill the bedbugs. Smash your own bedbugs, they don't even go on me.'

Lydia: 'It was only one time, what are you saying? Are you saying I'm dirty?'

Me: 'One went up your nose when you were asleep. I saw it with my own two eyes. He's probably built a house in your brain by now. He's probably planted a garden and bought a satellite dish, he go live there forever.'

Lydia: 'Gowayou!'

Mamma: 'Stop vexing your sister! Your hair's not long enough for cornrolls anyway. You can have low hair. And don't make squeeze-eyes at me.'

I just got low hair. Mario didn't even know what it was.

Mario: 'You mean a number one or a number two?'

He called it a number two! I swear by God! It was the funniest thing I've ever heard! Mario is dey touch. From today onward going I'm saving up all my hair until it's long enough for cornrolls, I don't care what Mamma says. Then I'll have the blood to pass any mission and they'll have to let me join the gang.

Number two is another name for a shit. I know, I didn't believe it either!

If you start from my tower, you go under the tunnel and past the little kids' school and some other houses, and then you'll get to the green. It's quite big. There's two football goals with no nets and a playground with swings and a roundabout and some other stuff. There's a little pirate ship and loads of springy things: a jeep on a spring and a motorbike on a spring and two ladybirds. You just sit on them and they bounce around. I don't go on them anymore because they're gay. Everybody agrees. They're just for babies. The swings are always broken from the dogbites.

The best thing is the climbing frame but you never get to go on it because it belongs to the Dell Farm Crew. They're always on it. They don't even play, they just sit there smoking fags and hooting the people when they go by. If you go on it after them it just smells of fags and there's too much broken glass everywhere. I just don't bother anymore. I'll only go on it when they invite me but if they offer me a fag I'll just say no thanks, I'm trying to give up, doctor's orders (it's the best way to get out of anything).

There's a sign next to the playground:

SAY **NO** TO STRANGERS

It doesn't even tell you what the question is. You just have to say no to whatever they ask you.

Me: 'What if they ask where's the hospital? What if they need your help?'

Jordan: 'Don't be gay. They never need your help. They just want to take you away in a van and shag you up the arse, innit.'

It felt very crazy. Nobody asked to sex me before. Most people just want your help. If I see a stranger I'll ask him first what he's looking for. If he gives a good answer then it's safe. He won't even try to sex me. Jordan is just dey touch.

Jordan: 'Come on, man, keep looking.'

So far I'd only found one beer bottle. Jordan had three. I wasn't really looking hard. Really I was looking for the murder weapon. If it's not by the river it could be here. There's always drug needles around the playground. They don't even try to bury them, they're just on the top. There could be a knife as well. It all depends how smart the killer is. If he's smart, he sent the murder weapon out to sea or buried it deep down underground. If he was high or in his bottle he could have just dropped it anywhere.

There's a hole in the playground where the twister used to be. Jordan set fire to it. It was ages ago, before I came here. The ground where it used to be is all black and burned like a lightning hit it. Jordan's always telling you the bad things he's done:

The biggest bad things Jordan has done
Set fire to the twister.
Drunk a whole bottle of vodka (it's like kill me quick).
Let down the tyres on the police car.
Put fireworks in the wheelie bin.
Kicked the teacher.
Threw a cat down the rubbish pipe.
T'iefed a Lucky Bag from the supermarket.
Chooked some people.
Called a grown-up a c—.
Smashed the beer bottles.

Jordan's hand around my neck was making me cough. I looked up in the sky for my pigeon to come shit on his head but no luck, they were all just flying past but not stopping. I only gave in to stop myself from coughing to death.

Jordan: 'You've gotta do it, man. I'm always doing everything. If you don't do it you're just a pussy.'

Me: 'I'm doing it, I'm doing it!'

I just wanted to go home but I had to wait for Lydia to come back from Dance Club. I should get a key. I don't care if Lydia's Year 9, it's not fair that she gets a key and I don't. I'm still the man of the house.

Jordan: 'I'll go first. Don't close your eyes, you've gotta watch every one. We're gonna smash the f— out of 'em.'

We had to smash them all. We couldn't even stop if a grown-up came, we had to keep throwing them until they were all smashed. It was the only way to get all the points. Jordan went first. I was waiting until last. If you only do the last one it isn't even a crime.

Jordan loves smashing the bottles, you could tell. His eyes go all big and shiny. He threw the first bottle up high. When it landed it made a mighty smash into a million pieces. You were scared but you loved it at the same time. He threw another one and another one. They all smashed all over path. You wanted to run but you couldn't even move. He even threw one from behind his back. That was the best time. Then it was my turn.

Jordan: 'Throw it high so it smashes better.'

Me: 'Do we have to pick up the broken bits?'

Jordan: 'Don't be gay, the council does it, that's their job. Just smash the f—er, man.'

I copied Jordan's style. I threw my bottle from over my head so it landed behind my back. It smashed all over the pavement. It was brutal. It made me feel crazy. Nobody even stopped us, they were all too scared to tell.

Me: 'How many points is that?'

Jordan: 'I'll give you ten.'

Me: 'How! That's not fair, you said a hundred!'

Jordan: 'Shut up man, you closed your eyes, you only get ten. You shouldn't be such a pussy.'

I told you, Jordan is a confusionist. You only can't rough him or he'll strangle you even more. I wanted to run when I saw Lydia coming down the path. It felt like she saved the day. She was still wearing her parrot costume. She just loves it, she doesn't even care who knows.

Jordan: 'Your sister's a numptie, man. She thinks she's a chicken.'

100

Me: 'It's not a chicken, it's a parrot.'

I only gave her a dirty blow on the arm for if Jordan was still watching.

Lydia: 'Ow! What did you do that for?'

Me: 'Sorry! It was an accident!'

You go to such lengths to keep us out. You blockade our favoured roosting sites with steel mesh and spikes. You shoot us with .22-calibre rifles where the law allows, poison us with strychnine, coat your windowsills with flypaper and watch us do the mashed potato as we try to unstick ourselves, have a good laugh at our expense. So undignified, I feel so stupid. I'm supposed to suck it up and pretend like it's all OK, just the food chain asserting itself, me below you above me, just the rules of the game.

You think you make the rules, that's the killer. Gets me every time. This stuff better not be toxic.

Volcanoes are just mountains with fire inside. The fire comes from rivers under the ground. They only erupt when the volcano god is angry. At least that's what the early-times people thought.

Mr Carroll: 'That's right, Harrison, people did use to think that.'

Me: 'But really it's Hell down there, isn't it sir.'

Mr Carroll: 'That's an interesting theory. It's definitely as hot as hell, that's for sure.'

Everybody was laughing at me. They don't believe in Hell around here. Asweh, they're in for a nasty surprise! They're going to get burned up like human toast!

In the early times they thought a fire god lived inside the volcano. He'd only stop throwing fire at them if they threw a virgin in the volcano for the god to eat. They thought there was a different god in everything. They thought there was a sky god and a tree god and a volcano god and a sea god. All their gods were angry all the time. They had to keep feeding them or they'd destroy them. The sea god would make a flood or the sky god would rain lightning on you or the tree god would fall on your house. They were always going to destroy you unless you fed them with virgins. Asweh, early-times people were very stupid. A virgin is a lady who isn't married yet. They're prized because they're so rare. Only the gods can eat them. Married ladies gave them the shits. Everybody agreed.

At afternoon Registration Poppy gave me a letter. I wasn't allowed to open it until I got home and I couldn't show it to anybody else. I made sure nobody was looking. I went in my room, closed the door and stood right in front of it so no invaders could break in. My belly went funny and sick for if it was a trick.

Do you like me?

yes ☐

no ☐

I just have to tick the box. I have to give the letter back to Poppy after the holiday. I don't know what will happen when I give it back. Asweh, I hope it was the right answer!

MAY

Today was the carnival. It was on the green. It was raining cats and dogs but everybody still came. All the umbrellas had cigarette names on them. The dancers were still dancing. Their feathers were so bright it still felt like the sun was out. One white lady was a peacock. All her make-ups was dripping down her face. It made her look like a broken puppet. It was very funny, the rain kept going in her smile and she had to spit it out. She never gave up though.

There were djembes. You had to dance, you couldn't help it. Even the white people and the old people were dancing. The girl from the never-normal flats was next to me. She did a little baby dance. She was hardly moving at all. She was still stiff. You only knew she was dancing if you looked at her feet. Her feet were tapping on the ground all stiff and shy. It's the only dance she knows.

I felt sorry for her. I wanted to teach her a real dance but there was no time, I'd miss all the fun things. I just pretended like her dance was still good, it was only her own style.

There were men on sticks, you know the sticks they stand on to make them go proper tall? It looked very hutious. It was too slippy, I kept suspecting them to fall down. I said a prayer inside my head so they wouldn't fall. Some of the stickmen were juggling at the same time. Juggling's when you throw a ball and catch it, except it's three balls and you never drop any. Asweh, it was brutal.

Me: 'Agnes would love them! I could learn juggling for when she comes. Where do they sell juggling balls?'

Mamma: 'You can just use tennis balls.'

Me: 'Will you buy some for me? I need three.'

Mamma: 'We'll see.'

Terry Takeaway stole a jar of hot-dog sausages from the raffle table and nobody even tried to catch him. He calls the hot-dog sausages Scooby Doo Cocks.

Terry Takeaway: 'They're for Asbo. He loves 'em, don't you boy.'

When Asbo came to see me Mamma got scared. I had to save the day.

Me: 'It's alright, he doesn't bite, he's lovely, look.'

Asbo went on his back for me to scratch his belly. He loves that. He even has a belly button, it looks like a tiny bum. Then it was time for Dance Club. They were all parrots. Lydia kept forgetting to smile. She was too busy concentrating on getting the moves right.

Me and Mamma: 'Go, Lydia! Give us a smile!'

She was even brilliant. She got all the moves right. I kept wishing Miquita would fall over but it was another girl who fell. She slipped and landed on her behind. The rest of them just kept going until the end. They only roughed her when the dance was finished, then everybody said she pissed herself because of the massive wet patch on her behind. It was only a lie. They knew what really happened because they saw it. But it's funnier to say they pissed themself. Pissing yourself is funnier than just falling over. Everybody agrees.

Smaller kids: 'Pissy pants, pissy pants!'

Girl: 'F— off!'

I won a binoculars with my raffle ticket. Asweh, it was a dope-fine piece of luck. They're army colour. They actually work even if they're just plastic. I looked at the whole world through them. They made everything close. I could see the satellite dishes on the flats and the cross on the real church and the bullet hole in the broken lamppost. I looked on the roofs for if the murder weapon was up there but I didn't see it. My pigeon was sitting on the roof of the Jubilee Centre, when he saw me he winked at me then he flew away, he was too fast to follow with the binoculars. I got dizzy from looking for him so I had to call it quits.

All the Dell Farm Crew were there but they didn't even talk to me. My new mission can wait, there's no business on carnival day. That's the best thing about carnival, everybody forgets their business for one day and just has fun. I hope Killa keeps Miquita, then she won't disturb me anymore. He was trying to burn her with his lighter. She tried to get away but he pulled her back. She was even laughing like she loved it. It felt crazy. Girls are stupid.

He only stopped when the police van went past. He went proper still and his face went all hard. I saw it through the binoculars. The whole crew all put their hoods up and went like statues. Nobody was laughing anymore. Then they all split.

When the police van went past the pissheads all threw their cans at it. The police van stopped. The pissheads got scared. They thought the policeman was going to come out and arrest them. They all went quiet. Then the police van carried on going and the pissheads all cheered like they'd won the war. Asweh, it was very funny. Binoculars are very useful for making things closer.

Lydia kept her parrot costume on all day. She made a parrot song for Agnes. Agnes loved it, her laughing was like a wave in the sea, when it landed on you it made you laugh as well. Nobody could even stop, it was too funny. Agnes can say Harri now. She can say all our names. Mamma and

Papa and Lydia and Grandma. She can even say her own name. We made her say all of them. She loved it. She said them all proper loud a hundred times. Asweh, it was very funny!

Mamma tried to make her say Harrison but she didn't want to. She just said Harri. Mamma didn't even get red-eyes, she was just smiling from ear to ear.

Agnes: **'Harri!'**

Mamma: 'That's it! Well done, my darling!'

Me: 'Take care with my ears! You'll make them fall off!'

Agnes: **'Harri!'**

Harri is her favourite. She loved saying it more than all the others, you could tell. She didn't want to stop. She was still saying Harri when the calling card ran out.

Agnes: **'Harri! Ha**

I can't wait until Agnes knows all the words, then I can tell her my best stories. The first one I'm going to tell her is about the man with the fake leg. He was on my aeroplane. He had a fake leg made from wood. It even had a foot with a real shoe on it. Before he went to sleep the man took his leg off and gave it to his wife to hold. The wife fell asleep holding it like it was a baby. It was very funny. It felt lovely. I pretended like the leg was a baby and the wife was her mamma.

If your leg fell off when you were alive, in Heaven it grows back. Asweh, Agnes will love that one!

There was no church today because of the broken glass and bad words. Mr Frimpong was nearly crying. He loves church the most from all of us. Mamma squeezed him to make him feel better. You thought his bones were going to turn to dust on the spot.

Mr Frimpong: 'It's senseless, that's what it is. No respect for anything.'

I was even glad at first, I'm tired of singing the church songs. They're always the same and Kofi Allotey isn't there to make funny words for them. The church isn't even a real church. It's just in the Jubilee Centre, in the room in the back behind Youth Club. It's only a church on Sunday, the rest of the time it's just for bingo and old people's stuff. Everybody wanted the wet patch on the roof to be Jesus but really it just looks like a hand with no fingers.

They smashed the windows through the cage. They wrote DFC all over the wall in mighty letters. Derek was trying to rub them off but they wouldn't rub off.

Mamma: 'What is DFC?'

Mr Frimpong: 'Who knows? Some code of theirs. Just nonsense.'

I didn't tell them what DFC really means. I pretended not to know.

Mr Frimpong: 'Will they be on CCTV?'

Derek: 'They'll have covered their faces. They're ignorant but they're not stupid.'

That's why Mamma won't let me get a hoodie, for if I cover my face. I don't even want to cover my face, I only want to keep my ears warm. I hate it when Mamma calls me a liar.

They tried to make it look like they put shit on the window but you knew it was only Snickers. The lumps were too square and you could see the peanuts sticking out, they weren't fooling anybody.

Me: 'We could go to the real church, the one where the dead boy had his funeral. It's only round the corner.'

Mamma: 'It's the wrong kind of church.'

Me: 'How?'

Mamma: 'Just because. They sing different songs. They're not the songs we know.'

Me: 'We can learn them. They might be better.'

Mamma: 'They're not better. We don't know them.'

Me: 'But I don't get it. It's even a real church. They had the dead boy's funeral there. It must be good.'

Mamma: 'It's just the wrong kind, that's all.'

Mr Frimpong: 'Bleddy Catholics. They want to give us all Aids so they can steal our land back again. It's true.'

I still don't get it. It has a cross and everything. It must be the right one if it has a cross.

I don't know why you have to sing songs every time. Sometimes you could play djembes instead or just pray. God's probably bored of the songs by now, he's heard them a million times already. That's probably why he makes earthquakes. If it was me I'd tell them sing me a new song I haven't heard before or I'll send you another earthquake. The same songs every time is just lazy.

Me: 'Do you want me to get my binoculars? They're only at home. Then I can look for clues.'

Derek: 'That's alright, Harri. I'll just clean this up.'

It wasn't my fault they ruined the church. If I was in the gang I could tell them about God. I could even save them. A gang can be for good things, not just for tricks. Where I used to live, me and Patrick Kuffour and Kofi Allotey and Eric Asamoah were always going on fine missions. We always took the empty Coke bottles back to Samson's Kabin. One time we even helped Patrick Kuffour's papa insulate his house. We searched all the streets and found all the boxes and broke the cardboard down to the right sizes. For our reward he gave us all a big bottle of Fanta. We had a drinking race and then we all did a big burp together like bullfrogs having a ruckus. Those kinds of missions are the best, when everybody helps and you get a reward after. Somebody should tell the Dell Farm Crew about them. I could pass on the message.

Lydia: 'Just stay away from them, they're trouble.'

Me: 'What about Miquita, she's even worse. She's always trying to suck me off and you don't even stop her.'

Lydia: 'That's different. It's different for girls, you don't understand. You need the right friends or they'll just rough you. Miquita's only bluffing, you can't take her serious.'

Me: 'If God saw what you did he'd take your eyes. I'm not going to be your guide dog when you go blind. I'll just pull you around on a string, it's your own fault if you can't keep up. I've got places to be, I'm not waiting for you.'

Lydia: 'It was only paint!'

Me: 'No it wasn't, it was blood.'

It was definitely blood on the clothes, that's why she put bleach on them. Both the two of us knew it. We watched the lie go up big and slow between us, then it burst like a spit bubble. They always burst before too long.

Lydia: 'Don't bring yourself, Harrison. It was Miquita's blood, OK?'

Me: 'How did her blood get there? She wasn't even cut.'

Lydia: 'It's not that kind of blood. It's a girl's blood. You don't know what you're talking about! Just go away!'

She ran to Mamma's room and shut the door in my face. I could hear her crying behind the door. It felt crazy. I wanted to turn the crying off but she had to learn her lesson. Doing something bad on purpose is worse than doing it by mistake. You can mend a mistake but on purpose doesn't just break you, it breaks the whole world bit by bit like the scissors on the rock. I didn't want to be the one who broke the whole world.

Me: 'You wouldn't have to cry if you weren't such a big liar! And you look stupid in that parrot costume! You can stop wearing it now, it smells! Carnival's finished!'

Lydia: 'Just f— off!'

Asweh, it just felt too crazy. My belly went all cold. I never suspected her to say it in a million years. I didn't even know what to do. I had to go on the balcony to get my breath back. I looked for my pigeon all over. Asweh, there were too many, they were too far away to see the colours. I even tried to tempt him with a Haribo Tangfastic but my pigeon still didn't come back. I don't think he ever will.

Kyle Barnes taught me the dirty finger trick. It's very easy: you just pretend like you're looking for something, like if they asked you for a penny, you search all your pockets as if you're looking for the penny. You have to pretend like you lost it and search for a long time. The longer you search, the funnier it will be at the end.

Then when you bring your hand out of your pocket, instead of giving them the thing you were supposed to be looking for, you show them your dirty finger instead. It's very funny.

I tried it on Manik. It tricked him. It was brutal. He had no idea I was going to bring my dirty finger out. He wasn't suspecting it in a million years. Don't forget, it only works with your dirty finger (that's the one in the middle that means the same as f— off).

Me: 'Got you!'

Manik: 'Shit, man! At least my trainers ain't manky, what did you do to them?'

My belly turned over. Everybody started laughing.

Everybody: 'What did you do that for? It's well gay!'

Me: 'How! No it's not!'

It's only lines. I drew them on to make my trainers look like Adidas. I did it with the marker pen. You're allowed to take them as long as you bring them back after the holiday.

I didn't breathe the poison in. I only breathed it in one time before my head went fuzzy. I didn't get high.

I made the lines proper straight, they weren't even wobbly or anything. They still look bo-styles from far away. They wouldn't stop laughing. It made me go red-eyes. I hate them.

Me: 'Quit it!'

Everybody: 'No can do, sorry! It's just too funny! You're classic! Asweh by God!'

They won't be laughing when I'm in the Dell Farm Crew. I'll make them kiss my trainers. They can kiss my arse as well.

Mamma says the CCTV cameras is just another way for God to watch you. If God's busy in another part of the world, like if he's making an earthquake or a tide, his cameras can still see you. That way he can never miss anything.

Me: 'But I thought God could see everywhere at the same time.'

Mamma: 'He can. The cameras are just for extra help. For the places where the devil is very strong. It's just to make you safer.'

Adjei, the devil must be mighty strong around here, there's cameras all over the place! There's one at both ends of the shops and outside the newsagent's. There's even three inside the supermarket just to stop Terry Takeaway stealing the beer. I'll have to put my coat over my head because I haven't got a hood. If I go fast enough the camera can't follow me, I'll just be like a spirit. That's what I was hoping for.

We were waiting for the right time. It had to be clear so we could get away without crashing into anybody. It was me and X-Fire and Dizzy and Killa. They were going to crash the target and I was going to run away with the prize.

Dizzy: 'Don't worry blud, you just stay with us, yeah? If it looks like it's getting f—ed up I'll give you the sign. Then you just get out of there, got it?'

Me: 'Got it.'

The sign is a nod. That's all I have to watch for. All I have to do is follow them. If they run, I run, it's easy. I'll just pretend I'm playing suicide bomber, then it won't even be hutious. I'll only fail the mission if I split before the end.

X-Fire was in charge of picking the target. It had to be somebody weaker, that way you could knock them down easily. They couldn't fight back and it was quicker. We had to keep our backs to the camera until X-Fire found a target. We pretended we were just hanging around. I felt in my pocket for my alligator tooth. I asked for the blood to make me go fast enough.

My pigeon was just walking around outside the news-agent's. I couldn't talk to him for if I missed my sign, I just watched him from the side of my eye. He had a big piece of bread in his mouth. There were two other birds following him, black and white ones. They wanted his bread. They wouldn't leave him alone. My pigeon kept running away but the other birds kept chasing him. One of them went right up and stole a piece of bread from his mouth! Asweh, it was very cheeky. I felt sorry for my pigeon. I wanted to kill the other birds.

But then you remembered they only wanted some bread. There was too much for the pigeon anyway. They just took it. They couldn't ask because they were only birds. You felt sorry for all of them then.

X-Fire: 'Here we go. This one'll do.'

Mr Frimpong was walking towards us. He was only past the supermarket. There was nobody else around him. That's when I knew Mr Frimpong was the target. I felt sick all over again. He only had one bag of shopping, I could see the bread sticking out. He's only skinny.

Mr Frimpong is the oldest person from church. That's when I knew why he sings louder than anybody else: it's because he's been waiting the longest for God to answer. He thinks God has forgotten him. I only knew it then. Then I loved him but it was too late to go back.

I hope I don't knock him over.

X-Fire: 'Let's do this shit. Go!'

We ran. Dizzy and Killa ran together. I just followed them. I put my coat over my head. I was only playing suicide bomber. I didn't care if I didn't hit anybody, I don't need the points. I just kept running. I didn't even want to see where I was going.

I couldn't stop. I just ran as fast as I could. My heart was going proper fast. I could feel the taste of metal and the wind rushing past. I just ran.

There was a mighty crash. I heard things falling. A bottle smashed. I felt the air change when the doors opened, I was at the other end of the shops. I just kept going. I didn't even want to see.

Me: 'It wasn't me it wasn't me it wasn't me!' (I just said it inside my head.)

I was going to crash into the railings. I put my coat down. The sun came smashing into my eyes. I was outside. I turned around.

Mr Frimpong was on the floor. His legs were bent in a funny shape. I'd never seen him in that shape before, he looked like a bug dying in the sun. It felt too crazy. His shopping was everywhere, his malt was all smashed. Dizzy was kicking his bread all over. His bread was all squashed. He jumped on it.

Killa kicked his eggs and they all went flying. I could see Mr Frimpong's face, he was all red-eyes and scared. I pretended like I knew what he was thinking: he was thinking where's God when you need him. I was thinking it as well. He was trying to slap the boys away but his

118

arms wouldn't reach. He was trying to get up but his legs wouldn't work. It was too hutious. Then X-Fire came. He had his scarf over his face. He searched Mr Frimpong's pockets and got his wallet. It felt like the craziest thing you've ever seen. He didn't even ask.

X-Fire: 'Give it up you old bastard or I'll stick you.'

I wanted to shit. I turned around and ran as fast as I could. I didn't look back anymore. I just had to get away.

It was my last chance. If you fail two missions you'll never get in. All you had to do was stay until the end. You just never knew the end would be so

X-Fire: 'Where the f— you going!?'

I pretended I was deaf. I just ran. I ran past the playground and the green and all the houses and I didn't stop until the tunnel. All my breath was gone. My belly felt like knives. I looked for my alligator tooth, it was still there in my pocket. I don't know why the blood never came.

I wish I was bigger.

It was those magpies again, they got in my way. Stupid creatures, they think I'm one of them, that I don't have anything better to do than squabble over scraps. I just wanted to get your attention, Harri, get you out of another mess. I'm trying to help you while I still can, I'm trying my best but there's only so much I can do from here. It's down to you, you have to keep your eyes open, watch for the cracks in the pavement. We gave you the map, it's inside you. The lines all point to the same place in the end, all you have to do is follow them. Home will always find you if you walk true and taller than those weeds. You can be a tree, you can be as big as you want to be.

Some mammas kill their baby before it's even born. They changed their mind and they don't want it anymore. Maybe they found out the baby was going to be bad when it grows up. It's easier to just stop it before the bad things get done. They just flush it down the toilet like a fish. It happened to Daniel Bevan. His mamma had a baby she didn't want anymore so she flushed it.

Me: 'I hope they wake up when they get to the sea.'

Daniel Bevan: 'No, they just stay dead. They just end up in the sewer and the rats eat them. I don't want a sister anyway, they're annoying.'

Daniel Bevan might die soon. He can't even run at all. Do you know what's an inhaler? It's a little can of special air. Daniel Bevan has one, he needs it to breathe because he has asthma. He has to breathe the air from the can because the air outside is too dirty for him. That's why he can't run. If his special air ever ran out he'd die.

He let me try his inhaler. It felt very cold. It tasted funny. It was brutal. I wanted it to make my voice go like a robot but it didn't work this time. If Daniel Bevan dies before me I can have his ruler. We even shook hands on it. It's bo-styles, it's even got its own calculator built in.

Daniel Bevan: 'What if you die before me? What can I have that was yours?'

Me: 'All my books. I've got loads. I've got one on reptiles

and one on creatures of the deep, and one on medieval. There's about twenty altogether.'

Daniel Bevan: 'Alright then. Deal.'

He can't go back on it now. If you shake hands you're not allowed to break it.

The best time was when Papa let me drive the pickup. We were coming back from the bamboo farm. I sat on his legs and did the steering. Papa just did the gears and pedals.

Every time he changes the gear we pretend it's the pickup doing a big fart.

Papa: 'Excuse me?'

Me: 'What did you have for breakfast?'

You still had to concentrate proper hard. It was very nervous. The steering wheel felt proper heavy. You just had to keep your eyes on the road in front of you.

Papa: 'Take time. Just keep it straight. Don't think about the other cars. I've got us. Just keep going straight.'

Every time I hit a bump in the road I got scared for if we were going to crash. I just kept proper quiet. I had to prove to Papa that I could steer good so next time he'd let me drive the whole way there and back. I only went wobbly one time. I nearly hit a grasscutter. Papa wanted me to go back and hit him but I couldn't turn the wheel around fast enough.

Papa: 'Next one you see, steer for his eyes. Then your mother can make some soup.'

Mamma doesn't know I drove the pickup on the road. If she knew it she'd kill me. It's only a secret for me and Papa. After that, every time we were in the pickup and we saw a grasscutter me and Papa laughed like crazy. Mamma and Lydia never even knew what we were laughing for. Asweh, it was the funniest thing you've ever seen.

I put my coat down the rubbish pipe. I waited until it was dark and snuck out proper quiet. I pretended like I was making a sacrifice. The coat was a virgin and I was giving her to the volcano god.

You have to dispose of the evidence or the police will trace you.

I threw my Mustang down as well. I didn't even want it anymore. It was only fair, they smashed Mr Frimpong's eggs. I was there, I saw the whole thing. The devil's too strong around here. Where I used to live, the devil only tempted me one time, when he told me to steal all the ice blocks from the Victory Chop Bar so we could have a water fight. I only listened to him until Osei chased us, then we gave them all back. The devil is stronger here because the buildings are too high. There's too many towers and they get in the way of the sky so God can't see so far. Asweh, it's very vexing!

I think the scars that go like ⫴ are better. From today onward going, I'll make all my scars like that. The ones that go ⫴ aren't even a scar yet. The stitches are still in. Connor Green explained it. It can't be a scar until the stitches are taken out. If the stitches are still in it's just a cut. It's very clear. I don't know why I didn't think of it before.

Do you know what's a superhero? They're special people who protect you. They have magic powers. They use them to fight the bad men. They're very great. They're a bit like Ananse except they never trick you, they only use their powers for good things.

Some superheroes are from another planet. Some of them were made in a factory. Some of them were born normal but they had an accident that gave them their powers. It's usually because of the radiation.

There's about a hundred superheroes in the whole world. Altaf knows all of them. He draws their picture. They're even better than his cars. Altaf can tell you all about any superhero. It's his favourite subject. Spiderman is a superhero. That's how he can stick like a spider.

Altaf: 'It's because he got bitten by a radioactive spider.'

Me: 'Cool!'

Every superhero has a favourite power. Some of them can fly and some of them can run proper fast. Some of them are bulletproof or have rays. They all have names that tell you what's their favourite power, like Spiderman because he can stick like a spider and Storm because she can make a storm and Wolverine because he fights like a wolverine (it's a kind of wolf with extra long claws for slicing).

We were talking about our own superheroes. What if we could make our own. Altaf has already thought of one, he showed me the picture. It even looked like a real superhero.

Altaf: 'He's called Snake Man. He changes into a snake and spits poison at the enemy.'

Me: 'He's bo-styles! Did you think of him yourself?'

Altaf: 'It's only the first drawing. I'm going to make his tongue better and give him a nemesis.'

Everybody calls Altaf gay because he's so quiet and he has girl's lips. He doesn't paint them, they're just very pink by accident. Sometimes they just call him Gay Lips. I pretended like his lips were his superpower, like if the enemy looks at them too long they go frozen into statues.

I can make a fart like a woodpecker. Asweh, it's true. The first time it happened was an accident. I was just walking along and I did one fart, but then it turned into lots of little farts all chasing it. Even Mamma loved it, she couldn't stop herself.

Mamma: 'You must have a woodpecker in your pant!'

Asweh, that's exactly what it sounded like! After that I tried to make every fart like a woodpecker. Sometimes it works better than other times. It's not a superpower, just a skill.

X-Fire made the gun sign at me. He was on the cafeteria steps when I went past. He made a gun with his finger and pointed it right at my head. I didn't know what to do. It felt very crazy. He looked like he was going to kill me and nobody could even stop him.

X-Fire: 'Pop!'

He shot the gun. My belly went all cold and the woodpecker fart just fell out. It wasn't as funny this time. I wanted somebody to come and jump in front of the bullet but then I remembered it wasn't a real gun. It was still hutious though.

Dizzy: 'Why'd you run out on us? We ain't gonna forget that shit, man.'

124

X-Fire: 'Keep your mouth shut, yeah Ghana? For serious.'

I wasn't even going to say anything, I know the rules already. A finger gun means if you tell you die. It felt crazy to be enemies, it was just too big. I don't even know how it happened. From today onward going I'm going to need eyes in the back of my head.

Terry Takeaway was kicking Asbo for donkey hours. He wouldn't stop. It just felt crazy. Asbo found some meat in the bushes. It was a leg from something. Terry Takeaway kept kicking him and kicking him to let go but he wouldn't let go. Asbo was crying but he wouldn't stop. I wanted to do something. I wanted to kill Terry Takeaway but he was too big. I couldn't do anything.

Then when we got closer it all started making sense. Terry Takeaway wasn't kicking Asbo, it was Asbo who was biting Terry Takeaway! It was very funny. Asbo was trying to pull the meat from the bushes but he got Terry Takeaway's foot instead. He wouldn't let go. It probably had the smell of meat on it. He probably thought it was a piece of the cow.

Terry Takeaway: 'Get off, get off! Asbo, leave it! Leave! Asbo!'

Terry Takeaway was wriggling and screaming but Asbo didn't listen. You thought he'd bite his foot clean off.

Terry Takeaway: 'Harri, help us out! Get a stick or something. Over there!'

Dean picked up a branch and wriggled it by Asbo's face. He got it right near his mouth. It was quite hutious. Asbo's teeth are like a shark. He got the branch so it was between Terry Takeaway's foot and Asbo's teeth, and then he had to let go. Terry Takeaway picked up the meat sharp-sharp and threw it back in the bushes. Asbo chased after it and Terry Takeaway got free. He was all red and sweating. He checked his feet to see if they were still on.

Terry Takeaway: 'Cheers, geezer. He just saw it and went crazy. Silly dog.'

Asbo came out of the bushes with the meat in his mouth like his forever favourite prize. He was very happy, you could tell. He ran away before we could steal the meat from him. All you could think about was the dead man in the bushes. You hoped the meat wasn't from him.

Me: 'Have you ever killed anybody?'

Terry Takeaway: 'Not lately. I hurt a few people's feelings though. Why, what you getting at?'

Me: 'Everybody around here wants to kill you. I don't get it. Will the police catch him?'

Terry Takeaway: 'Who?'

Dean: 'The one who killed the dead boy.'

Terry Takeaway: 'You're joking, they couldn't catch a cold.'

Me: 'That's what we thought. We're going to catch him instead.'

Dean: 'There's a reward.'

Terry Takeaway: 'Good luck with that.'

Dean: 'They should get the sniffer dogs in, dogs can smell everything innit. Dogs can even smell fear.'

We were both thinking it, you could tell, only I was quicker. I said it first:

Me: 'What if dogs could smell evil?'

Dean: 'That's what I was thinking.'

We did an experiment. Terry Takeaway helped us. He got Asbo on the lead so he wouldn't run off, then he just lay down eating his meat. He was enjoying his meat so much that he didn't notice what we were doing. I closed my eyes and filled my head up with killing thoughts, all blood and chooking and slicing and crushing and shooting and tearing and vampires. I pretended like I was the killer getting ready to go to work. I tried to squeeze all those bad feelings into a ball, as hard as it would go, then sharp-sharp I opened my eyes and threw the evil ball right at Asbo. I aimed for his nose. I did a little shout to make it stronger. It even worked, Asbo's ears went up and he looked at me all scared for a minute. That meant the ball had hit him. Now he knew what evil smelled like. Then he went back to eating his meat.

Me: 'Now if he ever smells a killer he'll remember and he'll make the same face.'

Terry Takeaway: 'He makes that face when he farts as well though.'

Me: 'But if he's looking at a person when he does it you know it's not farts, it's evil. It means that person's got killing thoughts. Then they're a suspect. You can tie them up with Asbo's lead until the police come.'

Terry Takeaway: 'Sounds like a plan.'

We got a chance to test it straight away: X-Fire and Dizzy and Killa were coming across the green. I wasn't even scared because Terry Takeaway was with us, he could destroy them. He used to be in the army before he got in his bottle. Me and Dean did a big jump to get Asbo's attention so Terry Takeaway could get the meat off him. He threw it back in the bushes. Asbo couldn't chase it this time because he was on the lead. He gave up looking for it when X-Fire bumped me. He's always bumping me. This time I even wanted him to, it meant he was close enough for Asbo to get a good sniff of him.

X-Fire: 'Get that dog away from me, man.'

Terry Takeaway: 'Watch where you're going then. What's your problem?'

Asbo got straight to work. He sniffed them all like they were more meat. We kept watching for if he made his evil face. If his ears went up or his eyes went sad, we'd know we were onto something serious. They tried to walk around him but Terry Takeaway pulled the lead so Asbo stayed in front of them. He wasn't finished yet. He jumped at Killa and made his eyes go all big. Asweh, it was too sweet! He was sniffing right in his nuts.

Killa: 'I ain't f—ing joking man, get him away!'

Killa got a screwdriver out of his pant. I saw it with my own two eyes.

Terry Takeaway: 'What you gonna do with that, play with yourself?'

X-Fire: 'Put it away, blud.'

Terry Takeaway: 'You best listen to your mate. Run on home before your ice cream melts, yeah?'

They just split. Asbo's ears were still up. I could even see the killing thoughts in the air, they were sticking to us like crazy moths after thunder. They wanted to kill us, you could tell. The test was a great success. It made more questions: if they wanted to kill everybody then what bit was meant for the dead boy? How could you tell one sin from another if they were all the same shape? Asweh, it's very hard sometimes being a detective, your head just gets filled up with questions all day. I wished I'd tied them up when I had the chance but I wasn't thinking straight.

We walked home with Terry Takeaway. Asbo ran in front of us. Sometimes he looked back to see if we were still coming. It was brutal.

Terry Takeaway: 'Does your mum want a kettle? Brand new, eight quid. It's got a filter and everything. They're twenty in the shops.'

Me: 'I don't think so. She doesn't agree with stealing things.'

Terry Takeaway: 'Good for her. Six quid? What about you, Copper Top?'

Dean: 'No thanks.'

Terry Takeaway: 'Suit yourself. Here Asbo, this way!'

If Asbo helps to catch the killer they'll give him a share of the reward. I bet he'll spend it on a big bone and a lifetime supply of belly scratches!

People who don't follow God are called non-believers. They're lost in the dark and they can't feel anything, they're just empty inside like a robot with the wires taken out. When something good happens they don't even feel it and they don't even know when they do something bad. Asweh, it must be very boring. A vampire is like that. A vampire has no soul or blood, that's why he's sad all the time.

Pastor Taylor: 'It's fear that makes them do such things. They're afraid of the truth of the eternal Promise of Christ. We must pity them and pray for them. We must forgive them their weakness. They're in God's hands now.'

Mr Frimpong: 'If I see them again I'll bang their heads together. Hooligans.'

It was very funny when Mr Frimpong said hooligans. He didn't mean it to sound so funny but it did. I had to bite my lips.

Church was proper quiet. Mr Frimpong didn't even sing. It didn't feel right. He wasn't even trying. That's what happens when you get knocked down, you stop trying so hard. Mr Frimpong showed us his knee, there was a big hole in it and poison all inside. He was very proud of it, you could tell.

Mr Frimpong: 'Have a look at that. That dressing's got silver in it, it's for the infection. Nobody tried to stop them, not one person. Why now?'

In England nobody helps you if you fall over. They can't tell if you're serious or if it's just a trick. It's too hard to know what's real. I even missed Mr Frimpong singing. It felt too crazy when it wasn't there. It's like when Agnes says goodbye to me, I can still feel her voice in my ear for a long time after. It even tickles. It's lovely.

Me: 'Goodbye Agnes!'

Agnes: **'Goobah!'**

Sometimes I can still feel it when I go to sleep.

Mamma: 'Harrison even had his coat stolen. Can you believe it? They don't care about anything.'

Mr Frimpong: 'I bet it was the same boys that got me. Hooligans.'

The window at church is fixed but you can still see where the bad words didn't come off properly. They're just hanging around like devil whispers waiting to trap you. I couldn't concentrate on praying because I kept remembering them. The prayer sounded right when Pastor Taylor said it but it came out wrong inside my head.

Me: 'Dear fucking God, please stop all the bad shit happening. Thanks a fucking lot. Amen.'

Asweh, lucky it was only in my head! My main superpower would be invisible. I get it from my alligator tooth. That's why Mr Frimpong never saw me when he got knocked down. I was there but he never knew it. My alligator tooth gave me invisible power, it's the only reason I can think of. I knew it was special, that's why Papa gave it to me.

Prossie and hooker and tutufo all mean the same. In England, if a girl has a tattoo it means she's a tutufo. Jordan's mamma has a tattoo of a scorpion on her shoulder. She doesn't even try to hide it, everyone can see it because she only wears a vest. It just feels too crazy. Somebody's mamma shouldn't have a tattoo, they should only be for men. Even a fierce one like a scorpion. If Mamma ever got a tattoo I'd just split. I'd go and live by the river. I'd only need a tent and a slingshot for catching squirrels.

You should see how far I can kick my new ball. Real skin footballs are much better than plastic. I can kick it right to the other end of the corridor and it doesn't even fly away, it stays low to the ground like a rocket. That's what Jordan calls it.

Jordan: 'This one's gonna be a rocket, man!'

Jordan blasted it at my legs. He did it proper hard to make it hurt. He loves it when he gets me. I try to jump out of the way but the ball always hits me, it's like it's magnetic or something. It's very vexing.

Jordan: 'Yes! Got you! Pussy! Quick, it's Fag Ash Lil! Pass it!'

Fag Ash Lil was coming in the door. I passed the ball to Jordan.

Jordan: 'Pretend you didn't see her.'

Fag Ash Lil lives on floor 2. She's called Fag Ash Lil because she picks up old fags from the ground. I've seen it with my own two eyes. She never smokes them, she just puts them in her pocket. She's the oldest person I've ever seen, at least two hundred years. When she was little there were no cars and every day was a war. She always wears the same dress with no coat or socks, even when it's raining, and her legs are very skinny like a bird. She can only say

Fag Ash Lil: 'Bloody hell!'

Asweh, she's proper hutious. She would kill me like that if she wanted. She's killed loads of children before but the police can't catch her because she's got magic that keeps them away from the terrible truth. I pretended like I didn't see her. I just kept my eyes on the ball. Fag Ash Lil pressed the button for the lift. I got ready to run.

Jordan blasted the ball at her. It hit her proper hard right on the legs. She wasn't suspecting it. You could even hear her bones cracking.

131

Fag Ash Lil: 'Bloody hell!'

Jordan: 'Sorry! It was an accident!'

The lift came and Fag Ash Lil got in. Jordan kicked the ball at her again. It hit her right in the face and bounced back out.

Jordan: 'Stupid old bastard!'

Fag Ash Lil was looking right at me before the doors closed, her eyes were all mad and blue. She thought it was me. It's not even fair, I only wanted to play passing. It just gets vexing when they blast it all the time. Now Fag Ash Lil is my nemesis (it's what Altaf calls the villian who always tries to destroy the superhero). I just hope my powers are stronger than hers.

Me: 'What did you do that for, she go kill us now!'

Jordan: 'Don't be gay, if she comes after us I'll just shank her, innit.'

Jordan showed me his knife. I didn't even see where it came from. I never suspected it in a million years. It has a green handle the same as the knives from Mamma's block. It's like her tomatoes knife. It even looks too deadly for tomatoes.

Jordan: 'This is my war knife. No one f—s with me, man. I'm telling you, when the war starts I'm gonna be ready for them.'

He was looking at the knife proper hard like it was his favourite thing. His eyes were all big. He showed me how to carry it so nobody can see. You just put it down your leg. You have to hold the handle or it will just fall through your trousers onto the floor. It works best if your trousers are elastic at the top. Otherwise you can just use your pocket.

Jordan: 'It's well sharp, look.'

He scratched the knife on the wall. He wrote cock with it like it was a pen, you could see the letters loud and clear.

Jordan: 'You should get one, you need it. I'll get one for you, my mum's got loads.'

Me: 'No thanks. I don't really need one.'

Jordan: 'Course you do, everyone needs one. Try and get one the same as mine, then we can be war brothers, innit. What's the matter, don't you wanna be brothers?'

He held the knife near my face. He twisted the blade around in the air like he was trying to open a lock with it. I felt like the lock. Everything went slow until he put the knife down again.

Jordan: 'Rarse, you should've seen your face, man! You were shitting yourself!'

Me: 'No I wasn't! You're not even funny!'

Everybody says there's a war but I haven't seen it yet. There's a hell of wars going on all the time:

Wars
Kids vs Teachers
Northwell Manor High vs Leabridge High
Dell Farm Crew vs Lewsey Hill Crew
Emos vs Sunshine
Turkey vs Russia
Arsenal vs Chelsea
Black vs White
Police vs Kids
God vs Allah
Chicken Joe's vs KFC
Cats vs Dogs
Aliens vs Predators

I haven't seen any of them. You'd know if there was a war because all the windows would be broken and the helicopters would have guns on them. The helicopters don't even have guns, just torchlights. I don't even think there's a war. I haven't seen it.

I don't even know what side I'm on. Nobody's told me yet. Vs just means against.

When Mamma was in the shower I got the tomato knife from the block. It was just a test. You had to be extra careful with the pointy end. I held it like an ironboy, I chooked the air like it was an enemy. I put it in my trousers. I walked around with it and pretended like there was a war. I pretended like God forgot me so I could do all the bad war things and not even have to feel it.

Me: 'There's a war! God has forgotten me! Papa has forgotten me! All the lights in the street are broken and the wolves are chasing us! It's every man for himself! (I only said it inside my head.)

I had to put the knife back in the end, it was getting too hutious. It's too sharp. I kept waiting to cut my own leg. You can't keep a knife in your trousers all the time, you might forget it's there and when you sit down it will go through your leg and come out the other side. If a war starts I'll just split instead, it's easier. I'm the best runner in the whole of Year 7, only Brett Shawcross can even catch me.

Ross Kelly is like that because somebody put acid in his milk when he was a baby. Everybody agrees. He always sticks his tongue out when he's writing his answers, he says it helps him concentrate but it just makes him look dey touch. I tried writing with my tongue sticking out: it didn't make me write any faster. It just made my tongue go proper frozen and dry.

If Ross Kelly calls Poppy Four Eyes again I'll push him out the window. I only let him look through my binoculars because he begged like a dog.

Me: 'It's Poppy's turn next!'

Ross Kelly: 'She don't need binoculars, she's got four eyes already.'

Poppy: 'Piss off!'

Me: 'Yeah, piss off, Skidmark!'

I went to the cafeteria window and Poppy stayed by the library stairs. Then she watched me through the binoculars. When I got back she had to say what I was doing.

Poppy: 'You were walking in slow motion. I could see you.'

Me: 'That wasn't slow motion, that was a robot.'

Poppy: 'Whatever. They both look the same to me.'

Me: 'I wasn't blurry or anything though? I looked close-up?'

Poppy: 'Yes.'

Me: 'See, I told you they were real.'

Poppy: 'I believe you, I believe you!'

I put my binoculars back in my bag for if they got broken. Nobody knows what they're really for, just me and Dean. I can't even tell Poppy about the case. I have to protect her for if the killer tries to hurt her to get to me. They're always doing that: they kidnap the detective's wife and cut her toes off one after another until the detective gives up. If Poppy asks, the binoculars are just for birds and distant games. It's safer like that. Poppy is my girlfriend now. It was easy. I didn't even have to ask her, I only had to tick the box.

So far I've collected five fingerprints. I've got Manik's, Connor Green's, Ross Kelly's, Altaf's, and Saleem Khan's. I asked for Chevon Brown's, Brett Shawcross's and Charmaine de Freitas's but they all told me to go f— myself.

Dean: 'We need innocent prints to compare to the killer's, so we can rule them out of the investigation.'

Me: 'Roger that, Captain. I'm on it like stink.'

I put all the sellotapes with the fingerprints on in my special hiding place with my alligator tooth. I folded them up in paper so they don't get any dirt or hairs on them. My room is now my headquarters. Nobody's allowed in without the password and I haven't even told anybody what the password is (it's pigeon, after my pigeon. Nobody else can find out if you only think it).

It isn't really a fingerprint's job to identify you. That's just an accident because everybody's pattern is different. A fingerprint is really just for feeling with. They're so you can tell the different textures and surfaces. Mr Tomlin told us.

Mr Tomlin: 'The fingerprint is made up of tiny ridges in the skin. When you brush your fingertips over a surface, it causes vibrations, and these friction ridges amplify the vibrations, making the signals to your sensory nerves stronger and allowing the brain to analyse the texture better.'

Me: 'So you can feel the close-up of things.'

Mr Tomlin: 'That's right.'

I couldn't burn my fingers so I decided just to freeze them instead. It was the next best way to make them go numb. I just wanted to see what Auntie Sonia's fingers feel like. I wanted to see if it was true about the close-up things. I got some snow from the bottom of the freezer and scraped a big pile into the bowl.

Me: 'Can you get frostbite from the freezer snow?'

Lydia: 'Advise yourself. Of course you can't.'

Me: 'But if I touched it for a really long time. Like for one whole hour. Then I might. I don't want them to die, I just want to freeze them for a little while. Don't let me freeze them too long, OK? Tell me when it's been half an hour, that should do it.'

It took donkey hours for my fingers to go numb. It even gave me pains. The cold was so cold it was burning. I kept wanting to take my fingers out but I had to leave them in for it to work. Lydia was watching Hollyoaks. The boy was kissing the other boy again. I just used the sick feeling it gave me for a distraction. I pretended I couldn't see my fingers. I pretended they didn't even belong to me.

Me: 'Are you counting?'

Lydia: 'Don't disturb! I'm watching this!'

When my fingers finally went numb it was like they just fell off. I couldn't even feel them anymore. Asweh, it felt very crazy. I got a melon and touched it. It even worked! I couldn't even feel the pattern on the outside. It was like my fingers weren't even made of skin anymore, it was like they were made of nothing. I swear by God, It was the craziest thing I've ever seen.

I tried the cushion on the sofa. I couldn't even feel the pattern. It's only lines but I couldn't even feel them. I was pressing proper hard but nothing happened. It was like I wasn't even there but just a spirit. I felt the feathers on Lydia's parrot costume. They didn't feel soft enough, they were too far away. I felt Lydia's face. I couldn't hardly feel it. I tried her nose and her lips and her cheek and her ear. I tried everything. It all felt far away, like she was just a dream.

Me: 'It feels crazy! You should try it.'

Lydia: 'Ho! Get off! It's cold!'

I tried to pick up a groundnut but it was too complicated. I kept missing. It was very funny. You can see your finger on the groundnut but you can't make it pick up. You just keep dropping it. It's proper vexing. It makes you feel very stupid. I only stopped when I forgot how long it had been. Lydia stopped counting donkey hours ago.

Me: 'The experiment was a complete success!'

Lydia: 'You're a complete retard!'

It was even hutious at first, you think the numbness will last forever. I felt sorry for Auntie Sonia then. I could still remember what the things felt like, I could use my memory to trick my fingers. But what happens if you tried to feel something brand new that you don't already know? I pretended like I was Auntie Sonia and I was in a new country where everything was brand new. I couldn't remember how anything feels because I haven't been there before. It was very hutious.

Me: 'What if it's night-time and all the light goes out and there's a fire, how will she find her way outside?'

Lydia: 'I don't know. It won't even happen.'

Me: 'What if it does happen? She'll get burned up like human toast.'

It even made me feel sick, I didn't want to think about it. When the numbness starts to run out it makes your fingers go all prickly. Asweh, it was a mighty relief. It meant they'd go back to normal. If I had to be numb forever it would just be too vexing. I'd have to pick everything up with my mouth instead like a dog. Everybody would call me Dogboy. I don't even want to think about it for if I make it come true.

Lydia's only vexed because she's not good enough to be a detective. She only wants to make hair when she grows up. All girls just want to make hair.

Me. 'My job's better. Detectives catch the bad guy and you can drive as fast as you like.'

Miquita: 'The detective don't get a gun though. The bad guy does. And he don't have to ask for what he wants, he just takes it. The detective's just an employee with a target on his back. I don't wanna work for no one, man.'

Miquita was ironing Lydia's hair. Mamma go sound her when she finds out.

Me: 'I bet it goes on fire.'

Lydia: 'How! No it won't.'

Me: 'I bet it does.'

Lydia: 'Don't disturb!'

Me: 'I can watch if I want.'

Lydia can't stop me watching. I'm the man of the house.

Lydia: 'Just don't burn me, OK?'

Miquita: 'Don't worry, man. I've done it enough times.'

Chanelle: 'Twice.'

Miquita: 'So? I'm well skilful, innit. My auntie taught me, she learned it in the pen.'

Miquita's auntie was a forger. It's when they buy something with a ticket except it isn't a real ticket, they actually drew it themself.

The whole thing takes donkey hours. When you iron the hair you only do a little bit at a time. You have to go proper slow so you don't make a fire, first one side then the other. It's very relaxing. I nearly fell asleep. We had to stop for a break. They pretended the apple juice was champagne.

I told you. Girls are very stupid.

It was very funny watching Lydia try to keep still. She was concentrating proper hard. She was even scared of the iron. When it came near her she closed her eyes up tight.

Lydia: 'Watch my ears.'

Miquita: 'Why, what are they doing?'

Lydia: 'Don't mess around.'

Lydia's hair was actually going flat. It happened right before our eyes. It looked bo-styles. Lydia was very happy, you could tell. She kept looking at herself in the mirror. She was falling in love with herself. Asweh, it was very funny.

Me: 'You want to kiss yourself. Go on, kiss yourself!'

Lydia: 'Don't disturb!'

Miquita: 'Keep still, man, or I'll burn you.'

She was holding the iron right next to Lydia's ear. There was smoke coming from it. Then Miquita's face went all hard. It came from nowhere. She wasn't laughing anymore.

Miquita: 'Are you with us?'

Lydia: 'What are you talking about?'

Miquita: 'You know what I'm talking about. You're either with us or against us, innit.'

The iron was right over Lydia's eye. It was nearly touching it. The smoke was going in her face. My belly went cold. Chanelle ate the last Oreo.

Chanelle: 'Don't, man, that ain't necessary. She knows the score, innit.'

Miquita: 'Shut up. Don't make me bounce you. You didn't see nothing. You don't know nothing, right?'

Everything went proper slow. Miquita was making the iron go near then pulling it away like a crazy game. I could feel Lydia's scared, it made me scared as well. I got ready like for an invader. I planned it in my head: get the knife from the block, chook the invader until they're blind, then push them outside and into the lift. One of us call the police. Chook them sharp-sharp so you don't have to feel it. It's only self-defence. Lydia closed her eyes. I could even smell the burning before it happened. It felt like all the birds fell out of the sky, dead.

Lydia: 'Please. I don't know anything. I'm with you, I'm with you.'

Lydia opened her eyes. She checked herself in the mirror: there was one tiny patch on her cheek gone shiny and red. She felt it proper slow like it was a kiss. I love waiting for the holes to grow back, the new skin makes you stronger. That's the best thing about cuts and burns.

Then Miquita's face just dropped. All the stiffness fell off and she was normal again. It happened proper quick. I even thought it was just a dream gone wrong.

Miquita: 'Keep looking to the front, yeah? It's gonna look well sick, believe. Just keep still, I don't wanna hurt you. You shouldn't have moved.'

Lydia: 'Sorry.'

I got my breath back. The world woke up again. When Lydia's hair was finished it actually looked bo-styles. It was proper flat and everything. It was worth the wait.

Me: 'Ho! It looks stupid! You look like a buffalo!' (I had to hoot her even if I didn't mean it. Telling a girl they look nice means you love them too much.)

Chanelle: 'No it don't, it looks wicked.'

Miquita: 'I'm too good! I can't help it!'

I got their fingerprints on a piece of sellotape. Chanelle gave me hers straight away but Miquita wouldn't cooperate. Then I remembered what Dean told me:

Dean: 'If they won't give you their finger, just get them to have a drink. Then the fingerprint will be on the glass. It's a piece of cake.'

Miquita thinks she's so clever. Who's laughing now! I didn't need Lydia's fingerprints. She's not a suspect, she's just my sister. She didn't even cry when the burning came true.

*   *   *

Lydia was killing her Dance Club costume. She had the scissors and she was slicing and cutting like a crazy shark. Her eyes were all wet and she kept stopping to pray. It felt like a crazy dream. You couldn't even move, you just had to keep watching for what would happen next. It was like the time Abena stuck the coat-hanger wire up her nose to make it go like an obruni nose (she thought that was how they got them that shape). Everybody knew it would never work, they were just waiting for something big to go wrong. It was like she'd lost her mind.

I kicked the door. I had to stop her before she got too crazy to come back from.

Lydia: 'Happy now?'

Me: 'What are you doing?'

Lydia: 'What does it look like? You won't believe it wasn't blood. You think I'm a liar. Do you believe me now?'

Me: 'Don't you want to keep it? I thought you loved it.'

Lydia: 'No I don't, it's stupid. I hate Dance Club anyway. It's all stupid.'

I didn't understand what was happening, I just helped her anyway. We took her parrot costume on the balcony. It was all in pieces like something dead. It was a long way to fall. When it hit the bottom it would all be over and you could start again. Both the two of us threw the pieces off. We watched them fall like big slow rain. Rain always washes the blood away in the end. There were some smaller kids down below. They let our raindrops fall on them and picked them up and made them back into feathers. They chased each other with them like crazy parrots and threw them like the lightest bombs.

Lydia: 'Don't tell anyone what I did, will you?'

Me: 'Do you know who it came from?'

Lydia: 'No, I swear to God. All I did was take the clothes to the launderette, that's it. It was only a test.'

Me: 'My coat wasn't stolen. I threw it down the rubbish pipe.'

Lydia: 'Why?'

Me: 'I don't have to tell you if you don't have to tell me.'

Lydia: 'Fine.'

Me: 'Jordan threw a cat down the rubbish pipe once.'

Lydia: 'No he didn't, he's just bluffing you. You're so gullible.'

We kept watching until the smaller kids gave up and threw the feathers down. All the landed pieces looked like dead bodies just asleep. I said a sorry inside my head but it wasn't sad anymore, it was strong. Strong to protect us from whatever came after, like an alligator tooth for all of us.

It's better if you don't see us coming, believe me. You have things you want to achieve, obligations to meet, all that human stuff. It's those things you do while you're pretending death isn't waiting around the corner that determine what look he'll have on his face when you bump into him. Carry on doing those things, knock yourselves out. Make your choices, answer your calls. Live the moments and the monuments will take care of themselves, carved from marble after you've gone or shaped in the clay of the still-living.

I got new trainers. They're called Diadora. Have you heard about them? Asweh, they're bo-styles. Mamma saw what I did to my Sports.

Mamma: 'What happened to your canvas? They're ruined.'

Me: 'I wanted Adidas.'

Lydia: 'It's not even straight. The lines are all wobbly. It looks gay.'

Me: 'Your face looks gay.'

Mamma: 'Ho! Enough with the gay! Nobody is gay!'

We went to the cancer shop. They sell trainers there as well. The Diadoras were the best. They were the only ones that fit me. It was a dope-fine piece of luck. They're white all over and the Diadora sign is blue. The Diadora sign looks like an arrow or something from space. You knew it would make you run superfast, you could tell straight away.

They don't even feel like foes. There's only a few small scratches on them. Their first owner took very good care of them. His feet just got too big. We tried to imagine what the first owner was like:

Lydia: 'I bet he was ugly and he had smelly feet with scabs all over them.'

Me: 'Don't bring yourself! They don't even smell. I bet he was the greatest at football and running.'

I pretended like he left some of his spirit inside the trainers and it will help me pass the ball straight and run for miles.

Lydia: 'Don't tell anybody where you bought them, they'll just rough you.'

Me: 'Just because they're from the cancer shop it doesn't mean they have cancer.'

Everybody says the things in the cancer shop have cancer. They're just stupid. My new trainers make me go faster than ever before. When I'm wearing them it feels like I could run forever and not even have to stop. I even tried them on the corridor where the floor's proper shiny and they made a mighty squeaky sound. It was too sweet.

It does sound like fuzzy-wuzzy. Only if you listen very carefully. It even works on Diadoras, not just nurse shoes.

Poppy loves my Diadoras. She thinks they're bo-styles. That's why we belong together, because we love the same things. We both love Diadoras and Michael Jackson and we both prefer the red grapes more than green. Having a girlfriend is easy. You just hold hands sometimes. That's your only duty. The rest of the time you can just have fun like normal. At breaktime me and Poppy sit on the steps outside the Science block. Sometimes she gives me missions. Sometimes I do the moonwalking for her or sing a song or tell a joke. Poppy loves it when I do something for her. Sometimes I want to play suicide bomber but Poppy wants me to stay with her. I don't even mind. I even want to stay.

At first I held Poppy's hand with my fingers flat and all together. Poppy hated it.

Poppy: 'That's for babies! This is the proper way, look.'

The proper way is to mix all your fingers up with the fingers of the other person. That way is more sexy. Girls just like it better. It makes your hand go proper sweaty but it still feels lovely. Only some of the rules for girlfriends are different around here. You can't chase them and make them fall over. It's banned. You just hold their hand instead. It's kinder like that.

Poppy let me try her glasses on. She only wears them for reading. They're not like old people's glasses, they're nice and small. She's still the most beautiful even when she's wearing them.

Me: 'I won't break them.'

Poppy: 'I know. They suit you. What do they look like?'

Me: 'It's quite crazy!'

When a normal person looks through glasses it makes the whole world go wobbly. Asweh, it's brutal. I couldn't see where I was going. I couldn't tell what was near and what was far away. When I walked around in them I felt seasick. I nearly crashed into the wall. Glasses only work if your eyes are broken already. If your eyes aren't broken they don't work. It was very funny. It was like looking at underwater.

Poppy: 'It only looks weird because you don't need glasses. It looks normal when I wear them.'

Me: 'I wish I needed glasses instead of you.'

Poppy: 'Ahh, that's sweet. Thank you.'

I wanted to tell her she was still the most beautiful. I wanted to tell her she was my yellow but there were too many people watching.

*   *   *

146

You can't see the lines but you know they're there. You just have to carry them in your head. The tunnel behind the shopping centre is one line. If you cross it you'll be slipping. I don't even go in that tunnel. It's just too hutious. It's always dark even when the sun's out and the water in the puddles is proper shitty and toxic.

The road going past my school is the next line. Behind it is no-go. The nearest I've been is the bus stop next to the hill. I've never been further than that.

The next line is the road at the end of the river. McDonald's is on the other side. I've never been there except with Mamma on the bus. If you go there on your own you'll be slipping. That road belongs to the Lewsey Hill Crew.

The last line is the train tracks. They're proper far away behind the river. I've never been that far. The train tracks is where they fight all the wars. It's the war ground. One time the Dell Farm Crew and Lewsey Hill Crew had a mighty ruckus there. There were a thousand people. They all had knives and baseball bats and swords. Some of them died. It was in the early times before I came here.

Jordan: 'They chopped off their arms and legs and everything. It was well sick. They're still there. You can see the arms and legs hanging up from the trees. They left them there as a warning.'

I don't know if it's true. I don't even know the way to the train tracks.

The lines make a square. Only if you stay in the square you'll be safe. That's your home. If you stay there they can't kill you. The best thing about home is all the places to hide in. If somebody's chasing you and you need to get away there's always somewhere to go. There's a hell of alleyways all next to each other. You just have to go down one of them and you're safe. They'll never catch you. You just have to steer right and keep running.

You can hide in the bushes on the green. They're big enough to cover you. There was a dead man in the bushes for a whole year and nobody saw him. They only found him when a dog went in there to chase a stick and came out with a hand instead.

You can also hide in the bins. Nobody will look for you in there because of the smell. As long as you can hold your breath you can hide in there forever.

The church is home for everybody. If you go in there they can't do anything, it's a sacred law. You can run into the shops. If you're a good climber you can climb on the garage or up a tree. They can still see you but they can't get you. They're too heavy to climb up there. They can only get you down with a rope. Home is safe for everybody. Just remember to lock the locks!

Dizzy saw me at the main gate. I wasn't suspecting it and that made it even better. Hometime is the best for chases.

Dizzy: 'Oi, pussy boy, I'm gonna kill you! You best run!'

I just started running. They never catch me, they're just too slow. Sometimes I run straight home, like if the hunger idey kill me. But if I want to make the chase last longer I go twisty like a snake. I ran past the staff car park to the spiky fence. I didn't go top speed. I wanted Dizzy to think he could catch me. I stopped at the sign:

NO CLIMBING.
SERIOUS RISK
OF INJURY

I waited for Dizzy to catch up to me. I held the fence like I was a prisoner. That made him go red-eyes even more. It was very funny.

Dizzy: 'Don't play with me, man. I'm gonna f— you up for that!'

I let him get closer and then I started running again. I ran along the fence and through the gate and down the hill towards the tunnel. When I turned around Dizzy was still at the top of the hill breathing proper hard like a broken tro-tro. He had to give up. Another hundred points to Harrison Opoku! I told you my Diadoras were the fastest!

I only started running for real when X-Fire joined in. He was coming across the road just as I came out of the tunnel. When he saw me he went proper red-eyes and came straight for me.

X-Fire: 'You're dead, you little prick!'

My blood went high. I ran for the church. I tried to get in but the door was locked. I ran on past the Jubilee Centre and the big library. I stayed in a straight line to go faster. I could hear X-Fire's feet smashing down behind me. I could feel his killing thoughts coming loose and filling the air like extra sharp rain.

X-Fire: 'I'll f—ing kill you!'

I got to the shops. The lady in the chair car was right in front of me, I nearly crashed into her. I only had one second to think. I did it before I even knew. I got up on the back of her chair car. I didn't even have time to feel crazy.

Chair car lady: 'What are you doing there? Get off!'

Me: 'I can't! Sorry!'

X-Fire was catching us. You wanted her to go faster but the engine was stuck. It was proper vexing. It even felt slower than walking. Everything stopped. You thought you'd just break down and die from the slowness.

Me: 'Hurry up, lady! Put your foot down!'

Chair car lady: 'Get out of it!'

Some smaller kids came running by the side of us. They thought it was a game. They showed me their dirty fingers when they went past.

Smaller kids: 'Dickhead!'

Chair car lady: 'Right! I'm not having this!'

The chair car lady hit the brakes and made me get off. I turned around quick for a peek behind me. X-Fire was stopped. Dizzy was caught up to him. Both the two of them were laughing like a maniac. Everybody was laughing.

Dizzy: 'Nice wheels, pussy boy! Do you need a licence for one of them?'

X-Fire: 'Oi, Ghana! Tell that pisshead next time I see his dog I'm gonna shank it!'

Then they just split to the shops and took all the evil away with them. I just felt proper vexed from the chase being over too quick. It was too easy. I waited for my breath to come back then I carried on running. I caught up to the chair car lady in no time. I waved to her on my way past.

Me: 'Thank you for the ride! Sorry for the commotion!'

Chair car lady: 'Piss off, you cheeky little bastard!'

In England they can never tell if it's a trick or serious. I think they get tricked too much and it makes them forget what the serious feels like. When I'm old my chair car will be faster for getaways and the tyres will be bigger so it can get over the bumps.

JUNE

Our base is the stairs outside my tower, the ones that go to floor 1. We're safe there. Only the junkies use them and they're too sleepy to even see us. Me and Dean were on a stake-out (it's just another word for when you're watching for the bad guys). We have to stay there until we see action, even if it takes all day and night. We had Cherry Coke and some Skips for if it took that long.

I was on binoculars duty and Dean was in charge of making the notes. He had to write down whatever I saw for evidence.

Dean: 'I tried getting my mum's phone but she needs it. The camera's shit on it anyway, it's only three megapixels. We'll just have to do it the old-fashioned way.'

I even like the old-fashioned way best. Have you tried Skips? They're dope-fine. They taste like prawn and the flavour actually goes fizzy on your tongue. It's brutal.

Me: 'Do I have to tell everything I see?'

Dean: 'No, just anything that looks suspicious. People acting guilty or doing something strange.'

Me: 'Does Jesus count?'

Dean: 'No, he's not a suspect. Killers don't use roller-blades, it's too conspicuous. They'd just be giving themselves away.'

Me: 'That's what I thought.'

Jesus was going past on his rollerblades. He never crashes. He's very graceful. He's only called Jesus because

153

he has a beard and long hair except it's grey. Everybody says he looks like how Jesus would look if he was still alive today. I still told it, we just didn't write it down:

Me: 'Jesus comes past the flats on his rollerblades. He nearly falls over a crack in the pavement but he saves himself just in time. He carries on going. A smaller kid shows him his dirty finger. Time?'

Dean: 'Eight minutes past twelve.'

Me: 'Copy that. No suspicious happenings. Detective Opoku goes back to looking.'

It feels brutal looking from our stake-out place. Nobody knows we're watching them. Especially with the binoculars you can see things you don't normally get to see. It's very relaxing. I saw that Jesus has a tattoo of a snake on his arm. I never knew that before. It felt lovely. I saw a baby tricycle on the roof of the bus stop. That felt lovely too.

I could see the basketball court but there was nobody inside. It felt sad to be empty and broken like that. I don't even know why.

The best time was when I saw the pigeon nest. They live on the windows of the Pikey House (it's just a big old house where the orphans used to live but it got burned down before I came here). I could actually see them sleeping on the windowsills. My pigeon wasn't there, but other pigeons kept coming and going. They were probably bringing dinner home for the wife and children.

Pigeon: 'I'm home! Chop time!'

Baby pigeons: 'Mmmm! Worms, my favourite!'

Dean: 'Forget about the pigeons! Focus, we've got a job to do. Unless you wanna write the notes.'

Me: 'OK, OK, I'm focusing!'

We were concentrating on the Chips n Tings van. It's always parked across the road from my tower. Everybody who gets their chop from there is a suspect because their burgers are so rank. You'd have to be a criminal just to eat them.

Dean: 'It's a front for drugs, I'm telling you. They hide them in the wrapper or inside the bun. I asked for chips from there one time and the geezer wouldn't even serve me. He said try McDonald's instead.'

Me: 'Did he have a gold tooth?'

Dean: 'No, but he was smoking a fag. If you smoked a fag inside a real chip van the council'd shut you down. Health and safety, innit. It's definitely dodgy.'

All the rogues hang around Chips n Tings at night, smoking and listening to music proper loud from inside their cars. You wouldn't drive all the way to a chip van if the chop was rank. I wouldn't even walk there even if the hunger idey kill me. I kept proper still so the binoculars wouldn't shake. I stayed low so we didn't give away our location. We were there donkey hours. My behind started to ache like crazy but I couldn't be the first one to move. I even started to like the pain, it meant I was a real detective.

Dean: 'Anything?'

Me: 'Not yet. Unknown white male came, bought a burger, went again. No signs of guilt.'

Dean: 'Keep 'em peeled.'

Me: 'Right you are, Guv. That's an affirmative on keeping 'em peeled.'

Signs of guilt include:
Ants in your pant
Talking too fast
Always looking around you like you've lost something
Smoking too much
Crying too much
Scratching
Biting your fingers

Spitting
Sudden bouts of violence
Uncontrolled gas (farting a lot)
Religious hysteria

Dean learned them all from TV. People can show some of those things and still be innocent, like ants in their pant because they need to greet the chief. We were only interested in people who showed three or more at the same time. Three is the magic number.

Dean: 'What about him? He's smoking and I think I just saw him bite his nails. Zoom in.'

I zoomed in.

Me: 'That's OK, it's only Terry Takeaway. He always smokes like that.'

Dean: 'Can you vouch for him though? I think he's a dodgy bastard. Keep looking.'

Me: 'He's only showing two signs and both the two of them are normal for him. He only stopped to get a light for his fag. I think he's safe.'

Dean: 'You sure about that?'

Me: 'I'm sure. He's my friend.'

That's when Terry Takeaway saw me. Asbo must have seen me first because he started pulling on his lead and when Terry Takeaway followed him he looked right up at our location. He made a cup out of his hands to make his voice go even bigger.

Terry Takeaway: **'Alright, Harri!'**

Terry Takeaway loves making you jump like that. He thinks it's very funny.

Dean: 'F— it, that's our cover blown. Mission aborted. Bollocks.'

Me: 'Sorry, Sarge, my mistake.'

Dean: 'Forget it. Next time I'm on the binoculars, yeah?'

Me: 'OK.'

Next time I'm going to wear a disguise so civilians don't spot me. You can buy fake nose and glasses from the market, they're only a quid. Civilians is every other person who isn't a criminal or a cop.

Me: 'He might not even still be here. If I killed somebody I'd just run away so the police don't catch me.'

Dean: 'They'll be watching the airports though. No, he'll probably just lie low till the police stop looking. Some other kid'll get killed soon and they'll have to concentrate on him. Then our killer can just come out of hiding and carry on like nothing happened.'

Me: 'That sucks.'

Dean: 'I know. But that's why we need the evidence, innit. We need to get our arses in gear, start collecting DNA. Blood, spit, shit even. Bogeys. Anything that came from a person that you can take away without 'em knowing. As long as you keep it in the fridge it won't go bad. All we need is some bags or something to put the samples in.'

Me: 'Hang on.'

I got a blackcurrant Chewit from my pocket. I put the Chewit in my mouth, then I got the best bogey I could find and put it in the empty wrapper. It was a perfect fit. There was plenty of room to fold it over so the bogey would stay nice and fresh.

Me: 'Perfect!'

I chucked the bogey bomb at Dean. He dodged it just in time. I gave him a Chewit and he did the same thing. He got a big bogey and wrapped it up in a bomb and chucked it at me. It would even work for shit if it was just a small piece. I don't know how to get human shit without the person it belongs to finding out. I don't even want to know! The Chief will have to pay us extra for that!

Me: 'What's DNA?'

Dean: 'It's a bit like a fingerprint but on the inside. All the cells in your body have a tiny label on them that only belongs to you. It's even on the shit cells and the spit cells, it's on all of 'em. You can only read it with a microscope.'

Me: 'What does it say?'

Dean: 'It's just a load of colours. But the order they go in's different for everyone, like my DNA could be green blue red green, and yours could be green blue green red, all times a million. And the order they go in decides if you'll be clever or fast and what colour eyes you'll have and what crimes you'll do. The DNA decides it all before you're even born.'

It felt brutal. That must be why I'm fast, because God knew I wanted to be fast. He gave me all the skills I wanted before I even asked for them. Asweh, DNA is a great invention. I wish I could see my colours, then I could see what other skills I'm going to learn in the future. I hope one of them's basketball. I got another bogey and looked at it through the wrong end of the binoculars but I couldn't see anything, the colours are buried too far down.

It's a shame the killer didn't see his colours in time. Then he could have found the colour for when he chooked the dead boy and painted it over with something else. Poppy does it all the time. She finishes painting her nails, then decides she doesn't like the colour after all, and starts all over again. Asweh, she should just stick to one colour or she'll be painting her nails forever and there'll be no time left over for loving me!

Lydia is in love with Samsung Galaxy. It's a kind of mobile phone. It's all she ever talks about. She thinks Auntie Sonia will buy her one for her birthday. I even heard her praying for it when she was in the bathroom. I waited for her to come out.

Me: 'I'm telling. You're not supposed to pray for a mobile phone!'

Lydia: 'Don't bring yourself! I can pray for what I like!'

Me: 'Devil-lover!'

Lydia: 'Bum-licker!'

Lydia won't even get a Samsung Galaxy, it's a hundred quid. If she gets a phone then I'll ask for a Playstation. Otherwise it won't be fair. Auntie Sonia loves us both the same.

I love listening to people talking on their mobile phone. You can hear them all over: walking along, waiting to pay in the supermarket, sitting in the playground. The best time is when you're on the bus, then they can't get away. You can hear everything. They talk about a hell of crazy things. I listen to them every time we go on the bus to the cancer shop (the driver sits behind bulletproof glass. It's brutal. That way he's safe from bullets and he won't get bitten if any animals run amok).

One time I heard a man talking about cheese. He was telling the person on the other side of the phone that he got the cheese for them.

Man on the phone: 'I got the cheese. I couldn't get camembear, they didn't have none. I had to get bree instead.'

Asweh, that's what he said! It was too funny. Another time I heard a girl talking about when she got her belly button pierced. She was telling how it went poison from the belly-button ring.

Girl on the phone: 'I know you're s'posed to bathe it. I did bathe it. Saltwater, yeah. It still went manky. There was pus coming out of it. I just took it out in the end, I couldn't be arsed with it. Can you get cancer in your belly button?'

I swear by God, you hear some very crazy things! It's very relaxing. Mamma says it's just jibber-jabber but I love it. I think it's very interesting. Just don't let them see you listening or they'll stop and then the fun is over.

Lydia: 'I'll only use it for emergencies. It's for you really, so you can know where I am the whole time. It's safer like that.'

Me: 'Liar. She only wants it so she can talk rudeness to Miquita.'

Lydia: 'How! No I don't.'

Mamma: 'What rudeness?'

Lydia: 'Nothing!'

Me: 'All about kissing boys.'

Mamma: 'Which boys?'

Auntie Sonia: 'Lydia has a boyfriend!'

Lydia: 'No I don't. He's just bluffing.'

Me: 'How did you hurt your nose?'

Auntie Sonia has a big bandage over her nose and her eye is all bruised a hell of different colours like a rainbow. She looks like she was in a war. I got ready to destroy whoever did it. I'd chook them with the toothy knife so it hurt extra bad.

Mamma: 'Yes, how did you hurt it? Tell us.'

Auntie Sonia: 'It was my own stupid fault. I was reaching for my suitcase on top of the wardrobe, I was looking for a dress. It slid off and hit me right on the nose. Broke it like that. I saw stars.'

Lydia: 'Silly thing!'

Mamma: 'You should be more careful.'

Auntie Sonia: 'I know.'

Auntie Sonia went proper quiet when Julius came back from greeting the chief. He made her sit on his lap like a baby. He was holding her arm like he was a handcuff, like for if she ran away. His hand can fit around her whole arm, that's how big it is. He thought we were still talking about Agnes (she has a fever but she won't die, God won't let it happen if we all promise to be good).

Julius: 'If she needs medicine, I can get the good stuff for her. None of those past-the-expire-date hand-me-downs. I have a friend in Legon, I can make a call for you.'

Mamma: 'We're fine. You've done enough for us already, thank you.'

Julius: 'Julius only wants to make people happy, eh?'

He did a big messy laugh and pulled Auntie Sonia's too-tights. Auntie Sonia nearly fell off the chair. You could see the line of her pant under her too-tights. It was quite disgusting.

Mamma: 'I've got to get to work. Come in the kitchen and I'll give you that tea bread.'

Me: 'I didn't know we had tea bread. Can I have some?'

Mamma: 'It's the last piece. I'll make some more tomorrow.'

I heard Mamma's secret drawer get opened and shut again. You can tell it's the secret drawer from the squeak. There's no tea bread in there, only a hell of money and Dairy Milk chocolate. I know because I looked this morning. I didn't take any.

Me: 'I observed no crumbs on the suspect's mouth when he came back from location: kitchen. My detective's nose smelled a rat.' (I only said it inside my head.)

Julius always splits in a hurry, he makes a big wind behind him. Auntie Sonia has to run after him like a dog. The

Julius wind made her face go stiff like the fart wind from the tube. It smells like kill-me-quick and the Persuader.

Mamma: 'Don't forget the lift's broken. Take care down those stairs, you don't want another accident.'

Auntie Sonia: 'Don't worry about me, I'm fine. What colour phone do you want?'

Mamma: 'No, Sonia. There's no need for that.'

Lydia: 'A red one.'

Auntie Sonia: 'I'll see what I can do.'

Lydia: 'Thank you!'

Me: 'Be careful of the puddles! People ease themself on the stairs.'

Lydia: 'Harri spits on them.'

Mamma: 'What's that now?'

Me: 'No I don't! Mamma, I swear by God!'

Julius: 'Come on, let's go!'

Julius was at the end of the corridor. He let the door swing back and just kept going. It nearly hit Auntie Sonia in the face. Asweh, two broken noses in one day would be a world record for unlucky! I couldn't get a fingerprint from the glass Julius used, the fumes from his kill-me-quick must have melted it. I smelled some close up one time and it burned the skin off my eyes. I was blind for one hour.

If Connor Green calls Poppy slack again I'll stick a compass in his leg. Connor Green said he saw Poppy's boobs. He said he's seen the boobs of every girl in Year 7.

Connor Green: 'It was when they had swimming. They let me in the changing room when the teacher weren't there and they all showed me. Fannies as well. It weren't even my idea, they just wanted to do it. You can ask them.'

Me: 'I will ask them.'

Connor Green: 'They won't admit it. They don't want you to know how slack they are.'

Connor Green's just a liar. He's never seen Poppy's boobs. He's only saying that because he wants to be her boyfriend. When he saw the message Poppy made for me his eyes went all dark. That's how I knew. He wanted the message to be for him, you could tell.

P.M.+H.O.
I.D.S.T.

It means me and Poppy belong together. That's what the top letters stand for: P.M. is for Poppy Morgan and H.O. is for Harrison Opoku. When you put + between them it means those two people go together like a sum. That's what Poppy told me.

Poppy: 'I.D.S.T. stands for If Destroyed Still True. That

means if somebody rubs them out, they still count. Nobody can destroy it, it lasts forever.'

Poppy wrote it on her desk. It was in English. Do you know what's Tippex? It's a special paint for crossing out your mistakes. It's white to be the same colour as the paper. If you make a mistake, you just paint over it with Tippex and start again. Then nobody has to see the mistake you made. It's very clever. I wish it worked with everything and not just writing.

Poppy: 'Now you write it. It's got to be as big as mine.'

Me: 'What if Mrs Bonner sees?'

Poppy: 'She won't. I'll cover it with my folder.'

Poppy held her folder in front while I wrote my message. You can't breathe the Tippex in because it's the same poison as in the marker pen. The brush is proper small. It's good for writing because you can get it quite neat. The only best thing is, when it's dry you can't rub it out. I wanted the whole world to see. I only had to keep it a secret until the Tippex was dry.

My hand was a bit wobbly because I had to go fast. It still looked bo-styles.

H.O.+P.M.
I.D.S.T.

My message was the same as hers except I put H.O. before P.M. I put my letters first because the message was from me. Everything else was the same. I covered it with my pencil case until the end of the lesson. I read it again before I left class. It felt brutal seeing it there. It felt important. Even Poppy thought so, she loved it, you could tell. She was smiling from ear to ear. Now everybody who sits at my desk will know me and Poppy belong to each other. You can't even take it back. It's the same as being married. It's better than that because you don't even have to sex them.

When you get married, everybody in your family, your mamma and papa and her mamma and papa, they all wait outside the sexing room. The husband and wife go in there and do it. They can only come out when they've done it. After they've done it, it means they're married in the eyes of God and it can never be broken. Then you have a big feast. But if a fish comes out of the girl's toto it means she's already done it with another boy. Then she's broken and you don't have to marry her, you can just send her back to her family. It's good news if the girl's ugly, but not so lucky if she was beautiful and you really wanted to keep her!

Connor Green: 'I seen this video once of a woman shagging a dog. I think it was an Alsatian. Is shagging a dog a sin in your country?'

Me: 'Shagging any animal's a sin, it could be a dog or a chicken or a worm, it doesn't matter. God will take your eyes for that.'

Connor Green: 'What about shagging a kid? That's the worst ever, it's got to be. What happens if you shag a kid, what will God do to you then?'

Me: 'Then he'll kill you in the worst ever way. Like all your skin will fall off and your brain will boil. Your eyes will go pop and your guts will fall out through your bumhole.'

Dean: 'Nasty!'

The never-normal girl is always scared like a little rabbit because her grandpa sexes her. That's what Dean said. She lives with her grandpa. He sexes her all day. That's why she walks funny. That's why she's quiet like a rabbit.

Me: 'Why doesn't she tell her mamma?'

Dean: 'Her mum's dead. It's just her and her granddad.'

Me: 'Why doesn't she tell the police then?'

Dean: 'If she told them they'd take her granddad away and then she'd have nowhere to live.'

Then I felt sorry for the never-normal girl. I wanted to say she could live with me except then everybody would think I loved her.

Connor Green: 'There's some people who just shag a hole in the wall. They make a hole in the wall and put their dick through it. It's usually in a toilet.'

Asweh, I didn't even believe it! It felt too crazy. They pretend the hole is a lady. Sometimes there's a lady on the other side of the wall. When she sees the man's bulla coming through the hole she kisses it.

Me: 'So what's the wall for?'

Connor Green: 'So they can't see each other.'

Me: 'Why, are they ugly?'

Connor Green: 'Usually.'

Me: 'Then why even sex them? Why not just sex the wall?'

Dean: 'Because they don't want people to think they're a pervert.'

Poppy would never even show Connor Green her boob. She thinks he's a spaz. Girls don't even like you if you're a spaz, they only like you if you're sexy. Asweh, Connor Green has never seen a boob, I'll bet you a million pounds.

People do ease themself on the stairs, you can smell it from a million miles away. You have to be careful not to go in the puddles. If you jump in a normal puddle you're only a retard but if you jump in a piss puddle it means you're made of piss.

If you land on a needle and it goes through your foot you'll get Aids. You have to go extra fast and still be very careful at the same time. It's a very difficult skill. It could be my next superpower.

I can't go in the lift anymore. Not ever again. Fag Ash Lil was in there. I didn't see her until it was too late. The door was already closed. She was behind me the whole time. She stared at me all the way up with her mad watery eyes. She wanted to kill me, you could tell. She thought it was me who kicked the ball at her.

It wasn't me, it was Jordan. I don't know why she thought it was me. I wasn't even shooting. I only wanted to play passing. The lift stopped.

Fag Ash Lil: 'Bloody hell!'

I thought I was going to die but the lift started again. It was just a false alarm. She only has to scratch me with her claws and I'll get poison. Then when I'm asleep she'll cut me up and make me into a pie. I wanted to say sorry but the words wouldn't come out. I couldn't even move. It was very hutious. I felt my alligator tooth in my pocket. I prayed for a second chance.

The lift was taking donkey hours. My belly was proper cold. I could feel Fag Ash Lil keep looking at me with her eyes all blue and hungry. If I turned around she'd spit poison in my face and take me away to her den. I don't even want to die yet. The lift stopped again.

Me: 'Bloody hell!'

When the doors opened, I swear by God, it was the mightiest relief! Fag Ash Lil got out. I watched for if she turned around but she just carried on walking. Then the doors closed again and I let a woodpecker fart out. I dedicated it to God and all the angels. Adjei, it was too close! From today onward going I can never go in the lift again. I can only use the stairs. The stairs are safe. If I run fast enough the pissy smell can't even catch me.

When the man who tells you the news on London Tonight makes his face go proper serious, you know you have to listen. You can tell he isn't lying. When he talks about the dead boy you know he misses him as well. You know he loves him. You just have to listen, it's your duty. Even Lydia agreed this time. She made me turn the sound up.

Newsman: 'It's three months today since he was fatally stabbed outside a fast-food restaurant, yet another victim of the knife-crime epidemic which continues to grip the capital. Police blame a fear of reprisals for the public's failure to come forward with information. Tonight we ask just what can be done to break the wall of silence, and encourage those with information to speak up. Your thoughts, please, the usual numbers at the bottom of your screen.'

Me: 'They should give them a prize. Just ask them what they want the most and then buy it for them. Then they'll talk. Like a new bike or a shitload of fireworks. Or if they had their favourite things already, then they wouldn't kill anybody because they'd be too happy. They wouldn't even think of it.'

Lydia: 'Who'll buy all the things?'

Me: 'The Queen. She's got plenty of money. She doesn't even need it all, she's old.'

Lydia: 'Write to the Queen then. Ask her for a new bike and see what she says.'

Me: 'I will. I'll email her. And I'll ask for a new face for you. Your old one's too ugly.'

Lydia: 'Don't bring yourself. Ask for a new brain for you. Yours is too soft.'

Me: 'Or a new behind for you. Yours is too fat. It looks like a bungalow.'

Lydia: 'Your head looks like a toilet.'

Me: 'Your head is a toilet. That's why it smells like shit.'

I waited for Lydia's turn but she was just watching the dead boy's picture on the TV. Her face was all sad like she knew him. She didn't know him. I knew him better than her.

Me: 'You can't suck him off, he's dead.'

Lydia: 'Advise yourself! I wasn't even thinking that. You're disgusting!'

168

He's even lucky. One kiss from Lydia would give you all the stupid germs in the world. I wonder what Heaven is really like. Is it different for kids than for grown-ups. Like would there still be somebody there telling him to come in from playing football when it got too dark. The dead boy could do the most tricks, he could flick the ball up with his heel and keep it up for donkey hours with both feet. He always aimed his shots for the corners like you're supposed to and he was even good at heading. He was good at everything. I wonder if there's dogs like Asbo who steal your ball. That would be funny. I hope in Heaven the animals can all talk, then they can tell you when they're happy so you don't have to guess. You can usually tell from the eyes but it only works on bigger animals, not pigeons or flies. Their eyes only look sad.

Newsman: 'That's all from us. Goodnight.'

Me: 'Goodnight!'

I always say it back. I don't care. When he says it I say it back to him.

Lydia: 'He's not even talking to you.'

Me: 'Yes he is, he's looking right at me.'

Lydia: 'But he can't see you. He doesn't know you're there.'

Me: 'I know that. I'm not stupid.'

Asweh, it always makes Lydia confused! I know he can't see me. But he's still talking to me or he wouldn't say it. It's the same when you talk to them on the phone, they can't see you but they're still talking to you. It's just fair. He said it to me so I say it back. Manners cost nothing, that's what Mamma says. It's Lydia who's stupid.

Me: 'Thank you! See you tomorrow!'

I used to chase the birds when I was little but I gave it up.
You can never catch them. The only ones you can catch
is chickens and they don't count because they're too easy.
There was a pigeon with only one leg. He was nearly as
lovely as mine. He could still walk quite good. He was just
hopping along the edge of the green looking for worms.

Me: 'Did you lose your leg in a pigeon war or did a cat
get it? Were you born like that? Don't worry, you're safe,
I'll tell you if I see any bad kids. I won't let them bash you.'

Pigeon: '   '

I know Jesus said I'm worth a hundred sparrows, but I
don't know what he thinks about pigeons. I think we're
both worth the same. Pigeons maybe more, because they
can fly and I can't. I love them with one leg or two.

There's grass now where the tree used to be. When the
tree fell down the men dug it up and filled the hole with
dirt. Now there's grass there. It's nearly covered already.
You can't even hardly see the dirt anymore. It's quite amazing. I don't know where the grass came from so quick, I
didn't see anybody plant it. It just grew there. It feels like
magic.

The seeds must have come down in the rain. It's the only
way I can think of.

I sat down on the new grass and listened to the wind
in the trees. When the wind blows through the leaves it
sounds just like the sea. I love it when the wind sounds like

the sea, it's very relaxing. Inside is too small sometimes, it makes me feel too squeezed up. I just wanted to stay outside with the sea and birds.

If Agnes dies I'll just swap places with her. She can have my life. I'll give it to her and I'll die instead. I wouldn't mind because I've already lived for a long time. Agnes has only lived for one year and some. I hope God lets me. I don't mind going to Heaven early. If he wants me to swap places, I will. I just hope I can try Haribo Horror Mix first (they're my favourite of all the Haribo styles. The sweets are all crazy shapes, like bats and spiders and ghosts. Mamma says it's against God but she just worries too much).

Mamma: 'Don't be silly. Agnes isn't going to die, she only has a fever.'

Me: 'Moses Agyeman's sister had a fever. She died.'

Mamma: 'That's not the same.'

Lydia: 'She only died because her mamma went to a juju doctor. Everybody knows it.'

I was still very scared. Anybody can die, even a baby. They die every day. The dead boy never hurt anybody and he got chooked to death. I saw the blood. His blood. If it can happen to him it can happen to anybody. I kept waiting for Agnes to say hello to me but it never came. She could only breathe and it didn't feel the same. It wasn't as loud as it should be. It was too fast and far away.

Grandma Ama: 'She'll be fine. God is watching over her.'

Me: 'Where's Papa?'

Grandma Ama: 'Working. Do you have a message for him?'

Me: 'Just tell him when he comes over to bring a blanket for Agnes. The blankets on the plane are too scratchy, they make you go electric.'

Grandma Ama: 'I'll tell him. Don't worry.'

When I put the phone down I could still hear Agnes breathing in my ear. I just wanted it to be louder. I don't even know why you have to die before you can get into Heaven, there should just be a door you can go through. Then you could come back and visit whenever you want, it would be like a holiday instead of forever. Forever's too long, it isn't even fair.

Sharks never sleep. They have to keep swimming or they'll die so they're not allowed to sleep at all, not even for one second. I think I read it in my Creatures of the Deep book or it might have just come from my dream. My dream was just black. It was a sea and I fell in. It was Dead, the same one Agnes would go to. All the ectopics and unwanteds were there, I could hear them crying and feel them bumping me when I swam past. I couldn't take any of them with me, it wasn't up to me. I just had to keep swimming like a shark. I heard Agnes calling to me:

Agnes: **'Harri!'**

but I wasn't allowed to stop. She was on her own. All I could do was keep swimming and hope one of the waves I made would reach her and pick her up. That was the only way to save her.

When I woke up my legs were tired from all the kicking. I just hoped I'd swum fast enough and made a big enough wave. They had a long way to go.

Papa taught me to swim in the sea at Kokrobite. It was after we delivered the chairs he made for the hotel by the beach. At first I was scared for if there were sharks but Papa knew how to chase them away if they came too close.

Papa: 'You just punch them on the nose. Their noses are extra ticklish. It makes them sneeze, then when their eyes are closed you just swim away. You'll be safe.'

Papa held my belly up, I just had to kick my legs. It was even easy. I loved making waves. It felt like the waves were pulling us together so we wouldn't get lost. Every time I thought I was going to fly away Papa just turned me around towards him and I was safe again. Asweh, the sea is even bigger than you can fit in your head. When I looked to the end of the sea it wasn't even hutious anymore, it was like looking at the place where I came from. Every time one of the fishing men jumped in the sea he made another splash that added to ours. They didn't stay apart like I thought they would, they all got mixed up like fingers in holding hands. They all became each other and the sea stretched back to the same shape It always was. It was very clever. The waves you make keep you together so you don't get lost. You just have to aim in the right direction and kick.

I woke up too fast to see you. You were there outside my window, I could feel it before I opened my eyes, but when I looked you were already flying away! Stay next time, I only want to talk to you. I only want to ask you if there really is a Hea

Pigeon: There is.

Me: Is the dead boy there? I knew it! What about Agnes, will she be OK? I don't want her to die as well. She doesn't like it on her own, she gets scared.

Pigeon: She'll be fine. We won't leave her on her own, I promise.

Me: How do I know you're telling the truth? What if you're just in my head?

Pigeon: Can you feel me in your belly?

Me: Sometimes, but it might just be from eating too fast or wishing too much.

Pigeon: No, it's me. Trust me, Harri, I wouldn't lie to you. Go back to sleep now.

Me: This time can I dream about you, that we're flying together like I'm the same as you? I want to do a shit on the bad guy's head, that would be brutal!

Pigeon: I'll see what I can do. Now close your eyes.

Brayden Campbell sneezes like a mouse. You think he'll do a massive sneeze because he's tough but when it comes out it's only a tiny little one. You can't even hear it. It hardly even makes a noise. Asweh, it's very funny!

Connor Green: 'It sounds like a mouse having an orgasm.'

You only can't laugh or he'll finish you. Orgasm is just another word for the sneeze of a mouse. It's my favourite word of today. I said it instead of God bless you.

Brayden Campbell: 'Ahchoo!'

Me: 'Orgasm!'

Brayden Campbell: 'F— off!'

Brayden Campbell is the toughest in Year 7. Nobody has ever beaten him. He's big and fast at the same time. His special move is the headlock. That's where they get your head under their arm so you can't see or breathe. He's also the best at real blows. Most people just hit the air but Brayden Campbell actually hits you. He punches like a man. I've seen it with my own two eyes. He punched Ross Kelly in the back of his head and spit came out his mouth. You could even hear where the punch landed. It was crazy. Brayden Campbell can knock you out with one punch.

Chevon Brown's the second toughest. He's not as big as Brayden but he's probably faster. He's never scared. He'll even kick you. He doesn't care if he kills you. He'll kick you in the belly or even the nuts.

Kyle Barnes just pushes you over all the time. He pushes you into the wall or the bushes. It's quite sneaky. Really it's cheating, he uses the world to defeat you. He just pushes you into whatever's there. The only way to beat him is to stay far away. If you're not close enough, he can't push you. He only pushes, it's the only move he knows. I could beat him. I'm too fast for him. He can't push me over because I'm never close enough.

Kyle Barnes: 'Come here so I can get you, pussy!'

Me: 'Sorry! No can do!'

I'm tougher than Gideon Hall as well. He's in the other half of Year 7. Everybody says Gideon Hall's proper tough but it's only because he has the most backup. When he's on his own he's weak. One time Gideon Hall wouldn't let me past. I just crashed into him with my elbow and he nearly fell over. He didn't even come after me. He isn't tough at all.

LaTrell beat a boy in Year 9. I never met him, I just heard about it. He actually broke the other boy's arm. The police even came.

Everybody: 'He just bent it till it snapped. It was well sick. You could see the bone sticking out and everything. The other kid can never play basketball again. He can't get his arm over his head no more, it won't even go straight.'

Dean's special move is the uppercut. It's when you punch somebody from down below. You move your hand from down to up and punch them under the chin. He's never used it. It's only for emergencies.

Dean: 'It's too dangerous, innit. It can give them brain damage. I only use it when I've got no choice.'

I don't really have a special move yet. I'm better at defence than attack. I'm still one of the toughest in Year 7, probably number four or three. I'm very fast. One time

Connor Green tried to slap me in the ear and I used my Tae Kwon Do block on him. It actually worked! Everybody saw it. Now they think I know Tae Kwon Do. Now they don't even try to fight me. They know I'll only block them or get away.

There was a ruckus at lunchtime. It was the best one so far. I didn't even think it was real until I saw her hair come out. I didn't even think girls could fight like that. It felt too crazy. It was Miquita and Chanelle. Nobody knew why they were fighting, we just had to watch. It was even hutious. Miquita actually punched Chanelle on the head, it was a proper dirty blow like a man. Then Chanelle got Miquita's hair. Miquita was screaming like a crazy witch.

Chanelle was just quiet. She was concentrating so hard. Her face was all pink and her eyes were proper fierce. She was mad.

Miquita: 'You f—ing skank! You ain't gonna tell shit!'

Then Miquita pulled Chanelle's hair. Some came out in her hands. She blew it out of her hands and it flew over everybody. They all screamed when it touched them, it was disgusting.

Everybody went into a circle to watch. Miquita's friends were all cheering her and telling her to kill Chanelle. Nobody was cheering for Chanelle. I felt sorry for her, it's not fair when they only cheer for one.

Chanelle made a bomb. She got into a ball and crashed into Miquita's belly. Miquita went flying. She nearly broke through the circle but the circle bounced her back into the middle. They wanted the fight to go on. They wanted to see somebody get killed. Miquita tried to dig her fingers into Chanelle's eyes. Chanelle closed her eyes so she couldn't dig them in. Then Miquita tried to pull Chanelle's ear off. That was the funniest bit. Everything stopped.

Chanelle: 'Earrings!'

Miquita let go of Chanelle's ear, then they started fighting again. Miquita got Chanelle's head in her arms. She was squeezing her head. Chanelle couldn't move. She was kicking. She tried to stamp on Miquita's feet but she couldn't see anything. You actually thought they were going to kill each other. You wanted them to stop. It wasn't funny anymore. Somebody was going to die. But everybody kept cheering them on.

Everybody: 'Kill her! Kill her!'

Some of the Dell Farm Crew were there. They were laughing. They loved it. Dizzy was taking a picture on his phone.

Dizzy: 'Rarse! You gonna die, bitch!'

Killa wasn't laughing. His face was just hard. He was worried for Miquita. He wanted her to win. He couldn't even watch anymore, he just split to the cafeteria.

X-Fire: 'Where you going, man? You should see this, innit. You made this shit.'

Killa: 'F— off, man. I didn't make nothing.'

Chanelle's behind was going to burst from her trousers. Some snot dripped on the floor and went on Miquita's shoes. They just kept going round and round. They were never going to stop. Miquita was trying to swing Chanelle around so she was in front of the cafeteria window. Everybody knew what was her plan.

Dizzy: 'Throw her through the window, man!'

She was going to do it. She was pulling Chanelle towards the window. Chanelle was pulling the other way. Her feet were dragging across the ground. It was like when you take a goat to the killing shed and the goat doesn't want to go. Chanelle was like that. She knew she was going to die. She was pulling and pulling. Miquita was dragging and dragging.

Miquita: 'This is what you get! You best keep your mouth shut, bitch!'

I wanted to close my eyes but I couldn't stop looking. It was just too brutal. I saw Lydia on the other side of the circle. She didn't know who to support, Miquita or Chanelle. She was just watching them both. Her face was all scared and stiff.

Then the teachers came. They broke through the circle and got Miquita and Chanelle and pulled them away. Everybody went quiet. They were disappointed, you could tell. They wanted to see somebody get killed. The teachers pushed us all away. The circle broke up and everybody split. It was very fast.

You could see the snot on the ground and some of Chanelle's hair like a crazy spiderweb. There was a fingernail. Somebody trod on it and crushed it before I could pick it up for evidence. I couldn't concentrate for the rest of the day, everybody was still thinking about the ruckus. Everybody acted out their favourite bits like a movie. Nobody could believe it was real. It was the best fight they'd ever seen. The best bit was when you thought somebody you didn't love would die, it made you feel invisible.

All the pool balls at Youth Club are broken. They all have holes in and they don't even roll right. People keep throwing them. You're not supposed to throw them but they still do. And some of the sticks don't even have an end. You can never hit the ball straight, it always goes wobbly. Asweh, it's proper vexing. The pool table smells of wet dust. There's a hell of burns on it from cigarettes. If you licked it you'd get a million germs. Even Nathan Boyd wouldn't dare to lick it.

Lydia went in first to see if X-Fire was in there. She looked around the corner. I crossed my fingers (it's quicker than praying when it's an emergency).

Me: 'Is it all clear?'

Lydia: 'Yes! Just come on or we'll be here all night.'

It was our only chance. X-Fire thinks he owns the table, nobody else ever gets a go when he's there. It's only when Derek isn't around. Derek's bigger than X-Fire, and he knows Tae Kwon Do. He taught me a forearm block. There's one that goes high to block a high attack and one that goes low to block a low attack. It's quite easy. Derek wouldn't teach me an attack for if I used it on Lydia. When somebody asks him to teach them an attack it's usually just to sound their sisters with. He only teaches defences.

We only played until the crazy balls got too vexing. Lydia wasn't even trying. She hit the white ball in the pocket on purpose just so she'd lose.

Lydia: 'Game over. You win.'

Me: 'Ho! You can't lose on purpose, it's cheating!'

Lydia: 'I can do what I want. It's a stupid game anyway.'

She only says that because she's no good. It doesn't mean you should give up. Mamma says giving up is a sin. It's the same as lying. It's even worse than that because it's lying to yourself.

When we came out I used my binoculars to check for enemies. Miquita and Killa were sitting on the wall. Miquita was smoking a fat cigarette and Killa had his hand down the back of her pant. It was quite disgusting. I wanted to puke.

Miquita: 'Hello, Juicy Fruit.'

Me: 'Gowayou.'

Miquita: 'Chlamydia, you want some?'

Miquita held her fag out for Lydia. The smoke smelled like BO. It made my heart go proper fast.

Lydia: 'No thanks.'

Miquita: 'She's a good girl, innit. And she knows when to keep her mouth shut, not like Chanelle. I had to bounce that bitch. Whatever she thinks she knows, she don't know shit. She's just an attention-seeker, that's all she is. She needs to grow up.'

You could see the lighter burns on Miquita's hands all shiny like wax. They weren't even for a good reason like Auntie Sonia's burns, they were just a trick. Killa only made them so Miquita would admire him. I even felt sorry for him then. I didn't even have to burn Poppy to make her admire me, I only had to make her laugh. Somebody should tell him, laughing is the best way to make them admire you. It's even easier than burning.

Killa: 'Stop looking at me, man. I'll break them f—ing things you don't put 'em down.'

His mouth just looked stupid through the binoculars. It was too close up to be angry anymore, it just looked like a cartoon. I don't even think Killa's hutious. He can't even spell his own name right. It should be Killer. His eyes were all sad from where the smoke was getting in them. I know how he feels, it's proper itchy.

Killa: 'I mean it, man, I ain't messing around. Just f— off.'

Killa stood up all red-eyes. I spun around sharp-sharp and started looking at the Jubilee Centre instead. You can still see the ghosts of the bad words on the wall, waiting to trap you. F— off and DFC and suck my balls. I felt Killa grab me from the back. I wasn't even suspecting it. He got my hands and squeezed them proper hard and made me drop the binoculars. He smashed them and smashed them against the wall until they were broken in a million pieces.

Killa: 'I f—ing told you. Don't f— with me, man.'

Derek: 'What's going on?'

Derek came out proper fast like thunder and Killa just split down the alley. Miquita went after him, her big fat behind was wobbling all over the place like a bag of crazy mice.

Me: 'You're paying for them! I'll tell the police you broke them!'

There's no way I can fix them, they're too far dead. Without the binoculars I'm just a civilian again.

Lydia: 'I'll buy you some more.'

Me: 'You'll never find them again. I got them at the carnival.'

Lydia: 'They don't have to be army colour.'

Me: 'I like army colour, it's better for hiding.'

Lydia: 'Who do you have to hide from?

Me: 'Nobody.'

Lydia: 'Let's just go home, it's getting late.'

<u>Signs of guilt include:</u>
Ants in your pant
Talking too fast
Always looking around you like you've lost something ✓
Smoking too much ✓
Crying too much
Scratching
Biting your fingers
Spitting ✓
Sudden bouts of violence ✓
Uncontrolled gas (farting a lot)
Religious hysteria

I put it in my notes for Dean:

Me: 'Detective Opoku observed four signs of guilt in suspect: Killa. He then obstructed Detective Opoku when he was doing his duty. Detective Opoku suggests we make him suspect number one. Beware: suspect's accomplice, Miquita Sinclair (aka Fat Hands, aka Miquita Shit Eater), is unlikely to cooperate. She's a bitch. Suggest we approach with caution. Over and out.'

Aka stands for also known as. It works for names you gave them and for names they gave themself.

All the women were very worried for if they couldn't get their meat anymore.

One woman: 'Where am I s'posed to get my meat from now? I always get my meat from Nish.'

Another woman: 'His meat's better. The butcher's meat's always tough. It's not as fresh.'

One woman: 'I know. What are we s'posed to do now?'

It was too late to do anything, they were already taking Nish away. He was shouting and screaming like an alien. He sounded mad. He didn't want to go. The policemen were pulling him and pulling him but he was hanging onto his van. He wouldn't let go of it. They had to pull his fingers off. I could hear them breaking. Asweh, it was very cruel.

Watch doctor: 'Leave him alone! Bully!'

Fruit man: 'About f—ing time! Send him home!'

It felt too crazy. It wasn't fair. He didn't even poison anybody. I wanted to help him but the policemen were in the way, they'd spray acid in my face.

Nish's wife fell over. The policeman pushed her, I saw it with my own two eyes. Her shoe fell off. I picked it up for her. She was crying. Her toenails were painted red. They looked crazy and lovely. Her lips were red as well. There was meat everywhere. People were stealing it. I wanted to kill them.

Noddy: 'Oi, put that back, you thieving bastard!'

Pisshead: 'F— off, baldy!'

More policemen came to stop the thieves. They locked up Nish's van so nobody could get inside. Then they took Nish and his wife away. They put chains on their arms. Both the two of them were crying now. It made my belly go cold. Nish is from Pakistan, I saw the flag in his van. It has a star and a moon, it's my second favourite flag after Ghana.

When there's a star on a flag it stands for freedom. The star points in all directions, it means you can go anywhere you want. That's why I love stars, because they stand for freedom.

Me: 'Did they poison somebody?'

Noddy: 'No, they didn't poison nobody.'

Me: 'Why are they taking them away? I don't get it.'

Lydia: 'Advise yourself. You're so lame.'

Noddy: 'They just lost their ticket, that's all.'

Me: 'What ticket?'

Dean's mamma: 'I never knew they was illegal. Their mince's better than the crap you get off the butcher's. His is all fatty.'

Noddy: 'I s'pose their luck had to run out sometime. Three pound please love. I can do you a discount if you buy another lot, three for four pound.'

Dean's mamma: 'Go on then.'

Dean's mamma was buying socks. You can get them with all different sports men on the top, like one playing tennis and one playing football and one riding a bike. I've even got them myself. I bet you a million pounds they're for Dean.

Me: 'What will happen to them now, will they send them back? Is there a market in Pakistan?'

Lydia: 'Of course there is, stupid. There's a market everywhere.'

Me: 'Do they have trains that go under the ground?'

Noddy: 'I don't know about that one.'

I hope they do. I hope Pakistan is as nice as here. If I had to go home I'd miss the tube the most. And my friends. Poppy likes it the most when I chase the clouds away for her. I just kept watching the cloud until it moved and the sun came out again. Poppy didn't believe it was me, she thought it was just the wind. I still think it was me.

Me: 'What ticket were they talking about? Have we got one?'

Lydia: 'He means a visa. He only said ticket because he thinks you're stupid. Oh, I forgot, you are stupid.'

Me: 'Is it the same visa Julius sells? I heard him talking on the phone one time. He said he can sell a visa for five hundred. Why doesn't Nish just buy one, then he can stay.'

Lydia: 'You can't really buy them. The ones Julius sells are no good.'

Me: 'Why, what's wrong with them?'

Lydia: 'They don't work, they're fakes. Forget about Julius, he's a crook. If you bought a chicken from him by the time you got home it would just be an egg again.

Me: 'Our visa works though, doesn't it?'

Lydia: 'Yes.'

Me: 'Are you sure?'

Lydia: 'Yes, I'm sure! Don't disturb!'

I hope our visa works. If they try to take us away I'll just go invisible, then when they can't see me I'll sneak up behind them and get their acid spray and spray them until they burn away to ashes. I wish I thought of it before Nish's wife got her head trod on.

The next time I see Dean I'll ask him how he likes his new socks. If I think they're bo-styles then so will he.

Connor Green says Mr Staines's real first name is Seaman. It's because he was in the navy. I don't even believe it. Mr Staines is too fat to be in the navy, he'd sink right down to the bottom. I can remember all my French now without looking in the book. I can make a whole conversation. Mr Staines even says my accent is very good. I only know one conversation. It's for when you meet somebody for the first time, to tell them who you are:

Me: 'Je m'appelle Harrison Opoku. J'ai onze ans. J'habite à Londres. J'ai deux soeurs. J'aime le football.'

Do you want to know what it means? It means, My name is Harrison Opoku. I'm eleven years old. I live in London. I have two sisters. I like football. It sounds better when you say it. Just writing it's not as much fun.

The first thing everybody would do if they went to France is go to the top of the Eiffel Tower and do a massive spit. We all agreed. Only Connor Green would do a piss instead.

Connor Green: 'Except the people at the bottom would probably try and catch it. They drink piss in France, innit. They think it makes them live longer. Thick bastards.'

Jordan was the first choice for a spit sample because he loves spitting so much. It wouldn't even be hard to get a sample, he'd just give it to me straight away.

Jordan: 'F— off man, I ain't spitting in that!'

Me: 'It's clean.'

Jordan: 'I don't care. What you want my spit for anyway, what you gonna do with it?'

I bit my lips to stop the smile coming. Lying is OK if it's for a good reason.

Me: 'It's for my Science project, to test how well germs survive in spit. You get loads of different spits and you put the germs in them, and the spit that kills the germs first is the special one. You could have a cure for something in your spit. It could make you a fortune.'

Jordan: 'I don't wanna be a cure, let 'em die, I don't give a f—. Just get it away from me, man.'

I threw the bottle in the bin. Another idea bites the dust! Adjei, nobody wants to help the investigation. It makes you feel like everybody's the bad guy except you. It's very lonely. I haven't even got a favourite gun yet. I haven't really thought about it. If I had to choose it would probably be a supersoaker. They sell them at the market. They only fire water. It's proper brutal, the water goes really far. You have to ask the person for permission before you soak them for if they don't like it, otherwise there'll be a ruckus. I'm going to get one in the summer holidays.

Jordan's favourite gun is a Glock.

Jordan: 'It's what all the toughest gangsters use. Have you seen it?'

Me: 'No. What's it like?'

Jordan: 'It's the sickest, man. It's the most powerful. If I shot you with a Glock it'd take your head off. It shoots dumb-dumbs, innit.'

Me: 'What the hell are they?'

Jordan: 'They're these special bullets that can go through walls and everything. It's well deadly. That's the first gun I'm gonna get when I've got the cash.'

Me: 'Me as well.'

Jordan: 'You can't have a Glock, it's mine. You didn't even know about it till I told you.'

Me: 'I still love it.'

Jordan: 'Yeah, well not as much as me. I love them the most.'

We were waiting for the bus to come. We were at the bus stop opposite the flats. If you wait inside the bus stop they can't even see you. You only jump out when the bus is coming, then it's a mighty surprise. They don't even have time to stop you.

You get ten points for every time you hit the bus anywhere. You get fifty points for hitting a window. If you hit the big window at the front where the driver sits it's a hundred points. If the window breaks it's a thousand.

If you hit the tyre and it goes down and the bus crashes it would be a million points but nobody has ever done it. It's next to impossible.

Jordan's better at throwing. He can get more power. It's only because he beat me to the smoothest stones. I only had pointy stones and they're not aerodynamic (aerodynamic means it flies through the air better. My stones weren't aerodynamic because they're too sharp).

Jordan has seen a Glock in real life. He even held it. It was one of his missions for the Dell Farm Crew. He had to bury a gun.

Jordan: 'They always keep a gun buried somewhere for when they need it. They've got loads of them all over the place, innit.'

Me: 'Why don't they just keep it in their house?'

Jordan: 'Don't be a retard, what if the police found it?'

Me: 'Did you shoot it?'

Jordan: 'No, there weren't no bullets in it. You keep the bullets somewhere else, you don't keep 'em with the gun. I still fired it though. I pulled the trigger and everything. It was well sick.'

Jordan loved it, you could tell. His eyes went all big. He says it's safer to bury the gun in somebody's garden because only they go in there. If you buried it on the green where lots of people go, it's a bigger chance that somebody will find it and take it away.

They don't even know the person who owns the garden. They don't even ask them. It's usually an old person. Then they don't know anything about it. If somebody asks them about a gun they don't know what they're talking about. It's just safer like that.

Jordan: 'You always bury it at night. You pick somewhere quiet where there's no streetlights and that. Only bury it a little way down, like next to a flower or a rock or something so you remember where you put it. You've gotta be well quick though; if you're followed it's game over, they'll kill you for giving the hiding place away. I only done it two times.'

Asweh, planting a gun just felt too crazy! At least if you're planting plants they'll grow into something. A gun doesn't even grow into anything. I pretended like I planted a gun and a lot of baby guns grew up from the ground. Then I sold them at the market.

Me: 'Get your baby guns here! Two pound a pound! Baby guns, nice and fresh!'

It was very funny. Planting a gun is the craziest thing I've ever heard of, I swear by almighty God.

You should always know where to find a gun if you're in a hurry, you never know when you'll need it. You'll mostly need it for a war or to do a robbery with. It makes the robbery easier.

Jordan: 'If they see a gun they won't give you no shit, innit, they'll be so scared they'll give you whatever you want. It's easy, man.'

You don't even have to shoot it, you only have to point it at them. The gun just makes everything easier.

Jordan: 'I can't wait to shoot someone though, man. I'd shoot them in the face, innit. I wanna see their head explode, that'd be wicked. I wanna see their eyes pop out and their brains splash all over the place. Bus!'

The bus was coming. We got ready. I had my stones in both hands. I waited for Jordan's command. My heart was going proper fast. I was aiming for the side, Jordan was aiming for the big window at the front. You're not allowed to run until you've thrown all your stones. I waited. The bus was slowing down.

I needed to break a window. I needed a thousand points to catch up.

Jordan: 'Now!'

We jumped out. Jordan threw his first stone. It hit the big window but it didn't smash. I threw all my stones together. I didn't even aim them, I just threw them as fast and as hard as I could. The first one missed but the second one hit the side and bounced off. There were people getting off the bus. They didn't even try to stop us.

Jordan: 'F—ers!'

Jordan threw his second stone. It whizzed past someone's head and hit the edge of the window. The bus driver got red-eyes, we could see him. It looked like he was going to burst out of his skin. Asweh, it was brutal. I only went cold when I saw Mamma coming. She was getting off the bus. She looked right at me. I don't even know how it happened, it was the worst luck ever.

Jordan: 'Leg it!'

We just ran. I was too scared to turn around. I wanted to puke. I didn't stop until we got to the tunnel. We got our breaths back.

Jordan: 'All mine hit. One on the window and one on the edge, a couple on the side. What about yours?'

Me: 'I don't know. One on the side I think, that's all.'

Jordan: 'You're shit, man! I win!'

Me: 'My stones were too sharp, that's the only reason.'

I didn't even care. I don't even need the points that much. We got to the other side of the tunnel. Mamma was waiting for us. My belly went cold again. Everything was finished.

Mamma: 'Ho! What do you think you're doing? Tell me I didn't just see that. What do you have to say?'

Me: 'Sorry, Mamma.'

Mamma: 'You stupid boy. I go sound you. Get yourself home right now.'

Mamma started pushing me. Jordan started laughing. I just wanted to die.

Mamma: 'And you'll stay away from this boy.'

Me: 'It was an accident. We were only playing around.'

Mamma: 'He's a waste of time. If I see you around this boy again there'll be big trouble.'

Mamma pushed me to the door of my tower. Just as I looked behind me the spit hit me in the face. I even felt it go in my eye.

Jordan: 'There's your sample, pussy boy!'

Jordan gave me the dirty finger, then Mamma. I wiped my eye with my sleeve before the germs got inside my brain. Now me and Jordan are enemies for life. It all happened too quick.

Me: 'Fuck off!'

I don't even know who I was aiming at, Jordan or Mamma. I didn't even care anymore. I could feel the words when they came out, they were all dry and sharp like knives. It was hutious but I couldn't stop it now.

Mamma: 'What did you just say? I go beat the black off you!'

Mamma sounded me. It made thunder in my ears like the sky god's birthday.

Mamma: 'Don't ever let me hear that word coming from your mouth again. I don't need your nonsense. Advise yourself, Harrison. Have a think about what you've done.'

I know what I did, I ruined everything. It's all broken and it's my fault. I knew it was true, I could feel it deep down. I should have been good. I should have been good but I let myself forget and now God's going to destroy us. He'll probably kill Agnes first just to teach me. I couldn't breathe right. I didn't even want to. I practised what it would feel like to be dead. I held my breath for as long as I could but it felt too crazy. It made my head go proper blurry and I had to start breathing again. I'd ask for a hell of air holes in my coffin. It would be easier, that's all. They could be the windows of the aeroplane.

Your superstitions tickle me, I see it all the time in the touch-
ing of buttons, the scattering of salt. It's kind of sweet, you
think if you dress death in costume and ritual he'll defect
to your side. You think you can distract him just by making
more of yourselves, keep chipping off the old block and
blind him with the splinters. So don't throw stones, we're
just doing what comes naturally. I puff out my neck feath-
ers, keep bowing. A bit of tail-dragging to bring her under
my spell. See these colours, this strong breast? Our chil-
dren will be champions, immune to all those —osises and
—coccuses that ravaged your forebears. That's it, put your
beak in mine, this will only take a few seconds. Bingo!

Seems like a lot of effort for scant reward, don't know
what you're supposed to feel. But I owe it to the boy. I owe
it to all of you, a cheap act of confederacy against the drip-
dripping of ill-captured sand. I detach myself from her and
strike for the setting sun.

There was a lovely breeze. The rain was all gone and the
stars were out. I went on the balcony to try and remember
what it felt like before Agnes was born. A star is just old
light. Google even says it. When you look at a star you're
just seeing a million years in the past. I didn't need to see
a million years, only two. I picked the star that looked
the best and asked it to show me. If I could feel what was
different then I'd know what bit was broken and how to

191

fix it. Then I could save us. I asked it with all my blood. I didn't blink for if it ruined it and I'd have to start again.

The best time was the blackout. All the light in our street went off. Me and Papa and Patrick Kuffour went around in the pickup filling everybody's lanterns with paraffin. It took us until late in the night to reach everybody. They all wanted to give us chop but we had to keep moving or we'd never get to everybody in time. Me and Patrick travelled in the back of the pickup like soldiers. It felt like we were on an important mission.

Patrick Kuffour: 'Watch the trees, there could be snipers. Be ready. We can't fail the mission or there'll be hell to pay.'

Me and Patrick were the askers. We'd ask the people if they needed paraffin and then Papa would fill them up from the gallon. Everybody stayed in the street. They didn't want to go to bed anymore. In the end we just had a big party. It was everybody's idea all together. Nobody thought of it first, we all thought of it at the same time.

A blackout always turns into a party. It's the best thing about them.

Everybody hung their lanterns from the windows and roofs and fences. They looked like stars all fallen down. We made them come back to life. People were dancing in the road to celebrate. I told Agnes the good news. She was still in Mamma's belly but I knew she could hear me.

Me: 'I fixed the stars for you! They'll be waiting for you when you come out!'

Mamma: 'Thank you, sweet thing!' (She did it in a tiny voice like it was Agnes who was talking.)

We got one swallow of beer for completing the mission. We pretended we were boozed. Patrick Kuffour did the best falling over, he went backwards over his wall and landed on his back, when I looked over the wall he was wriggling his arms and legs like a beetle upside down. Asweh, it was the funniest thing I've ever seen.

Then Mr Kuffour got his generator working and Mrs Kuffour and Mamma and Grandma Ama made cowpea stew for everybody. We all ate our stew around the lanterns with the moths disturbing our heads and the music blowing in from Mr Kuffour's transistor. It was dope-fine. The far-away music tickled your ears like a lovely breeze. Everybody forgot it was night-time. The girls played ampe, we threw cocoa pods at their legs to try and break their jumps. Then they ran out of wind and all fell on the ground in a big pile of sleepy leaves.

When the sun came up I felt sad and lucky all together. I wanted the night-time to go on forever. Everybody pretended to cry when Mr Kuffour turned his generator off. The music stopped quick quick and it was time to go home. I went to bed with a big smile on my face and the sun shining through my eyes made me all fed up with warm. Asweh, it was the forever best night I ever had. You just wanted it to stay. You wanted to always feel like that.

When I found that feeling I closed my eyes and let it fill me up again. Then I knew what I had to do. I closed the door proper carefully and put the key back. I sneaked past Mamma's room. Mamma and Lydia were snoring like the loveliest pigs. Papa would understand. He'd even agree with me. It was the only way to fix it.

I put my alligator tooth down the rubbish pipe. I heard it fall down to the bottom and disappear. It was an offering for the volcano god. It was a present for God himself. If I gave him my best good luck then he'd save us from all the bad things, the sickness and chooking and dead babies, he'd bring us all back together again. He'd have to or it wouldn't be fair. It was a good swap, nobody could say it wasn't. I knew it would work. Thank you pigeon for showing me the right star!

We were just walking past the church when X-Fire and Dizzy saw us. I knew they'd stop us, I didn't even try to run. I knew they'd make it quick or they'd be late for Registration. I just stepped on the church grass.

Me: 'Come on, they can't get you on here.'

Dean and Connor followed me. They just stood on the edge. They can't touch you if both feet are on sacred ground.

Dizzy: 'Do we look like we give a f—? We're too old for fairy stories, innit.'

Dizzy just kept going. He stamped all over the flowers. His face was ready for dirty blows. It was because I didn't have my alligator tooth anymore. It was part of the deal: God has to protect the others first, I can look after myself. I don't even mind. I got off the church grass and went back on the path.

Me: 'Leave them alone, it's nothing to do with them.'

Dizzy: 'Fine, whatever you say.'

Dizzy got me with two big dirty blows in the arm. I didn't even care. It didn't hurt. I only screamed for pretend so he'd leave Dean and Connor alone. Dizzy laughs like a stupid monkey.

Dizzy: 'Pussy boy.'

X-Fire: 'Come on, that's enough, he ain't worth it. Little prick.'

We waited for when they were near the tunnel then we all gave our dirty fingers to them. It was very funny.

Connor Green: 'Arse monkeys!'

Dean: 'Cock jockeys!'

Me: 'You hit like a girl!'

They didn't hear us. They can't even hurt me anymore. It was a trick all along. I knew it would be a trick.

Me: 'Shit-lickers!'

Dean read my notes, then I folded them away again quick quick before anybody saw. We were outside the assembly hall. We could see right up to the cafeteria steps. Only nothing was very big to your naked eyes. We need some more binoculars.

Dean: 'Four guilty signs is a lot but it still don't prove nothing. We won't get a confession unless we torture him and we ain't got the equipment. You need car batteries and wires and hammers and shit. I still think the best way's DNA. Could you get any samples?'

Me: 'No. I tried to get some spit from my friend Jordan but he wouldn't give it to me.'

Dean: 'What about piss?'

Me: 'I could get some from the hospital. If I got my Mamma's badge I could sneak into where they keep the sick people's piss. It's already cold, they keep it in the fridge.'

Dean: 'No, it's too dangerous, security's tighter than a duck's arse up there. Wait. What are they doing?'

Dizzy and Clipz and Killa were messing around by the cafeteria. Dizzy had Killa pushed up against the window and he was pretending to be a cop checking him for weapons. He made Killa spread his legs and put his hands up. His hands were flat on the glass to stop him falling over. All his fingers were touching the glass. All his fingerprints were captured in one place. Clipz was pointing an invisible gun to stop the suspect fleeing.

Dean: 'This is our chance. We have to do it now. What d'you reckon?'

My belly went all cold. My blood turned to metal. I was ready. I had to be. The plan was easy: I would be the runner because I'm the fastest. Dean would be the capturer. I got the sellotape out of my bag and gave it to him.

Dean: 'Just push him hard enough to distract him, give me time to collect the sample. If he chases you just run.'

Me: 'Copy that, it's a code red.' (That means time for action.)

We started walking towards the cafeteria nice and slow like nothing was happening. We had to do it now before they went away. I got up the steps. If they say anything just don't listen. Don't even stop. Dean went and stood by the window and pretended to be normal. I got right behind Killa, then I pushed him hard in the back. There wasn't enough time to be scared, I just bumped him and got ready to run.

Killa: 'What the f— you doing?'

Me: 'Batty boy! Batty boy!'

Dizzy: 'Get him!'

Dizzy and Clipz came after me. Killa just stood there all confused and red-eyes. Dean got to work with the sellotape, he stuck it where Killa's fingers touched the window, then he pulled it off again sharp-sharp and ran the other way back towards the assembly hall. Killa didn't know what to do or who to chase. He just kept looking in both directions like a rat lost in a tunnel.

Killa: 'What did you just do?'

He wiped his fingerprints off the window but it was already too late. He couldn't even stop us. We beat him at his own game.

Killa: 'Little prick!'

They all came after me. I just turned around and ran for the Science block. I got into Mr Tomlin's class. He was getting ready for the lesson, I could see the lemons all lined up. Somebody else was going to find out about the lemon battery. I wished it was me. I wished I could learn it all over again like it was still the first time.

Mr Tomlin: 'What's up, Harri? Why are you running?'

Me: 'Nothing. I got lost.'

Mr Tomlin: 'You'd lose your head if it wasn't screwed on.'

Me: 'I hope not!'

Killa and Dizzy were at the door. When they saw Mr Tomlin they stopped chasing me. Killa just kicked the door. It was all over, he should just admit it. The bad guys always lose in the end.

Killa: 'You're dead!'

Mr Tomlin: 'Breaktime's not over for another four minutes. Go and find someone else to annoy.'

Mr Tomlin was like my bulletproof. He blocked me from the bad guys' killing thoughts. I went superquick through the Science block and came out the other side before they even knew what hit them. I only have to dodge them at breaktimes and hometime. They can't even catch me with my eyes peeled.

We waited in Computer Club until everybody went home. Have you heard of YouTube? It's a place on the internet just for films of things eating each other. Dean showed me a snake eating a boy. He actually swallowed him altogether. It was in some dusty faraway place. The villagers all hit the snake with sticks until he puked the boy back up again. They didn't know if he was dead or just asleep. He was curled up tight in a cosy ball. There was a hell of slime all over him from the snake's belly but all his arms and legs were still on. He was smaller than us.

Dean: 'I want to see a snake eat a car, that'd be wicked. It's happened before.'

Me: 'I want to see a snake eat himself. Then he'd just disappear into nothing.'

Dean: 'Wicked.'

We waited until the coast was clear, then we got the sample out for inspection. Dean held the print up to the light.

Me: 'You can't really tell what it is. It's too messy. Damn it!'

Dean: 'I was in a hurry, innit. You should've done the collecting.'

I could still see some of the lines. They were nice and sharp around the middle but the outsides were all blurred into each other like they were moving when the picture was taken. There were two fingers and the edge of a thumb. We needed fatter sellotape.

Dean: 'Shit. Don't worry, at least we've got a copy now. Maybe the police computer can tidy it up. They can zoom in and everything. Do the honours then.'

Me: 'Okey-dokey, Boss.'

I stuck the sellotape to a page from my exercise book, then I folded it up and wrote the suspect's name on the front. Killa. I'm just going to keep it with the rest until we need it. It felt like the best kind of hutious, like I owned a piece of Killa's life. He can't hide forever, your finger-prints tell your story if you want them to or not. When the snake puked up the boy, it looked like he was being born. Maybe he was a snake boy and it was supposed to happen. Maybe he'll grow up to be Snake Man. I'm going to tell Altaf when I see him, he'd love it if it came true. So would I. Just type snake eats boy into YouTube and see for yourself. I guarantee it will blow your mind!

Agnes: 'Harri!'

Asweh, it was the best one so far, it made my ears go lovely and buzzing. It lasted donkey hours. I didn't even want it to stop.

Me: 'Hello Agnes! Are you feeling better?'

Grandma Ama: 'Say yes.'

Agnes: **'Yes!'**

Mamma was happy crying. It made Lydia join in.

Lydia: 'She's got her voice back anyway. Say Lydia.'

Agnes: **'Lyda!'**

Lydia: 'We love you!'

Me: 'We love you, Agnes!'

My belly felt lovely and warm from saving her. I wanted to happy cry as well but Lydia was looking so I had to hold it in.

Grandma Ama: 'She's fine. She woke up this morning asking for banana. She ate until she was fed up.'

Mamma: 'How is her temperature?'

Papa: 'It's normal. Everything's fine. Don't worry.'

Mamma: 'I just wish I was there.'

Papa: 'I know. I'll see you soon, OK?'

Me: 'Is the roof still OK?'

Papa: 'It's fine! We had a storm yesterday and it didn't even wobble!'

Me: 'Don't make anymore things, OK? Just sell what you have already. Then you can get here quicker. OK?'

Papa: 'OK.'

Me: 'Goodbye, Agnes!'

Agnes: **'Goobah!'**

Asweh, Agnes is the best shouter in the world. I pretended like it's her superpower. When she grows up she'll be called SuperShouter. I'll even let her be my sidekick (it's like a smaller superhero who roams around with the big super-hero, like his assistant and best friend).

I didn't tell Papa I lost my alligator tooth. I didn't want to ruin it all over again.

There was a big pile of passports on the table. Julius put them in his bag before I could look inside. I wondered what the pictures were like, if the people were smiling or if they had crazy hair or glasses or scars. I wondered if any of them looked like me.

Auntie Sonia: 'I put some credit in there for you. Pay as you go.'

Julius: 'Everything's pay as you go. Isn't that right now?' (Slap her behind.)

Lydia got a Samsung Galaxy for her birthday even if it's not until tomorrow. She was so happy she actually cried. She was screaming like a maniac. It was very annoying. The phone even has a camera.

Lydia: 'Say cheese!'

You have to say cheese when somebody snaps you, it's how you get the right face. Lydia kept snapping everything. Me smiling. Me driving my car. Mamma and Auntie Sonia squeezing each other. Auntie Sonia's tree. Julius drinking his kill-me-quick and looking hutious. The picture of Nana Acheampong on the wall in the kitchen. Through the spyhole in the door that just came out like a blur.

I was going to ask her to snap you but I then I remembered you don't like having your picture taken. Nobody else saw your shadow go past the window, I was the only one watching. Don't let them see you, I just want you to be mine. I like it better that way, that's all. If Mamma sees you she'll only take you away from me.

I got a remote-control car even if it wasn't my birthday. Asweh, it's so dope-fine, it goes superfast. You actually steer it with the remote control. There's no wires. It's like a beach buggy. There's no walls, just a frame so you can see the little man inside who drives it. It's red and silver and it goes a hundred miles an hour.

I was no good at driving it at first, I kept crashing into the wall.

Me: 'Stop snapping me, you're making me crash!'

Lydia: 'Stop crashing, you're making me snap you!'

Lucky there's a big bumper at the front so when you crash the car doesn't get smashed up. I practised in the corridor outside Auntie Sonia's flat. The car drives well on every type of ground. I tried it on the carpet and on the tiles and it went proper fast. The tyres are proper big with deep grips so it doesn't get stuck. I want to try it on every type of ground. Sand and mud and grass and everywhere. I bet it will be brilliant on the snow. I swear by God, as soon as the snow comes, I'll be the first one there. Then I'll have all the snow for myself before everybody's feet destroy it. I'm going to throw my first snowball at Vilis. I want to get him on the face. I swear by God, it will just be too sweet.

Do pigeons fly south for the winter?

I go wherever you go.

That's good! You can sit in the tree and watch me throw my snowballs.

Julius was fixing the Persuader, putting new tape on the grip where the old tape was all flaky from sweat and too much hitting. He did it proper slow and gentle like the bat was a one-leg pigeon and he was sticking a new leg on.

Me: 'Could you actually knock their head all the way off?'

Julius: 'I don't know about that, but you can definitely make a mess. You can give them brain damage if you do it right. One fellow, I pinged him on the head and his eyes went stupid straight away, it was like a light switching off. I broke his brain, you could tell. His voice went really slow and he started drooling, just from one little tap in the right place. The sweet spot. It's his own fault, he should pay his debts like everybody else. He's a vegetable now, he has to wear a napkin like a baby.'

Julius did a big messy laugh. Mamma just washed the plates faster like she was trying to scrub the sin off them. I'd rather be killed with the Persuader than with a knife. A knife's too sharp, it tears too much spirit up. A bat's rounder so more spirit stays together. Then you get to Heaven quicker and there's less mess for your Mamma to clear up. It doesn't matter if it breaks your brain, you'll get it back. It's the spirit that's most important.

Auntie Sonia's baby tree looked even smaller than before. The leaves were all shiny like a burn. It can't get rain if it's inside all the time. I fed it some water when nobody was looking. The water just disappeared between the stones in the pot, it didn't even grow.

I had to do a message for Mr Smith. I didn't want to do it. It might be a trick. Sometimes the teacher gives you a message just to test you.

Anthony Spiner: 'One time Mr Smith gave me a message. I opened it and guess what it said?'

Me: 'What?'

Anthony Spiner: 'Stop reading this message. That's all it said. It was a trick.'

Lincoln Garwood: 'That's sneaky, man. I hate Mr Smith, he's a dick.'

I didn't look at the message, I just took it straight to the front office. I didn't feel like being tricked, that's all. I saw her when I came back. I never met her before, I think she's in Year 10. She always wears a white head-tie. She was kneeling down on the floor. She even had a sheet. It was right there in the corridor. Her eyes were closed and everything. I had to stop.

I just watched her. It was very relaxing. I had to keep proper still. I had to be extra quiet or I'd ruin it. I tried not to breathe. I didn't want it to stop.

I could see her lips move but I couldn't hear the words. Sometimes she bent forward until her head was nearly on the ground. She made everything go proper slow. It made me sleepy just from watching it. I wanted to ask her what she was praying for but I swallowed the words back down again.

You knew it couldn't be bombs. You knew it had to be something good.

I just watched from behind the wall. There was nobody else around. It was the best kind of quiet. I even forgot about going back to class. I would have joined in but I didn't want to ruin it.

When the head-tie girl finished praying she opened her eyes and stood up. I turned around sharp-sharp and went back down the corridor. I tried not to make a sound. I didn't want her to see me. I didn't want her to know I was there for if it ruined it. I waited until she was gone, then I came back to life. I held my breath when I went past the bit she was praying in. I walked around the outside so I didn't tread on it.

When I got around the corner Killa was coming the other way. He saw me before I could do anything. He got me in the toilets. It happened too fast to stop it. He trapped me between the sinks. He had a craft knife from art and he was pointing it right at me.

Killa: 'I want my fingerprints back. They're mine. What did you do with them?'

203

Me: 'I threw them away, they didn't even stick properly. It was only a joke.'

Killa pushed me against the wall. My head banged proper loud off the paper-towels machine. The light coming through the window lit the edge of the knife up like the craziest sunshine, it made me go blind. I closed my eyes and got ready for the burning. Everything went quiet. The world stopped. When Killa's voice came back it was cracked like a lie. It always goes like that when you try to be hutious before your blood has caught up.

Killa: 'Don't mess with my shit, yeah? It's none of your business. You can't prove nothing anyway. Just drop it before you get yourself in some serious trouble, yeah?'

He pushed me proper hard into the paper-towels machine, then he split. I felt my head for blood but I couldn't find any. I just waited for my breath to come back. I was only a little bit wobbly. There was a black smudge on my shirt from Killa's dirty hands. They shouldn't be allowed to put their dirt on you. They shouldn't be allowed to step in someone else's quiet, it's just not fair. The wet in my pant was only sweat from where it was hot outside.

In England they celebrate summer coming by everybody opening their windows wide up and putting their music on proper loud. It's a tradition. That's how you know it's summer. You have to do it when the sun first comes out. Everybody does it together.

They put their flag out as well. If you have a flag, you have to put it out at the same time. Then everybody knows you belong there and summer has come.

The music's not all the same, it's all different kinds. When I got near the flats I could hear a hell of different musics all mixed up together. It felt lovely. It made me want to dance. I was smiling from ear to ear, I couldn't even help it.

I even joined in. I got the CD player from Mamma's room and put my Ofori Amponsah CD on. I played Broken Heart, it's my favourite. I wanted everybody to hear it. I opened my window and held the CD player outside.

Me: 'Hello! It's Harri! This is my music! I hope you like it!'

Then I got scared for if I dropped it so I took it back inside. I hope everybody heard my song, our CD player doesn't go so loud. Then Lydia needed it back. It's her birthday and she has two new CDs to listen to.

Lydia: 'Hurry up!'

Me: 'I'm bringing it! Keep your hair on!'

Mamma: 'Don't vex her. I'll give your piece of cake to the pigeons.'

Lydia's cake is only chocolate. I'm getting a Spiderman cake for my birthday. Lydia's presents from home came in a big box. I beat her to the door. We were both waiting proper carefully but Lydia had to go and greet the chief and that's when the door knocked. The postman gave the box to me. I was going to keep it at first. I only gave in because it's her birthday.

Lydia: 'Hands off! I go sound you!'

Me: 'In your dreams!'

I snapped it all on Lydia's phone: her holding the box. Her opening the box. Inside the box. There wasn't just one present, there were lots. There were two CDs from Abena, one of Michael Jackson and one of Kwaw Kese.

There were earrings from Grandma Ama. They were just circles. They were made of real gold (you can tell real gold by biting it. If there's no teeth marks left behind then it's real gold).

Lydia: 'Get my earrings out of your mouth, you're getting spit all on them!'

Me: 'Do you want me to test them or not?'

Lydia: 'Not!'

There was a picture of Agnes's hand. It looked lovely. It's very easy: they just put the paint on her hand and then held it on the paper. They helped Agnes write her name. It's the same way I learned to write my name: they just put the pencil in my hand and then moved it for me. The letters come out all lovely and wobbly like a spider wrote it.

Papa made Lydia a dancer from wood. I think it's supposed to be her. It looks just like her but not the face. He doesn't know she gave up dancing. She keeps forgetting to smile.

She started crying.

Me: 'I'll have it if you don't want it. I can swap it at school. I might even get a disco watch for it.'

Lydia: 'Don't disturb!'

Me: 'Why be like that?'

Mamma: 'She's missing her papa, that's all. Don't vex her.'

Me: 'Don't be sad. It's your birthday. Your nose is all snotty.'

Lydia: 'Shut up!'

Mamma: 'Harrison, just leave her.'

I had to make Lydia laugh. If I didn't make her laugh, the whole day would be finished. I thought of all the cheering-up words I've learned. I was going to try them all until one of them worked.

Me: 'Come on, sweetheart. Chin up.'

Nothing. Not even a tiny smile.

Me: 'Turn your frown upside down. You know it makes sense.'

Nothing again.

Me: '*You are my sunshine, my only sunshine.*
    You make me happy when things are gay.'

Mamma: 'Harrison! Enough with the gay.'

Lydia: 'Stop it.'

She made a little smile, I saw it. I was going to do it. I had to save the day. I just needed one more try.

206

Me: 'Rub a dub dub, no need to blub. I love you from the heart of my bottom.'

Lydia: 'Stop it!'

Me: 'Got you! I win!'

Lydia did a big laugh. She couldn't hold it in anymore. I love it when I save the day. I didn't even need the points. I let her keep them.

Me: 'Do you want my present? You have to follow me, it's outside.'

Lydia: 'Gowayou. I'm not falling for another trick.'

Me: 'It's not a trick, I promise.'

Mamma: 'Don't look at me, I have nothing to do with this.'

Me: 'Just come on, scaredy cat!'

In the end Lydia had to come, the secret got too big for her to forget. I went in front and she followed me. We both held our breaths when we went down the stairs.

Lydia: 'Where are we going?'

Me: 'You'll see. Just trust me.'

We got to the back of our tower, then I made us stop. Lydia looked all around for her present. She looked up in the trees and under the cars and in the windows. She even looked under the bin. She was very confused. She didn't even know what she was looking for. It felt brutal.

Lydia: 'Just give me my present and let's go! Where is it?'

Me: 'Right in front of you.'

They built a new ramp to the back of our tower so the wheelchairs can go up and down. We only saw it this morning when the council man came with his cement mixer. Dean dared me to climb inside it but I wasn't taking any chances, I knew it would be deadly sticky. I knew straight away what I was going to do. Aswch, holding the secret in all day nearly made me go crazy!

207

The cement was still wet. The council man was gone for his chop. If you were going to do it, it had to be now. You couldn't plan it any better.

Lydia: 'What am I supposed to be doing here?'

Me: 'Just jump. It'll be brutal. Your footprints will get stuck and when it dries they'll be trapped forever. Then the ramp will belong to us and the whole world will know it. Not just the ramp, the whole tower. You have to jump quite hard though. You have to mean it.'

Lydia: 'That's stupid. I'm not jumping in that.'

Me: 'Go on! It will only take one second! You put your footprints in it and I'll write your name next to them so everybody knows. We'll both do it. I'll go first.'

I got all my blood together and stood in the right place, then I did a proper powerful jump onto the ramp with both my feet in a line. I tried to focus all the weight of my body down into the cement.

Lydia: 'It looks like you're doing a shit.'

Me: 'It's the best way. Just watch me.'

I counted to ten. I did a little twist to squeeze the last of the footprints out into the cement, then I jumped back off the side so I didn't mess it up. It worked a treat. It was perfect. My footprints were there in the cement, lovely and straight and new. You could even see the Diadora sign from the bottom of my Diadoras. You could see all the patterns and everything. It felt brutal.

Me: 'It's quite hard to get out again. The cement wants to stick to you. You have to give it more blood when you jump off. Your turn.'

Lydia: 'You're so lame.'

Me: 'Just do it, lazy face! You can't give a present back if somebody plans it for you. It's like saying you hate them.'

Lydia: 'OK, OK!'

Lydia pretended to be red-eyes but she wasn't fooling anybody. She gave it as much blood as me. She went into the shitting shape and built a proper big jump up. She landed right next to my footprints. She even counted to ten, I could see her lips moving.

Me: 'Now give it a little twist.'

Lydia: 'I'm twisting, I'm twisting!'

She tried to jump back off the side but her feet got stuck and she nearly fell. She screamed like a baby.

Lydia: 'Help me, help me!'

Me: 'Don't panic, I've got you!'

I pulled her straight and lifted her out of the cement. Her footprints were there next to mine. They were nice and neat. All the lines were proper sharp like mine. She even loved it. Her eyes went all big before she could stop them.

Lydia: 'Quick and write the names before it goes too dry.'

I sat down next to the ramp and wrote both our names underneath the footprints. I had to push my finger quite hard to get the letters to come out. I could still read it. Asweh, it looked bo-styles:

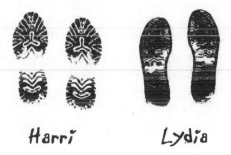

Harri   Lydia

Lydia was smiling from ear to ear.

Me: 'Happy birthday! I told you you'd love it!'

The cement on my finger looked like tea bread dough but it smelled like puke. If you don't get it off before it goes hard your finger will turn to stone. We washed off our shoes in a puddle, I used a stick to dig all the lumps out. Now the whole world knows about us. The footprints are there to tell everybody we were here. I can't wait until they dry. Guard them for me until they've gone hard, OK?

I will. Anyone wants to spoil your party they'll get more than they bargained for, I'll shit on anyone who gets too close. Do you want to know what I think? And I've been around long enough to have formed a few opinions. What your problem is, you all want to be the sea. But you're not the sea, you're just a raindrop. One of an endless number. If only you'd just accept it, things would be so much easier. Say it with me: I am a drop in the ocean. I am neighbour, nation, north and nowhere. I am one among many and we all fall together.

Or maybe I'm just a rat with wings and I don't know what I'm talking about.

I love it when you get a good surprise. Like the cement being there just waiting for us to write in it or like when you think somebody will be rubbish at something and then you find out they're actually brilliant at it. It was the same with Manik: nobody suspected him to be such a good goalie because he's so fat, but actually Manik's a brilliant goalie. It's impossible to score against him. Nothing ever gets past him. One time I kicked the ball at his head by accident and he didn't even move, he just kept on playing as if nothing happened. Only his eyes went watery, otherwise you wouldn't even know he'd been whacked in the head. After that we called him Superhands. He loves it, you can tell. Whenever we say it he smiles from ear to ear.

Everybody: 'Superhands saves it again! The boy's on fire!'

I didn't think Dean would be such a good climber because he has orange hair. I just didn't suspect it. But actually he's a brilliant climber. He's even as good as Patrick Kuffour (he can get on the roof of the comm. centre in three seconds flat. We all called him Monkey Blood).

Dean: 'Don't wory, I'll get it. I'm a wicked climber.'

We were playing gutter-to-gutter and I did a big banana shot and the ball landed on top of the garage. I didn't even know I could kick my new ball that far. It actually felt proud. Dean jumped on the wheelie bin then pulled himself onto the garage roof. It all happened proper fast.

211

He made it look easy. He threw the ball down and I caught it. When I looked up at him standing on the roof it made me go quite dizzy. The sun was in my eyes. I heard wings but I couldn't see where they were coming from.

Dean: 'Come up, it's alright. I'll pull you.'

Me: 'Somebody might steal the ball.'

Dean: 'Don't be a wuss!'

Me: 'I'm not! Come on, 9-all. All square, next goal wins.'

He didn't want to come down. He loved it too much up there, you could tell. He was walking up and down like the king. He was laughing at the face of danger.

Dean: 'Hey, what's this?'

He picked something up. It was all wrapped up like a parcel. It was wet from the roof puddles and oily. The wrapping looked like clothes torn up.

Dean: 'Shall I open it?'

Me: 'Open it!'

Dean: 'Do you really want me to open it though? What if it's anthrax or human teeth?'

Me: 'Just stop vexing me and open it!'

He unwrapped the wrapping. There was a wallet inside. I could see it was a wallet even with the sun in my eyes. It was blue with black velcro.

Me: 'Is there any money?'

Dean: 'Hang on, it's all sticky. I'm coming down.'

He climbed down off the garage and showed me the wallet. There were darker stains on it. It smelled of rain. He opened it up and checked all inside. There was no money. There was something stuck in one of the pockets, the rain had turned it into glue. Dean peeled it off proper carefully: it was a photograph. When I saw it my belly went proper cold.

Me: 'That's the dead boy!'

Dean: 'Do you reckon?'

Me: 'I swear by God! He's even got his Chelsea shirt on.'

The picture was proper small and stained where it got wet. The dead boy was with a white girl. You could only see their heads and shoulders. They were both smiling from ear to ear. I didn't even know he had a girlfriend. She was nearly as pretty as Poppy except one of her eyes was pointing the wrong way but it might have been on purpose for a joke. It felt proper sad. I pretended like the dead boy was trapped inside the picture and it was too late to get him out. I wished I'd been there when he was chooked. I'd chase the killer away before he even got that far. I'd shout proper loud for the police or throw a rock at him or freeze him with my breath. I don't know why nobody did anything.

Dean: 'I'd kung fu him in the knackers.'

Me: 'Me too.'

Dean let me hold the wallet. I felt the sticky and said a prayer inside my head. It just said sorry. That's all I could remember.

Me: 'What do you think the sticky could be? Do you think it's blood?'

Dean: 'It looks like it, or maybe oil. There might be a print in there somewhere. Let's get it back to the lab.'

I didn't make Dean say the password, it's only for civilians. We pushed my bed in front of the door for security. Dean held the wallet still and I put the sellotape on over the sticky bit. I stuck it down nice and gentle so there were no wrinkles, then I pulled it back proper slow. The sticky stuck to the sellotape. I held it up to the light. No patterns, just one big smudge of dark red. No prints, nothing for a match.

Dean: 'Never mind, it was a long shot. We've still got the DNA if it's blood.'

Me: 'Taste it and find out.'

Dean: 'I ain't tasting it, it might have Aids. Just hide it, yeah? The blood creeps me out.'

213

I got some blood on my finger. It was only sticky. I wanted to eat it so the spirit could live in me but I was too scared from the Aids. I waited until it was dark before I washed it off. I wanted it to stay but in the end it got too itchy.

The hole where the tree used to be is all the way gone. It's all covered now, not just with grass but a hell of plants and weeds as well. You'd never even know a hole used to be there. Asbo did a big shit on the new grass. It's his new favourite shitting place. When he saw me he wagged his tail so hard I thought his arse would fall off. He loves me because I talk to him in a soft voice. That's how they know you're their friend.

Terry Takeaway: 'Do you wanna take it? Here you go.'

Terry Takeaway gave Asbo's lead to me. He let me hold it and everything. Asbo's very strong. He couldn't wait for me, he just started walking straight away. I had to follow him or he'd just pull me over.

Terry Takeaway: 'Tell him heel, then he'll stop pulling.'

Me: 'Heel.'

Terry Takeaway: 'Louder than that. **Heel!**'

It worked. Asbo stopped pulling so hard. He slowed down and walked beside me.

Me: 'Good boy.'

Always tell a dog good boy when he does something good. Then he'll only do good things after that. They only know how good they are if you keep telling them. You have to tell them every time or they'll forget. Terry Takeaway showed me how to hold the lead the right way. If you hold it close to you, the dog has nowhere to go. Then he has to walk with you. If you hold the lead too far away, the dog will forget he's even on the lead and try to get away. In the end I was controlling Asbo. He stopped trying to get away. When I walked one way, Asbo came with me. When

I stopped he stopped as well. Asweh, it was brutal. It felt like I owned him. It felt like he belonged to me.

Me: 'Asbo, look for evil! Sniff it out, go on, boy! Find that evil smell!'

Asbo was looking all around like he was on a mission. He sniffed a man's leg when he went past. I watched his face: his ears didn't move and his eyes didn't go big. No evil there. We let Asbo off the lead. He ran away but he came straight back. Mostly he was just running in a circle. He loves to run even more than I do. Then we did some tricks.

Terry Takeaway: 'Sit.'

Asbo sat down. He just sat there looking at us. He was waiting for us to tell him something.

Terry Takeaway: 'Lie down.'

Asbo lay down on the grass. He was on his back. His tail was still wagging behind him. I could see all his nipples and his balls. He loved it, you could tell. It was all a game.

Terry Takeaway: 'Paw.'

That was the best one. Asbo gave me his paw. I shook hands with him. It was very funny. He even did his tricks for me. He loved it. When I told him to sit he sat. When I asked for his paw he gave it to me. It felt brutal. I just wanted him to be mine. Asweh, it was the funniest thing I've ever seen.

JULY

Fingerprints are just for feeling with and to help you hold onto things when they're wet. They don't really mean anything. If you didn't have fingerprints you could be anyone you wanted.

Eyebrows are there to keep the sweat out of your eyes. I always thought eyebrows were just for no reason but they're not, they keep the sweat and the rain away. If they weren't there the sweat and rain would get in your eyes and make you blind. Eyelashes are the same. They're to stop the dust getting in your eyes. And bugs as well.

All the things you think are just there for no reason are actually to help you or protect you from something. The hair on your head stops your brain getting too hot when it's hot out and too cold when it's cold out. Your hair is a lot cleverer than you thought. Everybody has the same defences. They all have eyebrows and fingernails and eyelashes. Their hair is all in the same places. That way they all have the same chance of surviving. It's what makes it fair. It wouldn't be fair otherwise.

Connor Green: 'Why do men have nipples then?'

Mr Tomlin: 'Because they'd look stupid without them. Next question.'

Connor Green got beaten to the joke by Mr Tomlin. He hated it. He tries to beat Mr Tomlin at jokes but Mr Tomlin is always too good for him.

Connor Green: 'How come when you're in the bath all the water doesn't go up your bumhole and drown you from the inside out?'

Mr Tomlin: 'Because the internal anal sphincter involuntarily contracts to occlude the anal canal. Any more?'

Connor Green: 'You said anal. You can't to say that to us, it's sex abuse.'

Mr Tomlin: 'Put a sock in it, Connor. Anybody else?'

Dean: 'Does your hair still grow after you're dead? My uncle says it does. And your fingernails. Is it true, sir?'

Mr Tomlin: 'No, that's a fallacy.'

Connor Green: 'Have you got happiness, sir?'

Mr Tomlin: 'Right, get out. Connor? Get out now, please.'

Connor Green: 'But sir, I only asked if you've got happiness.'

Mr Tomlin: **'OUT!'**

Connor had to go out of the class. His face went bright red like a crab. I was even glad Mr Tomlin roared at him. He's too annoying sometimes. Sometimes I just want him to shut up so the teacher can help us. You learn the most interesting things in Science.

Mr Tomlin says the space station is actually true. At first it just looked like a bright star but if you keep watching you can see it move. I only saw it one time because the sky is never dark enough, there's too many lights in the way from the streetlights and houses. On the space station they have to shit in a special tube that sucks it out into space. That's why the shuttle has windscreen wipers. Everybody agrees.

The floor outside my flat is perfect for driving my beach buggy. It's proper shiny. It makes the car go superfast. It makes you feel like you're going fast as well, even if you're just standing still. You have to remember to blink before you go dizzy.

I kept looking at Jordan's door. I was waiting for it to open. I made a little knock and pretended like it was an accident. The door opened. First Jordan didn't say anything, he just watched. He was watching for donkey hours. I kept crashing because his watching put me off. I just wanted him to ask for it already.

Jordan: 'Give us a go.'

It was all part of the plan but you had to make him wait a bit longer.

Me: 'In a minute.'

I just kept driving. I made him think I'd give him a go all along. I wanted to make him sorry. Then I'd be the winner for the last time. I could feel him watching me. I just kept driving. I pretended like he wasn't even there. Jordan was getting ants in his pant. It felt brutal. I wanted it to last forever.

Jordan: 'Come on, man, give us a go. You've had it ages.'

Me: 'You'll break it.'

Jordan: 'No I won't, I'm a wicked driver. I never crash.'

Me: 'We're not even friends anymore.'

Jordan: 'Who says? Come on, man.'

Me: 'Two more minutes.'

Jordan: 'One minute. I'll show you how to make it flip over, it's well sick.'

This is the bit I'd been waiting for. I had to make him want it proper bad. I had to make him beg. That way when I took it away it would hurt even more. I wanted to punish him. It was my duty.

Everything went dark and quiet. I could feel my heart going proper fast just waiting for the right time. I knew it would be brutal. I was by my door. It was perfect. I had to bite my lips to hold the laughing in.

Me: 'I can't, I've got to go in now. My dinner's ready.'

I picked up my car and went inside. I shut the door behind me. It felt brilliant. I did it sharp-sharp. He didn't even have time to suspect it. He didn't even know it was going to happen. It was perfect. Now I'm the winner forever.

Poppy doesn't need to wear make-ups because she already is beautiful. Miquita and Chanelle and all the others only have to wear it because they're ugly underneath. Miquita always wears green eyeshadow. It makes her look like a frog.

It makes her look like a skanky green fool but I didn't tell her. I just couldn't be bothered.

Miquita was putting her cherry lipstick on. My heart went proper fast. There was no going back.

Miquita: 'Are you ready for me then? Did you brush your teeth? No, I'm only joking, I know you're clean. You're a sweet boy, innit.'

Miquita's going to teach me how to kiss. Miquita has sucked off a hundred boys, she knows all the best ways to do it. If I know how to kiss properly then Poppy will never cut me for another boy.

I don't want Poppy to cut me. I want her to be my mine forever. It feels too good. The best bit is when I get to protect her from the bad things, like when I take the wasps away. Poppy's always grateful. When she smiles for me it makes my belly go lovely and warm.

It felt crazy already but you had to stay proper still. Just forget that you hate Miquita, just remember her big juicy behind and her big bouncy boobs and her expert lips. Just use her to get ready for the real thing. Lydia was even laughing. She loved it.

Lydia: *'I want a lover,*
        Not a Casanova.'
Me: 'Gowayou!'
Lydia: *'We will love every day.*
        You will be my lover.'
Me: 'Shut up! I go sound you!'

222

Miquita: 'Just hold still, Juicy Fruit. Relax.'

I was squeezed down on the sofa. Miquita sat on top of me. I couldn't get away even if I wanted to, she weighs a ton. She was licking her lips like a big crazy fish. I closed my eyes to make it go faster.

Miquita: 'Open your mouth a bit more, that's it. Relax, man. You're gonna like it, I promise.'

Everything went proper slow. I could feel Miquita getting closer. I could hear her breathing all hot in my face, then her boob was touching my arm. Then she kissed me right on the lips. It was quite soft. It was even not too bad until I felt her tongue go in.

Me: 'Nnngggtngg, yudiingsaanythnnngabouutnng!'

Miquita stopped. I got my breath back.

Miquita: 'What was that?'

Me: 'You didn't say anything about tongues!'

Miquita: 'But everyone likes the tongue. You gotta learn the best way or there's no point. Just go with it.'

Lydia: 'They're only Year 7, they don't need to know about tongues.'

Miquita: 'Shut up, man, what would you know? Just let me do my work, innit. Do you want your brother to be a batty boy?'

She put her tongue back in. It was all hot and slimy. Asweh, it was disgusting. I wriggled to get free but she just pushed me down harder. Miquita was making a horrible kissy groaning noise like a zombie in love. Her lips kept sucking. Her tongue was twisting around in my mouth like a nasty snake. I just thought about Poppy. I made her yellow fill me up like the sun. Then I felt somebody grab my hand. I pushed down on the sofa so they couldn't peel it off.

Lydia: 'Miquita.'

Miquita: 'Just relax, man. Give me it.'

She pinched my hand to make me let go, then she took it and put it down her pant. I could feel hair on my fingers. It

223

was all scratchy. It tickled. That's when it all got too crazy. I swear by God, I wanted to be sick. She peeled my fingers apart and stuck one up her toto. It felt wet and rubbery. She got another finger and another finger and she made my hand go up and down. Her lips kept sucking, her breath kept blowing hot up my nose. I couldn't even stop it. I don't even like cherry. My belly felt sick like the sea.

Me: 'Stoppih! Lyda, helllpe! Gehhheroff!'

Lydia: 'He's had enough. He keeps holding his breath.'

Miquita: 'I'll say when he's had enough, what are you gonna do, Chlamydia? Stop wriggling, man. I thought you wanted to learn.'

Me: 'I changed my mind. Get off me!'

I got all my blood and pushed her away. Miquita's eyes were all sleepy and stupid and she was breathing crazy like from a fight. Her jeans were open and she was still holding my hand down her pant. I pulled it out sharp-sharp while I had the chance. My skin was crawling with hair tickles and my fingers were all shiny from her toto. I just wanted to die.

Miquita: 'Not bad for a beginner. Don't lick my teeth though, girls don't like it. Wanna try again?'

Me: 'Go away, I'm not doing it anymore! Just piss off!'

I got away before she could hold me down again. I washed my lips and hands. When I tried to ease myself it came out all weird, I think she broke something. Lydia should have stopped her. I should have kept the locks locked. It was a bad idea. I don't even know how it happened. If Poppy finds out I sucked off another girl she'll cut me for sure.

Me: 'Stupid bitch. You're not even funny!'

Miquita was outside the bathroom. She was smiling like a stupid fat frog.

Miquita: 'We ain't finished yet, that was just the first lesson, innit. Did I make your willy go hard? Did you get a funny feeling down there?'

Me: 'No.'

Lydia: 'Don't say that, he's too young. Just leave him alone.'

Miquita: 'Who are you, his mum? Just 'cause you're tight, don't mean everyone's like you. You lot are so f—ing lame, man.'

Lydia: 'At least my boyfriend's not a murderer.'

Everything stopped. Lydia shut her mouth again sharp-sharp but it was too late, the words were already out, she couldn't get them back. Miquita's face went all stiff.

Miquita: 'What did you say?'

I thought Lydia was going to cry. She didn't move. She was trapped in the shock. Everybody was. I just didn't suspect it in a million years, it was too big to let out. It was the wrong kind of quiet and somebody had to break it. Mamma's never here when we need her.

Me: 'You shouldn't let them burn you.'

Miquita: 'What?'

Lydia felt the iron burn on her face where it was nearly faded away. She got my message and the blood I sent her. She woke up.

Lydia: 'You should just tell him to stop. Look at your hands, how could you let someone do that to you? That's just weak.'

Miquita buttoned up her jeans. You couldn't see her hands, they were moving too much. You couldn't hate her fat burny hands anymore, it didn't feel fair.

Miquita: 'Who you calling weak? You saw what I did to Chanelle.'

Me: 'She's not Chanelle, she's Lydia. And if you touch her again I'll chook you with the toothy knife. I'll get Julius to bash you, he's a real gangster.'

Lydia: 'No you won't. Just go home, Miquita. We don't want you here anymore.'

Miquita: 'Am I s'posed to care? You're just a stupid little bitch.'

I kept waiting for an earthquake but it never came. Miquita didn't know what to do, she just split proper quiet. I locked the locks behind her and got the Oreos from Mamma's secret drawer. It was a new packet. I let Lydia open them. The first one is always the tastiest.

I was just minding my own business, snacking on some sesame seeds the lady who drives the chair car put out. She likes to watch us eat from her kitchen window, she dreams of skinny-dipping in warm waters, dreams seahorses nibbling softly at her tender toes, winding their tiny prehensile tails around the soft perches of her nipples. Each to their own, I say, life's too short to think of your dreams as anything but blameless and bona fide.

They came from nowhere, I didn't have a chance to get ready. Four of them. First I feel a whuuump *at my back, of breaking air and collapsing space. Before I can turn around he's on top of me, the big male, he leans over my shoulder and sticks his black beak in my face, I see his beady eyes shining with dull intent, him and his cronies mean to make me pay for some perceived slight or another, maybe they don't like the way I walk but I'm pinned to the ground now, and his three accomplices form a triangle around me to bar my escape. I kick and bite and heave myself upward but two points of the triangle close in and there are three knives in my ribs now, three sets of claws digging at me like loose topsoil, I can feel myself being pulled apart, my pigeon skin slipping from its moorings. I make myself a nail bomb but the walls of the world are clamping shut and maybe I'm mortal after all. If I'm not here who looks after the boy?*

Me: **'Aaarrghhhhhhhh! Fuck off, magpies!'**

I ran and jumped through them and made them all fly away. My pigeon was just sitting on the grass, he looked proper scared and sorry for himself. I wanted to cry but I couldn't see any blood or broken bits.

Me: 'Are you alright?'

Pigeon: ' '

I went to pick him up but he split before I could catch him, he just flew up to the roof of the never-normal flats, he was still working and everything was alright. Asweh, it was a mighty relief!

Me: 'Be careful, pigeon, they might still come after you. Keep your eyes peeled. I'll come and see you when I get home from school, OK?'

Pigeon: 'OK. You're a good boy, Harri. Thank you for saving me.' (He only said it inside my head.)

Girls love it when you give them presents. It means you're serious about them. Girls always want you to be serious about them, otherwise they worry too much and it's not fun anymore. I gave Poppy a Jelly Ring. It was my secret sorry for kissing Miquita. She put it on her finger. I never asked her to, she just did it anyway.

Poppy: 'Thank you!'

Me: 'Don't mention it!'

Then she ate it.

I don't even want to kiss Poppy. I don't want to kiss anybody anymore, not after Miquita nearly broke my bulla. I'll only kiss Poppy if she asks me for it. If I win Sports Day she'll probably want to kiss me then. I'll just do it if I have to but not on the lips.

Clipz: 'Oi, batty boy! You shagged her yet? Want me to show you how?'

We just walked past. I didn't even look at him. I don't even want to sit on the top steps, there's nothing special about them. I prefer the Science block steps, you can see just as much and Poppy's there to share it with. The top steps aren't even worth it.

Four hundred metres is one whole lap around the running track. It looks quite far. I touched my lane for good luck. I saw Brett Shawcross do it. Me and Brett Shawcross were the favourites. Nobody knew who'd win from us, they couldn't decide. They wanted both the two of us to win but it's impossible. Only one can be the winner.

Brett Shawcross: 'You can have silver. I'm gonna get gold.'

Me: 'Good luck.'

Brett Shawcross: 'I don't need luck, I'm gonna cane you.'

There's no medals, you just get a certificate. I only have to win to prove I'm the best runner and because I told Papa I would.

Lincoln Garwood was in lane one. He was going to cheat, he told us. He knows he'll never win because the hat he has to wear to keep his dreadlocks in is too heavy. It will only slow him down and make him look gay. He even said it himself.

Lincoln Garwood: 'I'm just too slow, man. I don't wanna look gay.'

He didn't want to come last so he made a plan: he was going to fall on purpose and make it look like he twisted his ankle. We all promised not to tell.

We waited for the whistle. It was very nervous. I could feel my heart beating like crazy. There were lots of people watching. Not just my friends but some of the mammas and papas.

Only not Mamma. She was at work again. She said she'd pray for me to win but I don't know if she'll remember.

I didn't want to let them down. I wanted to make it the best race ever.

All the runners were just standing around. Some of them were scared. Kyle Barnes was chewing chewing gum. Saleem Khan was picking his nose. Brett Shawcross thought he was a real runner, he was shaking his legs like the real runners do it before the race. He looked proper serious like he had to win. Asweh, it was very funny.

Mr Kenny: 'Ready!'

You had to get in the ready shape. It's down on one knee with your arms straight in front. It made it feel more important. You didn't want to mess up. Everybody went proper quiet.

Mr Kenny: 'Set!'

That's the same as ready except you know it's going to start very soon. You have to hold it proper still. Somebody farted. Everybody laughed.

Mr Kenny: 'Go!'

Mr Kenny blew the whistle and we all started running. Lincoln Garwood fell straight away. I saw him trip himself up. It even looked real. He rolled over holding his foot. I heard the scream behind me. I kept on running.

Me and Brett Shawcross were in front. Everybody else was behind us. I was in lane 4 and Brett Shawcross was in lane 6. I didn't know which one was the luckiest. It was very close. We were both trying our hardest, you could tell. It felt brutal. Brett Shawcross has Nikes. I only have Diadoras but I was still in front. I just looked straight ahead. I wanted to win more than anything.

Kyle Barnes gave up. He ran out of wind and fell over. Everybody else was miles behind.

Everything went proper quiet. It felt like I was in slow motion even if I knew I was going fast. My legs were burning, it didn't feel like a race anymore, I was running for my life. If they caught me they'd tear me into little pieces. I just had to get away. I just had to win or it was all over.

When I went round the last bend I thought I was going to fall off, I had to slow down to stay in my lane. When

I got onto the last straight I could go fast again but my breath was running out. I started going dizzy. I remembered the spirit in my trainers. I said a quick prayer inside my head:

Me: 'Spirit, give me your blood! Give me your quickness! Don't let me die!'

I could see the finish line. I was nearly there. Poppy was waiting for me, she was clapping me home. It was like the biggest energy. I felt the spirit come into my lungs. I made my legs go higher, my arms swish faster. I was Usain Bolt, I was Superman. I was still alive and they could never catch me. I blew my last breath out and stretched for the line. Brett Shawcross crashed into me and we both fell over. I closed my eyes and waited for the whistle.

Mr Kenny: 'First place, Opoku! Shawcross second!'

I won! Asweh, I couldn't believe it! I wanted to shout **'Yes!'** but I had no breath left. I just lay on my back. The sky was so dizzy and the clouds were all racing around. My head was all itchy. I just wanted to watch the sky and sleep. I just wanted to go around again.

Brett Shawcross: 'Well done. Good race.'

I could feel the biggest smile grow over my face like God just painted it there with a tickly brush. It was the dope-finest kind of sick I ever felt. I'm the fastest in Year 7. It's even official. I can't wait to tell Papa. When I stood up again everybody wanted to shake my hand, even Brett Shawcross and Mr Kenny. Poppy squeezed me for the longest time. Asweh, it felt like I was the king. Everybody admired me and nobody was waiting for me at the gate, they know they can't touch me until the spell wears off. Asweh, I wish every day was just like this!

Auntie Sonia will have to hide in the boat. If they find her they'll throw her over the side to the sharks. That's what happens: first they cut you so the sharks can smell your blood, then they throw you in the sea to get eaten. A feeding frenzy is when all the sharks come together and fight over you. When they're finished all that's left is your bones and a blood slick.

Mamma: 'You don't have to go anywhere. You can stay here until you find somewhere else.'

Auntie Sonia: 'And have Julius coming around here making trouble for everybody? I don't want to get you any more involved than you are already.'

Mamma: 'It's too late for that. It has been ever since I took his money.'

Auntie Sonia: 'I should never have told you about him.'

Mamma: 'How else would I have made it here? Should I have planted a plane ticket tree? I'd still be at home putting my coins in a Milo tin, ten pesewa here, fifty there. I made the choice, nobody forced me. I did it for me, for these children. As long as I pay my debt they're safe and sound. They grow up to reach further than I could ever carry them. I'm here now, let me help you. Just tell me what you need.'

Auntie Sonia: 'Your stove. I can feel the old me growing back.'

Mamma: 'It's about time. I missed her.'

Auntie Sonia rubbed her fingers all sad and slow. I waited for the black and shiny to fall away like dead paint and the new old patterns to come back. If a skink gets his tail bitten off he just grows a new one, I read it in my reptiles book. A skink is well lucky.

Mamma: 'You can't keep running forever.'

Auntie Sonia: 'No, but I could hop back to where I started and try again; this time I'll pay the extra fifty dollars to get a boat with a driver knows the difference between fishermen and the coastguard. I tell you, you don't want to know what a Libyan jail smells like, I still dream about that smell. Adjei, my leg's itching like crazy! Pass me that pen.'

Auntie Sonia's foot is in plaster up to the knee. I think it was the Persuader but Lydia thinks Julius ran over it in his car. Whoever's right gets a hundred points. Auntie Sonia isn't telling. She just says it was her fault for not getting out of the way. She let me draw a picture on the plaster, I tried to draw my pigeon for good luck but it came out more like a duck.

Auntie Sonia: 'Anyway he'd never let me leave, I know too much. I should count my blessings, at least I can get decent painkillers, I've been eating Percocets like they were M&Ms, feels like I'm in the States again, it's great. Can I have those back please, Doctor? Thank you!'

I had to give the crutches back. They were making me dizzy anyway. I opened the door for Auntie Sonia and checked the corridor for enemies. The coast was clear.

Auntie Sonia: 'Have you seen what they did to your door?'

We all looked where Auntie Sonia was looking. It was there in big letters scratched into the wood:

DEAD

The letters were all sharp and skinny where they were written by a knife instead of a pen. My belly went cold before I could stop it.

Auntie Sonia: 'Who did that?'

Me: 'Probably a junkie. There's millions of them around here.'

I followed the word with my fingers to feel for a clue. It was only for pretend: I knew already who did it and who it was meant for. Jordan's always writing warnings with his war knife, it shows the enemy he means business and freaks them out. At least I'm not scared of the stringy bits on the banana. I always eat them. Jordan always pulls them off. It's only banana string, it can't even hurt you. Jordan's not even that tough. I got a splinter from the A but it didn't hurt.

Lydia: 'You should see what they wrote on the stairs. I F—ed God Up The Arse.' (She only whispered it for if Mamma sounded us.)

Auntie Sonia: 'Lydia!'

Lydia: 'I'm just telling it.'

Me: 'Who'll feed your tree if you go away?'

Auntie Sonia: 'I can take it with me, it's only plastic.'

Asweh, it even made me feel sick. I never knew the tree was plastic. I thought it was a real tree. It was a mean trick.

Me: 'Why do they make trees from plastic? It's just crazy.'

Auntie Sonia: 'They're easier to look after. Real trees need food and the right kind of weather. You can take a plastic tree anywhere and it doesn't die if you forget to feed it. They're for people who can't be trusted with a living tree.'

Mamma: 'Don't say that.'

Auntie Sonia: 'You know it's true.'

It's actually a good idea when you think about it. It's safer than a real tree. A plastic tree is only a lie if it pretends to be a real tree, if you know it's plastic then it can't be a lie.

*   *   *

Some superheroes were born that way. Superman came from a planet where everybody had powers. Storm and Cyclops and Iceman had the X-gene all along.

Altaf: 'It's just in their blood from when they're born. They started showing their powers when they were still babies.'

Me: 'Wicked!'

Altaf: 'I like it better when they were born normal. Like Spiderman, he was just normal until the spider bit him. He didn't even want to be special. He just wanted to get on with his life. But then when he got his powers he realised he needed them all along.'

Me: 'How?'

Altaf: 'He needed to be strong for when the bad crimes started happening. He didn't even know they were coming but God knew all along. God sent the spider to make him ready. I wish it would happen all the time like that. I could have saved my papa then.'

Me: 'Why, what happened to him?'

Altaf: 'He died in the war.'

Me: 'Did you see it? Did the helicopters have guns on them?'

Altaf: 'I don't know, I didn't see them, we ran away before the Ethiopians came. I heard the tanks though. They were well loud, it was like an earthquake. My papa was going to follow us when the fighting finished but he got hit with a rocket. They weren't trying to get him, he just got in the way. He just went into smoke. If I had my powers I could catch the rocket but it wasn't my turn yet. I didn't even know about superheroes then, nobody told me until I came here.'

Altaf went back to his drawing. It looked like half a man and half a lion. I bet he calls it Lion Man. Altaf is the best drawrer by far.

Me: 'You should give him night eyes. Lions can see in the dark.'

235

Altaf: 'I'm going to.'

Me: 'Guess what: Snake Man is real, I saw him.'

Altaf: 'Where?'

Me: 'It was on YouTube. I actually saw him being born. Just type in snake eats boy and you'll see it. Don't worry, he spits him back out again. It's the greatest thing you've ever seen. I knew it was real.'

Altaf: 'Wicked!'

I like it better when they're born normal. Then it could happen to anybody. It could even happen to me, I just need to meet a radioactive spider or eat the right poison. I'd ask for invisible, flying, mind-reading and superstrength. They're the best powers for winning wars and catching the killer. I won't have a costume though, it would just bring attention on myself. The costumes just look gay.

I hope we don't get homework in the big holiday. That would suck. Everybody agreed.

Connor Green: 'That would suck arse.'

Kyle Barnes: 'Definitely.'

Me: 'Too right. It would suck bigtime.'

When something sucks it means it's the worst. It comes from America. We made a spell. It was me and Dean and Connor Green and Kyle Barnes.

Dean: 'If we don't step on any cracks for the rest of term, then the holidays will be sunny every day and we won't get any homework. Agreed?'

All of us: 'Agreed!'

The first one to step on a crack gets their head flushed down the toilet. If you only do tiny penguin steps you can stop yourself before you get to the crack. It's safer like that. The big holiday will be brilliant. We're going to the zoo first. Papa and Agnes and Grandma Ama will be here by then. Sometimes you even get to feed the penguins. Agnes is going to laugh her head off, she's never seen one before. Agnes gives the best cuddles even when she puts her finger in your nose.

Then I'm going on a mighty long bike ride. It will just be me and Dean. We'll ride our new bikes that we bought with the reward. We'll leave early in the morning and we won't come back until it's proper dark. We're going to ride all around London, to the Eye and the palace and the dinosaur museum.

Dean: 'We can hide in the T-Rex ribs, then we can jump out when they close up for the night and we'll have the place all to ourselves. That'd be wicked.'

Me: 'Yeah, that would be well good, especially if everything comes alive.'

Dean: 'We don't want the T-Rex to come to life though, he'd eat the shit out of us.'

Me: 'Too right!'

We borrowed Lydia's phone. I only didn't tell her because it's classified police business. I was in charge of filming. I pointed the camera at Dean. I got ready to snap if the dead boy's spirit came back. We were checking the basketball court because the dead boy used to hang out there. It was my idea to try and catch his spirit on camera. A piece of the dead person's spirit always stays in the places he knew, even if his soul has already gone to Heaven. It might only be a tiny piece but sometimes if you look hard enough you can feel it.

Me: 'It's like when you go in a puddle and then when you come out you make a footprint on dry land. For as long as it takes for the footprint to dry up and disappear, that's how long your spirit stays on the ground. It's the same when you die, except it lasts a lot longer because your whole body and all your feelings and thoughts were there, and they weigh a lot more than just a footprint.'

Dean: 'I get it, I get it. Just hurry up.'

I held the dead boy's picture for extra energy. I said a prayer inside my head for him to find us. If we could bring him back just long enough for him to tell us what happened, if he could give us the name of who chooked him, then we'd have all the proof we needed and he could rest in peace for ever after.

Me: 'Are you feeling anything yet?'

Dean: 'Yeah, f—ing stupid. It's not working, man. Come on, let's go.'

Me: 'Keep trying. Pretend like you're the dead boy. Pretend like you can feel what he felt and see what he saw. It works better if you concentrate.'

The dead boy was brilliant at basketball. One time he scored a basket from one end of the court to the other. Asweh, it was a one in a million shot. You'll never see one like that again. Everybody said it was a fluke but he just smiled like he planned it all along. He didn't even bluff about it, he just carried on playing. X-Fire kept calling him a poser but he didn't even listen to him. When X-Fire and Killa started pushing him he just pushed them back. He wasn't scared of anything.

X-Fire: 'F—ing poser. Anyone could've made that shot.'

Dead boy: 'Go on then, let's see you make it.'

X-Fire: 'F— off, man, don't be fronting me.'

Killa: 'We'll f—ing batter you.'

Dead boy: 'Easy now, children. Play nice, yeah?'

I was watching from outside. I could see it all happening through the fence. First X-Fire pushed the dead boy, then Killa pushed him. Then the dead boy pushed Killa, then X-Fire pushed the dead boy again. They were all red-eyes by now. The pushing just got faster. It felt quite crazy. The dead boy pushed Killa so hard he fell back and his T-shirt got twisted and you could see the handle of the screwdriver sticking out from the back of his pant. You could even hear the slaps. Nobody was going to stop, it was like somebody pressed the wrong button and now they had to keep pushing until they ran out of batteries. All the other players just stood and watched. Most of them were smaller kids like me. They only stopped when one of them tried to steal the dead boy's bike. He had to chase after him to get his bike back.

Killa: 'That's what I thought, pussy boy!'

X-Fire: 'Run away!'

I thought it was all over but then the dead boy came back on his bike. He got a big drink from his water bottle and spat it all on Killa's back. It went all on his T-shirt and everywhere.

Dead boy: 'You're the f—ing pussy, pussy boy!'

Then he rode away. Killa was proper red-eyes. The water was dripping off him. One of the smaller kids threw the basketball at him.

Smaller kid: 'Pussy boy!'

That's when I knew somebody was going to get killed. I just ran away sharp-sharp before it was me. It was ages ago, when I first came here. Now the basketball court is nearly always empty. Somebody tore all the nets up and tried to set the posts on fire. A basket without a net just doesn't feel the same.

Dean was lying on the ground under the basket. His eyes were closed and his arms were spread out from his sides like an angel.

Dean: 'I'm telling you, I'm not getting anything!'

Me: 'It's because he didn't know you, his spirit doesn't trust if you're friendly or not. It's OK, spirit, he's with me. We only want to help.'

X-Fire: 'What you two batty boys doing? You been eating retard sandwiches again?'

X-Fire and Dizzy blocked the gate. Killa was behind the fence, Miquita was hanging onto him like a tree. I dropped Lydia's phone through the fence quick quick so the grass would hide it.

Dizzy: 'Don't you know you're trespassing? You'll have to pay the tax now, innit. How much you got?'

Dean: 'Nothing.'

Dizzy: 'Don't make me hurt you.'

Dizzy made Dean empty his pockets. All he had was 63p

and two Black Jacks. Dizzy took it all. I couldn't stop it, there was nowhere to go.

Dizzy: 'What about your trainers?'

Dean: 'What about them?'

Dizzy: 'Just take them off before I batter you. I ain't messing around, man.'

Dean took his trainers off. His socks had a tennis man on them. It was too late to ask if they were his favourite. He emptied his trainers out but he wasn't hiding anything.

X-Fire: 'What about you, Ghana? What you hiding?'

Me: 'Nothing.'

My belly went all cold. I held onto the dead boy's wallet in my pocket. I couldn't get the picture back in in time.

Dizzy: 'What you got there?'

Dizzy got my arm and pulled it. I tried to dig it further down. I pressed proper hard and pushed all my fingers together to make them like glue. I could see the dead boy's face, he was smiling and alive. Nobody was going to ruin it. I only had to let go when Dizzy stamped on my foot. He got his hand in my pocket before I could stop him and got the wallet out. The picture fell on the floor.

Dizzy: 'What's this? There better be some cash in here.'

Dizzy went through the wallet but it was empty. He just threw it away like it was only rubbish, like it never belonged to anybody. Killa saw the dead boy's picture on the floor. He came and picked it up. Everything went quiet. Killa's face went all stiff. He just stared at the picture like he was trying to make it disappear.

Killa: 'Where'd you get this?'

Dean: 'We found it.'

Miquita: 'It's alright. It's only a picture, it don't mean nothing.'

Killa: 'What the f— do you know? You don't know shit.'

Miquita: 'I'm just saying, babes.'

Killa: 'Get off me.'

Killa pushed Miquita away. She bounced off the fence. It was her own fault for loving him too much. Dean put his trainers back on. The air was thick and full of killing thoughts. I was sinking in a black sea, that's what it felt like. Killa just kept staring at the dead boy's picture. I thought it was going to catch fire in his hands.

X-Fire: 'F—ing sort it out, man. Just get rid of it, yeah? Just f—ing go.'

Killa: 'What if I don't want to? This shit's gone too far, man. It's over.'

X-Fire: 'I say when it's over. Don't pussy out on us now, you got us in this shit. Just give me the f—ing thing and go!'

X-Fire took the picture from Killa and kicked his behind to make him split. Miquita followed after him but he pushed her away. He was nearly crying. When he got to the road he started running, his elbows were sticking out like a girl. I even felt sorry for him, he was sharper than I remembered. Everybody's sharper when they're running away.

X-Fire burned the dead boy's picture with his lighter. His spirit made the quickest sparks, you could never catch them. The smoke just got lost in the air. There was nowhere to go.

X-Fire: 'Dizzy, cover the gate, man. They ain't going nowhere.'

Dizzy blocked us. I looked for a big enough hole to escape through but everything was too close. Me and Dean stayed together. X-Fire came for us, he wasn't even redeyes anymore. He'd made up his mind. He reached in the back of his pant. I knew it would be a war knife. All the windows of all the houses were empty, nobody was going to save us. X-Fire put his hood up.

I saw you coming out of the sun. Please pigeon, help us!

Lydia: 'Get away from him! I called the police!'

Asweh, my heart nearly jumped out of my skin! I turned around: Lydia was outside the fence. She was filming the whole thing on her phone, she must have found where I dropped it. She must have known I needed her.

X-Fire: 'Get her!'

Me: 'Run!'

Dizzy went after my sister. All I could do was pray. I saw you do the shit, saw it drop right past X-Fire's face. He had to jump out of the way of it and that's when me and Dean dodged him and made it through the hole Dizzy left.

X-Fire: 'I'm gonna f—ing kill you!'

We didn't have time to believe him, we just ran. I could see Lydia ahead of me, I just followed her. I couldn't let her get lost. My mouth tasted like rain. Just keep going, don't stop. If you stop moving everything will fall down. I made one look behind me sharp-sharp. X-Fire was gone and so was Dizzy. I kept on running to make it stick. We only slowed down when we reached the shops.

Lydia: 'The library! Quick!'

We ran into the big library, we had to be safe there. We got up the stairs to the computers. Lydia showed us the film. She got everything: Killa looking sorry and X-Fire burning the dead boy's picture. She got us away just in time.

Dean: 'Don't delete it, will you.'

Lydia: 'I won't. What have you been messing in?'

Me: 'We were only doing our duty.'

Lydia: 'Mamma go sound you.'

Lydia emailed the video to Abena for extra security. It took donkey hours to send. We waited for long enough to be safe. When we got home I locked all the locks and drank a whole glass of water with my eyes open. It didn't even feel like I was easing myself on a cloud anymore. I knew it was just the bubbles from the bleach.

I could have done more but I'm still stiff from that run-in with the magpies. I could have saved you but it's not my place. It's like the Boss always says: they're just meat loosely wrapped around a blazing star. We don't mourn the wrapping once it's discarded, we celebrate the freeing of the star. We tow it to its rightful place with the ropes he spun, set it to shine upon the peeling paint of a past life, to light a bereaved mother's journey back to her god.

The rain keeps falling, the sea keeps rising, you keep going. You keep going out of spite or with magnificent defiance, you keep going through steely instinct or by cotton-wool consensus, you keep going because you're made that way. You keep going, and we love you for it.

We miss you when you're gone.

Connor Green stood on a crack. He did it on purpose, he just jumped right on it. Now the spell's broken and the summer holidays will be ruined and it's Connor Green's fault. We all gave him one dirty blow on the arm. He even let us do it. He said he didn't care.

Kyle Barnes: 'You dick! What'd you do that for?'

Connor Green: ''Cause I felt like it. So what? There's not really a spell, it's just bullshit.'

Kyle Barnes: 'You're bullshit.'

Connor Green: 'Yeah, well, I know something you don't. I know who killed that kid.'

Nathan Boyd: 'What kid?'

Connor Green: 'The one who got stabbed outside Chicken Joe's, who d'you think? I seen it happen.'

My belly went proper cold. Everything stopped moving, even my blood.

Connor Green: 'For real. I was driving past. I seen the kid get stabbed and I seen Jermaine Bent running away. I seen the knife and everything.'

Kyle Barnes: 'Why didn't you tell the cops then?'

Connor Green: 'F— off, I ain't getting stabbed. They can do their own dirty work.'

Nathan Boyd: 'I don't believe you. Whose car were you in?'

Connor Green: 'My brother's.'

Kyle Barnes: 'What car's he got?'

245

Connor Green: 'A Beemer. Five series.'

That's when we knew he must be lying. Connor's brother can't have a BMW, he isn't even rich enough. Connor only wears Reebok Trail Burst. Nathan Boyd started sniffing the air. Everybody got ready to laugh.

Nathan Boyd: 'I can smell something. Can you smell something? What is it, dogshit? No, it's not dogshit. Cowshit? No, hang on. It could be horseshit.'

Connor Green: 'Just f— off, man.'

Nathan Boyd: 'I know what it is, it's **bullshit!**'

I couldn't believe it, it was too hard. I kept hoping there was another Jermaine Bent who wasn't Killa, then it wouldn't have to be real and I could go back to normal. I wanted to fix it so bad I couldn't even pick it up for if it broke all over again. Maybe I don't have what it takes to be a detective after all. Maybe it's just too risky.

Have you ever played rounders? Asweh, it sucks. I hate it so much. It's too hard to hit the ball. The bat's too small and it's the wrong shape. I can never hit it. I wish I had the Persuader, at least it's big enough. You want to be the batter because it's the best bit, you wait donkey hours for your turn and then you can't even hit the ball. It's proper vexing. Everybody was supporting me.

Everybody: 'Come on Harri, you can do it!'

I just wanted to hit the ball far like Brett Shawcross. He makes it look easy. I couldn't even hit it one time. Asweh, it gave me red-eyes like crazy. In the end I just fielded. All you do is wait for the ball to come near you. If it comes near you, you try and catch it. It's boring. The ball never came near me the whole time. I just stopped trying. I sat down until Mr Kenny made me run around the field.

Mr Kenny: 'Opoku, get up! One lap!'

Nobody knew about my plan. It had to be a secret or it wouldn't work. I waited until I was too far away for them to see me then I squeezed through the hole in the fence. If I eat the crab apples I'll get all the superpowers I need. Then I'll be protected. It was Altaf who gave me the idea. I got tired of waiting for a radioactive spider to come bite me so I'm going to use the magic poison fruits instead. Then the bad guys can't defeat me and I'll be safe the whole summer.

First I checked the trees for asasabonsam. I looked for their legs hanging down from the branches. The coast was clear. The trees weren't even big enough to hold them, the branches were too skinny. The forest felt proper slow. I was all on my own. The air smelled like rain. I couldn't see the birds, only hear them chatting high up above my head.

Me: 'Hello, pigeon, is that you? Keep a lookout for me, OK?'

Pigeon: 'Will do!'

The forest is a lot smaller than I thought. I could see all the way through to the other side, the road and houses behind. I wanted to be the first person to come here but somebody was there before me: there were broken bottles on the ground and a hell of sweet wrappers all muddy and stiff. It was very vexing. I wanted to be the first. I went in deeper. I picked the two best-looking apples from the best tree. They were only small. It's only poison for the others, for me it's a meteor. It's the only way to get my powers.

I sat on a broken tree trunk. It was lovely and quiet. I thought of all the important things I had to do and all the power I'd need, I did one big breath then I bit the first apple.

I swear by God, it was the most disgusting thing I've ever tasted! I wanted to spit but I had to swallow it for the spell to work. I put my hand over my mouth so I couldn't spit it out. I closed my eyes and chewed. My belly felt crazy. I needed all my blood just to get it down. I swallowed the whole thing, all except the seeds. I opened my eyes. Everything was grey and I felt like puking. I did another big breath and bit the second apple. I had to try very hard. I had to concentrate and forget about the sickness and the taste. It took donkey hours but I just kept chewing and swallowing, chewing and swallowing. I only did a spit at the very end to take the taste away.

My belly felt proper bad after. I couldn't stand up yet. I wanted to shit but I held it in for if I shit all the powers back out again. I waited. I kept going cold then hot again. It must be the powers going into my blood. I needed it to work. I needed the protection and to make them pay for what they did. I did a big woodpecker fart. It was wet at the end but it didn't escape. I wasn't ShitHisPantsMan, I was UnstoppableMan. When I came out of the forest I was still wobbly. Mr Kenny was waiting for me.

Mr Kenny: 'Where've you been?'

Me: 'I felt sick, sir.'

Nathan Boyd: 'He was smoking a fag in the woods.'

Connor Green: 'He was having a wank.'

Me: 'No I wasn't.'

Mr Kenny: 'That's enough.'

Mr Kenny let me sit out the rest of the game. Rounders is boring anyway. I never hit the ball because the bat's the wrong shape. They should make it more flat. I don't know why nobody thought of it yet.

The war was here. It was real, you just knew it. There was smoke everywhere, it was thick black and it filled up the whole sky. You could feel the fire from miles away. Everybody went to watch the playground die.

Dean: 'I thought it was a plane crash at first. I wish it was, that'd be wicked.'

Somebody set the swings on fire. That's where most of the smoke was coming from. The rubber smell from the seats got in my nose, I couldn't smell anything else. You know when a smell is so big it even makes you laugh? Well that's what it felt like. You only couldn't laugh because all the grown-ups were watching. The fire was a disaster and you had to be serious.

Dean's mamma: 'It's them bloody kids that done it. I saw 'em in there when I come back from the chemist's. They were trying to light it then.'

Lady with big arms: 'When was that?'

Dean's mamma: 'Just now. I was coming back from the chemist's. I knew they were up to something.'

Manik's papa: 'Little bastards.'

The climbing frame was on fire as well. All the metal was gone black and the rope from the net was burned off and dying. The fire was very hot. When I got close it made me go proper itchy. It felt lovely and sleepy. It was the biggest fire I've ever seen.

Some smaller kids were playing a game to see who could get the closest. They all ran to the fire and the one who got closest before they ran away again was the winner. It looked brutal. I wanted to play but I had to show respect. When you're Year 7 you have to set an example. Everybody just watched the fire. They didn't even want to talk anymore, they just wanted to watch. They couldn't help it. They were stuck there. The playground was dying but nobody was trying to save it. They knew they couldn't do anything, it was too hot and beautiful. They knew the fire would always win. It was brilliant and sad and hutious all at the same time.

Whenever a new person came along somebody had to tell them the story so far, about the kids who started the fire. Then the new person would say something like:

New person: 'Little f—ers'

and they they'd just watch like everybody else. It was like having a secret except you were allowed to tell everybody. It was like having a secret between all of us. It made you feel like you were together, like you knew everybody, even if you've never talked to them before and you don't know their name. They were all on your side. It's the best thing about a war.

Lydia snapped the fire. All I could see in the picture was black smoke.

Me: 'Ho, you can't even see the fire! Try again!'

Lydia: 'Don't disturb! It'll melt my phone!'

Me: 'No it won't. Snap the pirate ship before it sinks!'

Lydia: 'No, I'm going, the smoke's killing my eyes. Are you coming?'

Me: 'No, I'm staying. I'll walk home with Dean.'

Lydia: 'Be careful then. Don't let them follow you.'

Me: 'I won't!'

I only wanted to snap the pirate ship before it sank forever. I just wanted to be there for when the playground died, so it knew I was there and that I loved it until the end.

Terry Takeaway: 'Alright little man. What happened here?'

Me: 'Just a fire. Asbo! Hello, boy! Good boy! Good boy, Asbo!'

Asbo jumped up and licked my face. It was proper funny, even when his tongue went in my mouth. In the big holiday I'm going to teach him to hunt for spirits.

Terry Takeaway: 'Wanna buy some DVDs? I've got some good ones, there's one with zombies somewhere.'

Me: 'No thanks. If you buy a pirate DVD the money goes to Osama Bin Laden. We learned it at school.'

Terry Takeaway: 'Suit yourself.'

Then the fire engine came. I heard the siren from miles away. It drove right across the green. Everybody was proper vexed when they turned the siren off because they wanted to hear it in close-up.

Fireman: 'Everyone stay back.'

But everybody kept going closer again. They couldn't help it. The smaller kids were the bravest. They never listened to the firemen, they just kept going nearer. They just loved being with the firemen, you could tell. They wanted to help. They wanted to be them.

One of the smaller kids tried to lift up the hose but he couldn't even move it because it was way too heavy. He started crying. That was the funniest bit.

Fireman: 'Alright matey, I've got it. You can help next time, yeah?'

The water came out superquick like a bullet. The firemen were very skilful, they put the whole fire out in one minute. When the fire was gone the playground just looked nasty. It was all black where the burning was. It just looked dirty and dead. It made you feel dead as well. It even made you wish the fire was back so it would hide all the dirt again.

Everybody cheered the fire engine away. I was sad to see them go. We didn't know when we'd get to see them in action again.

Dean: 'If I knew they'd be so quick I'd've made some more fires for them to put out.'

Dean's mamma: 'Yeah, and you'd get my foot up your arse for your trouble.'

Dean: 'I was only joking!'

Now the fire was gone I could see things I couldn't see before, sad and crazy things that felt like they shouldn't even be there. I saw a piece of dead rope from the cargo net. It was all black and shiny from the fire. It looked just like a snake. I kept suspecting it to move and slide away under the wood chippings. I saw a dead penny buried in the ground by the ladybird. I pretended like it was a shit the ladybird made. The ladybird was so scared by the fire that he shit himself. It made me feel sorry for him even if I knew he was just plastic. His head was all bent and melted from the heat.

The smaller kids started playing a new game where they dared each other to pick up the burnt woodchips. They were still proper hot. Nobody could hold them for longer than two seconds. I saw Killa through the smoke. He was on his own. He'd just been watching the fire like everybody else. He picked up a woodchip, wrapped his hand around it and just stood there holding it, waiting for it to burn his fingers. He was even loving it, he didn't care. He kept holding the woodchip for donkey hours, I didn't start counting from the beginning but I got to 28 before he dropped it again. The secret is to make your fist as tight as it will go. Then he just put his hands in his pockets and walked away not looking at anybody. It was like he was as sad as me, even if he only used the climbing frame for hooting.

Then the light came back on. The smoke started blowing away and I remembered it was daytime. I didn't feel sleepy anymore. People started going home. Me and Dean wanted to stay, even if it meant the playground was dead. It was too late to change anything, it just felt too important to leave yet. We had to see what came up from under the ashes, any powers or important news or any dead things that used to be hidden.

A smaller kid was still crying.

Smaller kid: 'Now I can't go on the slide anymore.'

Smaller kid's mamma: 'Don't worry, they'll build another one. It'll be even better than the old one, you'll see.'

I hoped the new slide would be the longest in the world. I hoped it took forever to get to the bottom. When it only lasts one second it's just too vexing, I remember from before I was too big for slides. I only wanted to be small again enough for one more go.

I took a walk around the ruins of the playground, let the soot stain my orange feet black. I was hoping the flames might bring a concession, a last-minute change of plan. I was hoping to singe my wings in the embers but it didn't work, I'm still here and whole. Still got a job to do. No rest for the wicked, and all that.

We prefer it when you walk around instead of through us. We like to be left in peace while we're eating and performing our courtship rituals. We ask only for the same rights as you: we just want to live our lives, make a place for ourselves, room to shit and room to sleep, room to raise our children. Don't poison us just because we make a mess. You make a mess, too. There's enough of everything to go round if we all stick to our fair share.

Leave us be and there'll be no trouble. Be kind to us and we'll return the favour when the time for favours comes. Until then, peace be with you.

Me and Dean and Lydia all walked to school together for extra security. It didn't even feel like the war would come today, it was the last day before summer and it made an unbreakable spell. It was lovely and hot. Everybody was smiling from ear to ear. We had to shout along with them. We couldn't hold it in.

Me and Dean: **'It's the last day! We're nearly free!'**

Lydia: 'Ow! Don't shout right in my ear!'

Me: **'Aaarrghhhhhh!'** (That was me doing a big shout in Lydia's ear.)

In Geography Mr Carroll put the fan on. It was already blowing when we came in. It was a dope-fine surprise. Everybody went crazy when they saw it. We all took turns to air ourselves, the cold wind felt lovely.

Some of us made a dare to air our private parts. None of us really did it, we just lifted our shirts and aired our bellies instead. The cold wind on our bellies was the sweetest feeling of all.

Kyle Barnes: 'Look, Daniel's nipples are going hard! Pervert.'

Daniel Bevan: 'Shut up, no they're not.'

Brayden Campbell: 'He's got wood. Look, Charmaine. Touch Daniel's wood.'

Charmaine de Freitas: 'Piss off!'

Everybody was wearing their ties around their heads. They all pretended they were ninjas. The Year 11s wrote all on their shirts. Their friends wrote their names and messages for good luck. It was the last time they'd ever wear that shirt. They were never going to school again, it was finished forever. You have to cover the shirt with good luck to take on your journey to the world. It's a tradition. It felt lovely. I can't wait until I do it.

GOOD LUCK   KEEP IT REAL   spud

NORTHWELL MANOR TILL I DIE   TYRONE

TAKE IT EASY   GET RICH OR DIE TRYIN   naomi

DFC   FUCK SCHOOL   LEWSEY HILL R. PUSSIES

FUCK DA POLICE   LEON   IN DROG WE TRUST

Damon   MR PERRY SUCKS DOGS COCKS

JUST ENOUGH EDUCATION TO PERFORM   Cherise

CHEESE TITS   RUFUS   RUFUS

repeat after me: DO YOU WANT FRIES WITH THAT?

ONE LOVE

DON'T PAY TAX, SELL DRUGS INSTEAD

SEE YOU AT THE JOB CENTRE   FASAR   TWAT   Donovan

hair by Toni & Guy, personality by Ronald McDonald

MALACHI

FREAK KNOBJUNKIE   GINGER   Zaida

ME LUV YOU LONG TIME   TOMORROW IS THE FIRST DAY

OF THE REST OF YOUR LIFE – AND IT'S GONNA SUCK ARSE

Don't worry, be happy!   MUUMBE

NOTHING SPECIAL   E.M.+S.T. 4 EVA   Kieron

I'm the only gay in the village   VIRGIN

Get high naturally: climb a tree   Everyone's a cunt except me

LIVE YOUR DREAM

MARVIN P. IS PENG-A-LENG!

PRACTISE RANDOM KINDNESS

NOT A UNIFORM

Be warned: the future doesn't need you!   MOTAHIR

crack whore in training   NATASHA VICKY C. INDIA

SMOKIN HOT

God used to be my co-pilot but we crashed in the

mountains and I had to eat him

NOBODY CARES   Jack   GOONER

I TOLD YOU YOU'D GO BLIND   I STINK OF JIZZ

MUNTER   BUY MORE CRAP   Lester

HEAVEN IS A HALFPIPE   HUSTLER   MATT

we are all made of stars   SIMONE   Corinne

SPOON   Where's the bitches?

JASON B. FUCKED MY MUM

NINJAS AGAINST EMO

bite my shiny metal ass!   Michael D.   BIG WORDS

Too cool for school!

WILL FELCH FOR BACARDI BREEZERS

everything will be OK!

Every time I didn't say I love you I was lying   Nahid

I LOVE POKI BUM WANKS   SLUT

Everybody was watching from the window. The Year 11s got let out before us. Some of them threw their jumpers up in the trees. Some of them brought supersoakers and water bombs and there was a big water fight. They were soaking each other. It looked brutal. Sometimes it turned into a ruckus, then it was even funnier. We couldn't wait to be let out. We were all going to run around like a dog. We started singing at five minutes left.

Everybody: '*We want freedom! We want freedom!*'

It was Kyle Barnes's idea. Everybody joined in, even the scared ones. Asweh, it was brutal. We were all banging on our desks like in a crazy movie.

Everybody: '*Out! Out! Out! Out!*'

In the end Mr Carroll gave up. He had to let us out or there'd be a riot.

Mr Carroll: 'Go on then. Everyone have a great holiday. Stay out of trouble!'

Everybody: 'We will!'

You forgot all about no running on the stairs. Your legs just wanted to get out, you just had to follow them. It was like a race for the future. First one outside would own the summer.

Everybody put their ties around their heads and drank the rain. Me and Poppy walked to the gate together. We were holding hands the proper way, it was very sexy. My heart was going proper fast. Poppy was more beautiful than before. It was even scary. It sounds crazy but it's true, it was like I remembered how beautiful she was and it made me scared. My belly turned over like an aeroplane.

Me: 'Have a nice holiday.'

Poppy: 'And you. Are you going back to Ghana?'

Me: 'No. I'm going to the zoo though. Do you want to come?'

Poppy: 'I can't, I'm going to Spain.'

Me: 'Forever?'

Poppy: 'No, only two weeks.'

Me: 'Are you coming back to this school?'

Poppy: 'Of course I am. Are you?'

Me: 'I think so.'

Poppy: 'That's good.'

I wanted to tell her I loved her but it wouldn't come out. It felt too big. Even the word. It felt too big and stupid to say it now. I had to keep it in my belly for later. I had to swallow it back down.

Poppy: 'Will you text me?'

Me: 'OK.'

Poppy wrote her number on my hand. Her pen was purple and tickly. It felt lovely like the best good luck message. I didn't tell her I haven't got a phone. I'll just borrow Lydia's phone, she'll have to let me. I might ask for a phone for my birthday instead of a Playstation. It's only one month away. I don't care if it has a camera as long as I can talk to Poppy with it. I never want her to cut me, it

That's when Poppy kissed me. I didn't have time to get ready. She just kissed me there and then, right on the lips. It felt lovely. I wasn't even scared this time. It was warm and not too wet. I didn't get any tongue. Her breath smelled like Orange Tic Tacs. I forgot all about Miquita, it didn't even mean anything.

I just closed my eyes and followed Poppy. Her lips were very soft. It was very relaxing. It made me want to go to sleep forever. I squeezed my legs a bit to stop my bulla tickling.

Connor Green: 'Hey, look, now Harri's got wood! What's going on, is it I've Got Wood Day or something? Have a word with yourself!'

Connor Green was throwing spitwads at us. We had to stop. It was like waking up after a lovely dream when you didn't even want to wake up.

Poppy: 'Piss off, Connor.'

We were at the gate. Poppy's mamma was waiting for her. I wished her car would blow up so I could walk Poppy home.

Poppy: 'Bye then.'

Me: 'Bye.'

Poppy waved to me through the window. I waved to her. It didn't even feel gay, it felt like the best thing to do. That's why people wave to each other, because it makes them belong. It tells the whole world. I licked my lips. I could still taste Poppy's breath on them. It was the only superpower I needed.

Dean says to wait until Monday before we tell the police. We need to get all our evidence together and work out what to say. Dean has to decide what games to get with his Playstation and we have to tell our mammas. They'll have to come to the police station with us for if the cops don't believe our story. Dean says we might get a tour, I hope they show us the torture room. They'll just hold Killa's head in a bucket of water until he admits it. In England you get TV in jail and the pool balls even roll straight. It's better than being dead. We just have to stay alive until Monday, then everything will be alright.

It was raining faster now. I did a big breath and got ready to run. I was going to count how long it takes to get home.

If I get home before seven minutes it means Poppy won't forget me AND we solved the case.

I started just moving my arms to warm them up. I made them go faster and faster. I could feel my blood getting stronger. When I was ready I started running.

I ran fast. I ran down the hill and through the tunnel. I shouted:

Me: 'Poppy I love you!'

It made a mighty echo. Nobody else heard it.

I ran past the real church. I ran past the cross.

I ran past the Jubilee.

I ran past the CCTV camera. I let it snap me for luck.

I ran past the other pigeons. I pretended they called hello to me.

Me: 'Pigeons I love you!'

It didn't even feel stupid, it felt brilliant. I ran past the playground and the dead climbing frame. I was running superfast. I was going faster than I've ever gone, my feet were just a blur. Nobody could ever catch me, I was going to break the world record.

I ran past the lady in the chair car. She didn't even see me coming! I ran past the houses and the little kids' school. My legs were getting tired but I didn't slow down. I even went faster. My lips still tickled from where Poppy's kiss had been. My powers were growing inside me. I ran past a tree in a cage.

Me: 'Tree I love you!'

I kicked a Coke can out of the way. I nearly fell but I didn't fall. I could see the flats. I was nearly home. The stairs would be safe. When I got to the stairs the spell would come true.

I ran through the tunnel. My breath was nearly gone, I couldn't get the words out anymore. I just made a noise instead:

Me: **'Aaaaaaahhhhhhhhhhh!'**

Asweh, it made the best echo ever. There was nobody else to ruin it.

I ran past the flats and around the corner to the stairs. I had no breath left. I stopped. The sweat was itching on my face. It felt like less than seven minutes, it felt like only five. I did it! The stairs were lovely and cool. I only had to go up the stairs and I'd be home and dry. I was going to drink a lovely big glass of water all in one go. The tap in the kitchen is safe.

I didn't see him. He came out of nowhere. He was waiting for me. I should have seen him but I wasn't paying attention. You need eyes in the back of your head.

He didn't say anything. His eyes gave it all away: he just wanted to destroy me and there was nothing I could do to stop it. I couldn't get out of the way, he was too fast. He just bumped me and ran away. I didn't even see it go in. I thought it was a trick until I fell over. I've never been chooked before. It just felt too crazy.

I could smell the piss. I had to lie down. All I could think was how I didn't want to die. All I could say was:

Me: 'Mamma.'

It only came out like a whisper. It wasn't even loud enough. Mamma was at work. Papa was too far away, he'd never hear it.

Hold on, I'm coming. Hold on.

I held onto my belly for if I lost myself. My hands were wet. My foot went in a piss puddle, the piss all went up my trousers. I could see the rain. All the raindrops were crashing into each other. They were going in slow motion. I don't even have a favourite, I love all of them the same.

It was too cold and everything was itchy, all I could taste now was metal. It didn't even feel sharp, it just felt like a surprise. I wasn't suspecting it. I only saw the handle for one second, it could be green or brown. It could be a dream except when I opened my eyes there was a bigger puddle and it wasn't piss, it was me. I looked up, you were perched there on the railing watching me, your pink eyes weren't dead but full of love like a battery. I wanted to laugh but it hurt too much.

Me: 'You came. I knew you would.'

Pigeon: 'Don't worry, you'll be going home soon. When it's time to go I'll show you the way.'

Me: 'Can't I stay here?'

Pigeon: 'It's not up to me. You've been called home.'

Me: 'It hurts. Do you work for God?'

Pigeon: 'I'm sorry if it hurts. It won't be long now.'

Me: 'I like your feet. They're nice and scratchy. I like all your colours.'

Pigeon: 'Thank you. I like you too, I always did. There's nothing to be scared of.'

Me: 'Tell Agnes my story, the one about the man on the plane with the fake leg. You'll have to wait until she's old enough to know the words.'

Pigeon: 'We'll tell her, don't worry.'

Me: 'She'll love that one. I'm thirsty.'

Pigeon: 'I know. Just relax. Everything's going to be alright.'

You could see the blood. It was darker than you thought. It just felt too crazy, I couldn't keep my eyes open. I just wanted to remember, if I could remember it would be alright. Agnes's tiny fat fingers and face. I couldn't see it anymore. All babies look the same.

ACKNOWLEDGEMENTS

My foremost thanks to Maureen, Mark and Karina for listening and believing. Thanks to Julius, Ali, Jordan, Kevin, Joyce, Lily, Justin, and everyone who helped along the way, and to Mark Linkous for the inspirational music.

Thank you David Llewelyn for getting the ball rolling. Special thanks to Jo Unwin for your patience and support, and to all at Conville and Walsh. Thanks to Helen Garnons-Williams, Erica Jarnes and all at Bloomsbury for your wisdom and dedication. And to the children and their families, my deepest gratitude and sympathy.

www.damilolataylortrust.com
www.familiesutd.com

PIGEON ENGLISH

STEPHEN KELMAN

A reading guide

ABOUT THE BOOK

Newly arrived from Ghana with his mother and older sister, eleven-year-old Harrison Opoku lives on the ninth floor of a block of flats on an inner-city housing estate. The second best runner in the whole of Year 7, Harri races through his new life in his personalised trainers – the Adidas stripes drawn on with marker pen – blissfully unaware of the very real threat all around him.

With equal fascination for the local gang – the Dell Farm Crew – and the pigeon who visits his balcony, Harri absorbs the many strange elements of his new life in England: watching, listening, and learning the tricks of inner-city survival.

But when a boy is knifed to death on the high street and a police appeal for witnesses draws only silence, Harri decides to start a murder investigation of his own. In doing so, he unwittingly endangers the fragile web his mother has spun around her family to try and keep them safe.

A story of innocence and experience, hope and harsh reality, *Pigeon English* is a spellbinding portrayal of a boy balancing on the edge of manhood and of the forces around him that try to shape the way he falls.

FOR DISCUSSION

1 *Pigeon English* is written from an eleven-year-old boy's point of view but is not a children's novel. How do 'adult' issues appear? Discuss particular scenes and characters.

2 What is the significance of the pigeon?

3 Harri's father and sister Agnes still live in Ghana, and we hear their story through a phone line. Why do you think Stephen Kelman chooses to separate the family in this way?

4 Discuss the social forces at work on Lydia, Harri's older sister. How does she compare to her friend Miquita?

5 Stephen Kelman was inspired by true events in writing this novel. Does this make a difference to the way you read it?

6 Harri is new to the UK. How do you think this informs his perspective on his neighbourhood? How are his attitudes and beliefs different from those of his peers? How are they the same?

7 Harri makes lists and diagrams to explain what he has learnt about his new life in the UK. What effect do his explanations have on you as a reader?

8   How old would you say the members of the Dell Farm Crew are? How do the way they are described and the names they go by affect the way you perceive them?

9   Discuss Harri and his friends' attitude to violence. Is it surprising?

10 How present are male role models in this story?

11 How well do you think Harri and Lydia's mother has protected them from the danger in their neighbourhood? Is there anything else she could do? What would you do in her situation?

12 Discuss the importance of the characters' physical environment on their behaviour and attitudes.

13 Discuss the ending of the novel.

14 Has the novel in any way changed the way you think about youth gangs, knife crime or urban poverty?

SUGGESTED FURTHER READING

Paddy Clarke Ha Ha Ha by Roddy Doyle
The Brief Wondrous Life of Oscar Wao by Junot Díaz
Vernon God Little by DBC Pierre
The Catcher in the Rye by JD Salinger
Lord of the Flies by William Golding

A Q&A WITH THE AUTHOR

1. When did you realise you wanted to be a writer?

I first realised I wanted to be a writer at a very young age, probably six or seven years old. I remember being a very keen reader at that age, and it's something that, as far back as I know, I've always wanted to do. I just feel very lucky now that I have the chance to fulfil a lifelong dream.

2. What was the inspiration for Pigeon English?

I think a large part of the inspiration for *Pigeon English* was the recent press that the UK's children, especially those that live in deprived areas, have gotten. There's a lot of noise around about knife crime and violence among the nation's children at the moment and, having grown up myself in a housing estate which is much like the one that features in the book, I wanted to show the positive aspects of these children's lives and tell their stories in a way that I think hadn't necessarily been told before.

3. Who is your favourite character in Pigeon English?

I love all the characters in *Pigeon English* – they all have their own unique voices, their own spirits – but I'd have to say Harrison, the main character. We see the world through his eyes, he's the narrator of the story and I love him; he has so much exuberance, so much curiosity for the world, and I think writing him was an inspiration to me. He's a character that I've taken with me and he's a good kid, I'm very fond of him.

4. How do you research your characters and stories?

I think it depends on which story you're telling. With *Pigeon English* I was lucky that a lot of the material came from my own experience, my own background, so I had that knowledge to draw on. Many of the characters in the book are based on people I knew growing up or have known in adult life. Also I think that having your ears and eyes open, watching the news and reading the press – just being aware of the stories that are around you and the people that around you – can often help you develop a story in an authentic and original way.

5. What was the first book you loved?

The first book I remember falling in love with was probably *The Adventures of Tom Sawyer* by Mark Twain. I remember being given a copy by my grandparents when I was six or seven. It's the first book I remember reading over and over again, and also the first book that made me think, 'I would like to do that.'

6. Can you give us a hint about your next novel?

I can tell you that it's based on a real-life character I know, an Indian man who has a very unusual hobby: he's a serial world record breaker in bizarre and wonderful feats of physical endurance and strength. The book is part biography of him and part novel, and I hope to have it finished in the near future.

A NOTE ON THE AUTHOR

Stephen Kelman was born in Luton in 1976. After finishing his degree he worked variously as a warehouse operative, a careworker, and in marketing and local government administration. He decided to pursue his writing seriously in 2005, and has completed several feature screenplays since then. *Pigeon English* is his first novel; he is currently working on his second.

A NOTE ON THE TYPE

The text of this book is set in Linotype Sabon, named after the type founder, Jacques Sabon. It was designed by Jan Tschichold and jointly developed by Linotype, Monotype and Stempel, in response to a need for a typeface to be available in identical form for mechanical hot-metal composition and hand composition using foundry type.

Tschichold based his design for Sabon roman on a font engraved by Garamond, and Sabon italic on a font by Granjon. It was first used in 1966 and has proved an enduring modern classic.